Search
for Sky

Searching for Sky

JILLIAN CANTOR

BLOOMSBURY

LONDON   NEW DELHI   NEW YORK   SYDNEY

Bloomsbury Publishing, London, New Delhi, New York and Sydney

First published in Great Britain in July 2014 by
Bloomsbury Publishing Plc
50 Bedford Square, London WC1B 3DP

First published in the USA in May 2014 by
Bloomsbury Children's Books
1385 Broadway, New York, New York 10018

www.bloomsbury.com

A CIP catalogue record for this book is available from the British Library

ISBN 978 1 4088 4664 3

Printed and bound in Great Britain by CPI Group (UK) Ltd, Croydon CR0 4YY

13 5 7 9 10 8 6 4 2

For Grandma Bea, in loving memory

And hand in hand, on the edge of the sand,
They danced by the light of the moon.
—Edward Lear

1

ON THE AFTERNOON OF MY sixteenth birthday, River spears a fish. "Happy birthday," he says, and he's grinning as he holds the fish out in front of me. It is large, the length of River's wide, outstretched arms, and I'm both surprised and impressed by his catch. He is, too, I can tell, because he's still grinning as he places the fish on Cleaning Rock and begins to scale it with a sharp stone.

It has been weeks since we have eaten fish, and this one will certainly be enough to last us for a few days. Truthfully, I am the better fish spearer of the two of us, but today River insisted he would catch me one. I was doubtful when he left this morning because lately, the fish have been coming less and less, even for me. But here River has gone and pulled it off, just as he said he would.

"What a catch," I say to him now. "How'd you get her?"

He shrugs a little, smiles at me, then uses the jagged tool to cut a line down the fish's belly. "I went past Rocks," he says.

"River"—I shake my head—"you promised you wouldn't."
Past Rocks, Ocean grows deeper, cooler, darker, and the water
pulls you hard, so if you aren't careful, you could easily be
swept out, swept away into the deep, great nothingness that lies
beyond us.

He shrugs again. "It's your birthday," he says. "And besides,
I'm starving."

I can't stay mad at him, because I'm starving, too. When one
of us doesn't spear a fish or catch a bird or a rabbit in my traps,
we eat purple flowers, blue berries, and green leaves that we keep
stocked inside Shelter for emergencies. Every plant in our world
is valuable in that it can be eaten, drunk, or used in Shelter in
some way. Except for the mushrooms. Now, we know better.

For the past three days we've eaten mostly purple flowers
and drunk warm coconut milk, and we were still hungry last
night when we crawled into Shelter and curled up together to
go to sleep, the way we have now for so long, both of us lying on
our rabbit pelt mats on our sides, our backs touching. I almost
can't remember sleeping any other way, without the warm feel
of River's back hugging mine. I almost can't remember what it
was like when my mother and Helmut were still here.

The air is cooler this afternoon but heavy, and the moisture
beads against the skin of my bare shoulders. It will rain soon. I
can smell it, the dewy scent of salt water rising, even by Cleaning Rock. I hope it won't rain before the darkness falls, before it
is time to eat the fish.

"Well," River says as he slices the head off the fish with one
swift motion of the jagged stone. He grins again, so pleased

with this fish, with himself for bringing it back to me. My birthday gift. "Do you feel any different today, Sky? Older?"

I shake my head. And for a moment, I consider telling him how, this morning, as I came out of Falls, I noticed how much my body, without my rabbit pelt, looked the way my mother's had looked once. *I am sixteen now, not at all a child anymore*, I'd thought. Then I remembered all the things my mother had said I'd feel someday for River, and I began to wonder if that someday was today. But I didn't say anything to him when I'd made it back to Shelter, and he announced he planned on bringing back a fish for my birthday, and I don't say anything to him now. I'm not sure why not, because River and I tell each other everything, and we have for as far back as I can remember.

"Come on," River says, picking up what remains of the large fish. It is missing scales, a head, a tail, and guts, and my stomach rumbles in anticipation of our feast. "Let's clean her off at Falls and get the fire going." He looks up at the sky, which is filling fast with thick gray-and-white clouds. "We should eat her now, before the rain ruins your birthday, all right?"

I nod and stand up to follow him. Cleaning Rock, where we clean and prepare our food, is about halfway between Ocean and Shelter, and Falls is only twenty paces down Grassy Hill from Shelter, so we can hear the soft rushing of the water even as we sleep. Shelter is a cover of palm fronds woven low and held between two tall trees. Someone—maybe my mother, Petal, or River's father, Helmut, or maybe both of them together—braided the fronds so tightly that the ground beneath them always remains cool and dry. Even in the heaviest of storms or heat, we are comfortable in Shelter, where we lie on soft rabbit pelt mats and cover ourselves with soft rabbit pelt blankets.

We walk by Shelter now, then the twenty paces down Grassy Hill to Falls. River holds the fish up high above his head, careful not to drop her, and then I stand at the edge of the clear, cool water that shares River's name while he wades in, ankle deep, to clean the fish under the water that rushes down from Falls.

River is so tall now, taller than me by at least two heads, and his shoulders are wide and strong, the way I remember Helmut's being. His straight blond hair hangs nearly to his waist but is tied back in a braid, and his cheeks, once smooth and dark like mine, are now lightening with blond hair. *It won't be long before a full beard grows in, like Helmut's*, I think, and I'm not sure why that thought makes me sad. Once, not so long ago, I was the taller one.

———•———

River and I live on Island, in a great blue-green expanse of water that my mother once told me was called *the Pacific*, but we just call it Ocean. I've lived here nearly my entire life, and I don't remember or know of anything else, if there is anything else. My mother sometimes, late at night, would whisper things in my ear about a place called California, where, she said, the people were cold and broken, skeletons.

"What's a skeleton?" I asked her once, when I was much younger, maybe six or seven.

"A skeleton?" she said, her voice rising softly in the darkness of Shelter but still in a whisper so she wouldn't wake Helmut. Instinctively I knew that he would be mad at her for telling me this, for talking about this other place somewhere, another world, away from Island. "A skeleton is just your bones," she said. "Nothing else."

I imagined bones walking around in some otherworldly place, tall and harsh and frightening, and I began to cry.

"Oh, Sky," my mother said, holding my body to hers tightly so I could feel the warmth of skin, of her life. So much more than a skeleton. "It was just a metaphor. I don't mean actual skeletons."

But I didn't understand what she meant by a metaphor, and sometimes, even now, I picture that very far away across Ocean, there is this other world where people like River and me walk around without their skin, their hearts, their souls. And then I walk to the edge of Ocean and stare out as far as I can. All I see is blue, blue, blue, until that point where the water meets the sky, and then the blue softens a shade. Beyond us, there is nothing but water and sky, I tell myself.

———·———

"Come on," River says to me now, his wet toes curling on the grassy edge. He holds the fish out in front of him, and she is pink and bloodless, ready to be cooked.

We walk back up Grassy Hill, just past Shelter to Fire Pit, where we cook our food and we sit for warmth when we need to. It's the only place we ever start fires on Island. Near Shelter would be too dangerous, and on Beach was always forbidden by Helmut. Even now that he's gone, River and I abide by his rules, except for the one River broke this morning, about swimming out past Rocks.

5

River starts a fire with our fire stones, and the orange flames leap out of Fire Pit. He takes our searing stick out of its hole and glances at me.

"You better let me," I tell him, and he nods and hands me both the stick and the thick, slippery fish. The last fish River cooked over the fire he left it too long, too close to the flame, and the meat began to smoke and burn. We ate it, but the black meat made us both feel sick.

I push the stick through the fish and then hook it on top of Fire Pit. I stare into the glow of the flame, watching the meat slowly turn from pink to a silvery white. River is across Fire Pit from me, and his face looks younger in the glow, the way I remember him looking as a little boy, still shorter than me, running across the sand, laughing, as I chased after him.

In the distance, I hear the first rumble of thunder, soft and not at all menacing, but I look away from River and turn the fish, willing it to cook faster, before the rain comes.

River glances anxiously up at the sky, and the first cool drops begin to fall, splashing against his cheeks. "Good enough," he says, pulling the stick from atop Fire Pit and holding on to it tightly. The rain comes down faster, harder, extinguishing the fire. We run to get out of the rain, and by the time we are inside Shelter with the fish, my hair hangs damp, falling out of the braid and tangling down my back.

But I'm too hungry to care, and River and I pull at the meat of the fish and put it in our mouths, chewing so fast we are barely tasting how delicious it is. Outside Shelter a torrent of rain floods our world, dampening Fire Pit, Cleaning Rock, and Grassy Hill. Inside Shelter, it's only River and me and dinner.

We are dry and warm, our bellies finally losing that horrible, hungry ache.

We both eat until we can eat no more, and then suddenly I'm so tired. I lie down on my rabbit pelt mat, and River lies down beside me. He's on his opposite side, so it's not the warmth of his back touching mine, as it usually does, but his front, and he wraps his arms around me tightly in a hug.

"Thank you for the birthday fish," I murmur, and I try not to think about my last birthday, when my mother was still here and she gave me the armband made of pink shells she'd dug from the sand. *It's a bracelet*, she told me, and I had never seen anything like it before, something pretty whose sole purpose was for decorating your arm. Helmut didn't approve. I could tell by the way he frowned as he watched her place it on my wrist.

"Sky," River whispers in my hair now. I'm almost asleep, my mother and Helmut so close that I can almost touch them. River's voice is hazy and raw, and I wonder if he's almost asleep, too.

"Hmm?" I whisper back.

"I saw something today."

"What?" I ask him. I am so warm and full and tired that I can barely move my lips to make a sound. I think about my mother's bracelet, the way the pale pink shells feel cool and smooth against the bare flesh of my arm.

"A boat," River says, just as I am on the cusp of dreaming. "I think I saw a boat."

2

THERE ARE VERY FEW THINGS I know about my life before I came to Island, and even less that I know about my mother's life before that. But this much I do know. She came here on a boat. *We* came here on a boat.

I was one or maybe two. And River was three or maybe four. My mother and Helmut and The Others Who We Never Met were all on this boat, and they didn't mean to come here. I don't know what they meant to do, but I am pretty sure Island was an accident because sometimes my mother would talk about The Others Who We Never Met and The Accident, and tears would well in her eyes, but whenever I'd ask her for more details, she'd press her lips together tightly.

"It doesn't matter now," Helmut would say. "We are all more happy here anyway. Just the four of us. Aren't we, Petal?" He would look to my mother for approval, and she would give it with a nod, a smile, and the quick disappearance of her tears.

I don't remember the boat we came on, or what happened to

it, or how we got here. In my mind, I have always been here. Island is my home. The blue, blue, blue stretch of the water into the sky. The warm grains of sand between my toes. Soft Grassy Hill by Falls. The cool water of Falls that cleanses me each day. Helmut, my mother, River. And now, only River.

I'm not sure I know what a boat looks like, or that it's even a real thing. Or if it is, I imagine it like the stars, the one hanging just below the moon that my mother told me is Venus. The morning star and evening star, a distant, glowing planet, she said. It is so far away it's not something I believe to be anything more than what I can see: the smallest dot of twinkling yellow against the pale blue light of dusk.

———•———

The next morning, when I wake up, River is gone, and I'm in Shelter all alone. I make a notch in Tree of Days, as I do every morning. Then I walk to Bathroom Tree and squat over Pee Hole to relieve myself.

River still isn't at Shelter when I get back, so I walk down to Beach. Beach is in the opposite direction from Falls, and about three times the distance. Shelter is on the highest point of Island, so when the storms come and Ocean floods Beach, Shelter still stays dry and safe.

When I step onto Beach now, the sand is still damp from last night's storm, and River stands there, at the edge of Ocean, ankle deep in blue, blue water. For a moment, I stare at the arch of his back, his wide, strong shoulders, before I walk down to the water's edge to join him.

"Maybe you were wrong," I say.

River turns to look at me. His face is blank like the sand. Any trace of yesterday's smile is gone. "Good morning to you, too."

"About the boat, I mean."

"I know what you mean." He turns back to Ocean, staring hard out across the horizon. Still, all that I see is blue water meets blue sky. The waves crest whiter today in the aftermath of the storm, and it comforts me to think that even if there was this boat that River thought he saw, the storm might have swept it away, taken it back out into Ocean, beyond our reach. "I wasn't wrong," he tells me, shaking his head.

River is older than me, less than two years, but still. Sometimes he uses this, as if it makes him so much wiser. As if he remembers so much more about some other life than I do. I remember nothing before Island. And I don't think River really does, either.

"Come on, Riv," I say now. "I'm going to check the traps. Are you coming?"

He shakes his head, and I leave him standing there by the edge of the water, watching for something I don't even believe is real.

———•———

Our animal traps were first set by Helmut. They are strong and made of palm wood. He made them so long ago that I have no idea how he made them or how he knew to set them. But now they exist, something real, just like every other part of my life on Island.

As I walk from trap to trap, I think about River, standing there at the edge of Ocean, looking faraway and serious. River is what Helmut always called a dreamer, which I took as a bad thing. My mother always said, "Oh, hush, Helmut. Leave the boy be."

I know that Helmut was not my father, that my real father died before I was born. But Helmut was mostly kind to me, as if he were my real father. "You," Helmut told me, "are the practical one. My son wouldn't survive a day here on his own." And so Helmut showed me how to set the traps, bait them with old fish for birds, leaves for rabbits, and then check them each morning. When I was younger, I used to go with him every morning to check them. Now that he's gone, I'm still the trap keeper. The practical one.

But maybe Helmut wasn't being fair, I think now as I walk from trap to trap through the thick, wide green palms that scratch against my bare legs. Helmut would've been proud of River's fish yesterday, even if River did go beyond Rocks. It was a stupid thing to do, but even though he wouldn't have admitted it, I think deep down Helmut would've thought it brave.

Then I imagine his thick face turning red with anger if he could see River now, standing at the edge of Ocean, thinking about this boat instead of checking traps with me.

All the traps are empty today, and I'm grateful River caught such a big fish yesterday so that we will still have more to eat than flowers.

———◆———

Back outside Shelter, I find River just returned from Falls, his blond hair loose and hanging wet down his brown back, drops of water still beading his forehead. He sits down in front of me, and I comb through his hair with my fingers, then braid it, tying the ends in a knot, the way my mother taught me.

"I'm going back beyond Rocks," River announces when I'm finished.

"To look for this boat?" I say, hands on my hips, frowning at him the way I'm certain Helmut would've.

"The traps empty again?" he asks. I nod. "Then we need more fish." He grabs his spear from Tool Tree and begins walking the path toward Beach. I imagine him there beyond Rocks, swept into the thick current, never to come back here to me. As practical as I might be, I don't want to be alone. It's almost too much that my mother has been gone now for nearly a year. I can't lose River, too.

"Riv, wait," I call after him. I grab my own spear from Tool Tree. "I'm coming with you."

He grins, and he holds out his hand for me to take. I do, and we head down the path toward Ocean together, holding on to our spears and each other.

———•———

If you walk down Beach fifty paces, there's a small cove encased by Rocks. This was what Helmut and my mother always called Fishing Cove, and it was where Helmut taught both River and me how to spear fish. Part of the trick in catching them is moving softly, lightly, and so it's not really River's fault that he's not as good at it as I am. I'm smaller and lighter than he is. The air whispers more softly around the thinner space of my body. The fish don't hear me coming as often as they hear him.

Also, I'm fast with the spear, maybe faster than River. A fish rarely gets by me alive.

I am determined today to catch fish in Fishing Cove so then River won't have a reason to climb over Rocks and swim beyond them. But River runs through the cove, splashing water, warning the fish. "River!" I yell at him, but either he doesn't hear me or he pretends not to, and soon I watch him climb over Rocks and start swimming beyond them.

I hesitate for a moment before removing my rabbit pelt, but then I watch River move farther beyond Rocks, and I take my pelt off, leave it on the sand, and quickly run in the water.

I climb over Rocks and begin swimming toward him. The water has grown suddenly deeper, and only River's blond head bobs above the surface.

"River," I call as I swim to catch him, "this is too deep to fish. You're going to drown."

His head is bobbing, his hands waving in the air, his fingertips reaching for the sky. I turn the corner, so Island is behind me now, wide-open Ocean in front of me. I have never been this far from Island before; I've never gone around the bend of it, never seen what's beyond. It makes me nervous, and I want to get back to Beach as quickly as possible. So I swim faster to catch him, before Ocean takes him under, away from me.

"You idiot," I say as I grab his shoulders and pull him toward me. "You can't come out this far. You know it's too dangerous."

"Sky," he shouts. "Look." He points out to the horizon, or the place where the horizon should be, and there in the distance is something large and white, unfamiliar. "The boat. It's closer than it was yesterday." His voice is thick with something. Fear. Excitement. I'm not sure which.

"How do you know that's a boat?"

"I just know," he says.

"That's not a boat," I say, though I'm unsure. Maybe it is.

His head is still bobbing, and I'm holding on tightly to his shoulders. He waves his arms in the air, higher, higher.

"What are you doing?" I ask.

"If we can see the boat, then maybe it can see us," he says.

I let go and start swimming back toward Fishing Cove. It takes him a few minutes, but then he seems to notice I've left him, and I hear him calling after me. "Hey, Sky, wait. Where are you going?"

I hear him swimming behind me now, fierce, broad strokes, and he catches up to me. It's not fair that his arms are stronger, his legs longer, that he can move through water faster than me.

He catches the length of my hair first, tugging on my braid. I don't stop swimming, so then he catches me by the shoulders and pulls me toward him. We are in shallower water now, just by the edge of Rocks, and he pulls me close to him in a hug. I am suddenly aware of the absence of my rabbit pelt, the feel of his large hands against my back, and I try to pull away, but he doesn't let me.

"Sky." He whispers my name, so I can barely hear it over the crashing of the water against Rocks. "Don't be mad."

"What would Helmut say?"

He shakes his head. "He's not here," he says, and I can't tell if he's angry or sad. Or if I've hurt his feelings. "That's the point, isn't it?" he says. His arms hold tightly against my back as the water bobs us up and down and up and down, and I notice the way his hands feel—warmth touching my bare, wet skin. The salty water beads across his broad forehead. "Don't you ever wonder if there's anything else out there?" he asks me.

"Skeletons," I say. He raises his eyebrows, and I know he's confused, but I don't even try to explain. "Never mind." I yank hard enough so I'm out of his grip. Then I climb over Rocks and wade to Beach, and I quickly pull my rabbit pelt back over my head, not wanting River to see me here, out of the water, without it.

3

I AM SO ANGRY WITH River that I run from Fishing Cove and take a long, quiet cleanse in Falls to calm myself down. Then I take a long walk along the grassy banks of the stretch of inland water that shares River's name. He is like that water, calm and beautiful and deep. I remember this now, and I soften. And I am no longer mad by the time I make my way back to Shelter at dusk, where I find yesterday's fish, rotting.

We fell asleep in the storm last night, neither one of us taking the time to climb down to Falls to store the fish in Cooler, the giant hole Helmut and my mother once dug where the air inside is dark and cold. Inside Shelter, it's too warm to store cooked fish, and everything has absorbed the rotting stench now, even our rabbit pelt mats.

I'm tempted to yell at River as he takes the remains of the fish down to Beach for Ocean to take back. I'm tempted to tell him that it's his fault the fish has gone bad. *You are the practical one*, Helmut told me, and I realize it's my fault as much as his, if not more. I was too preoccupied with looking for him when I woke up this morning, and I should've noticed and taken the fish to Cooler then.

"Purple flowers tonight," River says when every trace of the fish is gone, except the rancid smell. He sighs and reaches for the box fashioned out of wood where we keep our extra supplies. His voice is soft, no trace of anger or anything else, and no more mention of the boat, either. The boat, I reason with myself, if it even is a boat, is far out on the horizon. It'll disappear, the way it did that other time just before Helmut and my mother died. That was nearly a year ago, and only Helmut saw it then. River and I have seen no sign of anything since. And then, today, even if it was there, there was no way it could've seen River's flailing arms, his bobbing head. No way.

River hands me a flower, and I chew on it slowly. The petals melt in my mouth, but not in that good, satisfying way that the fish had the night before. They are too sweet, too thin. I chew them because I know I have to, not because I want to.

"You're not still mad, are you?" River asks tentatively.

River is always so worried about what I'm thinking about him, and this is part of what makes me so happy that he's here. He doesn't ever ignore me, the way I would sometimes watch Helmut do with my mother when they were mad at each other. Sometimes I wished my mother would push Helmut, hard. Just shove him across his wide chest and see if he tumbled over. Just like that. She never did, of course. And River is not like his father, I remind myself for the hundredth time. None of us thought so, least of all Helmut.

"Well"—River pokes my leg with the stem of his flower—"are

17

you? Still mad, Skyblue?" His voice hangs easily on his nick-name for me, what he's called me in moments like this one since he was six years old.

I shake my head. "No," I say. "You know I can't stay mad at you." I don't ask him where he was all afternoon, what he was doing, because I don't want him to talk about the boat again. And then I tell myself, even if it was a boat, this thing he saw. *Even if it was?* So what? That means nothing for me, for us.

I swallow back the too-sweet taste of the flowers, and also my fear, as I remember the look on River's face when he said it: *Don't you ever wonder if there's anything else out there?*

What's there to wonder? There's Ocean and Beach, Grassy Hill and Falls, Fishing Cove and Shelter. River and me. At night the yellow glow of a million tiny stars against the round black sky, River's back against mine, warm and strong.

"Good," River whispers now into my hair as we lie on our mats, our bellies empty and still with hunger. River kisses the back of my head and then turns his normal way. Our backs touch, the way Ocean hugs Beach. And before I know it, I'm asleep.

4

I'M STARTLED AWAKE BY AN unfamiliar noise. A sound I can't place. I hear it, and I sit up, suddenly startled, sweating, breathing hard. The air is calm and black; it's still night. I squint for my eyes to adjust to the darkness, and I realize River has heard the noise, too, maybe before I did, because he's already up, sitting at the entrance to Shelter, his fishing spear resting uneasily in his hand.

"River," I whisper, "what is it?"

"Shhh." He puts his finger to his lips, and we listen in the blackness. We're so used to the sounds of Island: giant green birds that cry, even at night, and sometimes owls hooting, too. Falls rushing twenty paces down Grassy Hill. In the distance, the roar of Ocean. Sometimes, the breath of thunder, the slap of rain. Rabbits rustling in the trees, or the snap of a wooden trap as we catch one. The whirring of insects in the hottest months. But this is something altogether different.

It sounds like Helmut talking, from somewhere far away, although something about it isn't quite Helmut. I wonder if Ocean has finally brought him back, the way we always wished and thought it would. And if it brought him, then did it also bring my mother? I listen hard for the soft whisper of her voice. I don't hear it, but I hear the not-quite-Helmut again, though I can't tell what he's saying. River reaches across the ground for my hand and holds on tight.

"Over here, mate," the not-quite-Helmut's voice yells, and the words are so different from any Helmut had ever spoken that I don't think it's actually him. Then, the sound of something else. Palm fronds moving, or being ripped away?

"River?" I whisper, and I start to panic.

"Shhh," he says again, pulling me close, wrapping his arms around me. My head is against his chest. His skin is warm against my cheek. I hear his breath, his heart. It keeps on beating, faster, faster.

The roof of Shelter shakes hard, and I jump. River pulls me closer. Then a round close moon catches on my face, the yellow light making me unable to see anything at all.

"Jesus Christ," the not-quite-Helmut's voice says. "Jeremy," he shouts. "Jeremy, mate, you have to see this."

I turn my head into River's chest and close my eyes, willing the moon to go away, the voice to go away. River's heart beats faster and faster and faster.

"They're kids," the voice says, and it feels a little farther now. "Two of them."

"River," I whisper into his chest, my voice shaking. "We need to run."

You are the practical one, Helmut told me.

River's body is still, and he doesn't respond. "River," I whisper again, "run."

I tear out of Shelter into the night. My body knows the way even in the darkness, twenty paces down Grassy Hill, but in my rush now, my fear, I forget the rules. That there is no running in the darkness, and now I run too fast and I stumble, tripping down Grassy Hill, scraping my leg on a rock.

It hurts, but I keep running, around the corner, letting the rush of Falls be my guide. When I reach it, I sit on Bathing Rock, just next to Falls, hanging my leg under the cool water, cleansing it. It stings, and when my hand reaches to soothe it, it comes back sticky with what feels like blood. I can't hear the voice now over the sound of the rushing water, but I don't hear the sound of River coming, either.

I sit there for a little while, waiting. My leg aches, but I think it stops bleeding. In the morning, I know River will wade across the water here and bring back an aloe leaf for me, and then it will feel better. But as the darkness begins to fade into a blue-orange glow, I'm still sitting on Bathing Rock alone. Just below the moon, I see it there, the morning star, Venus, still bright, even when it's almost day.

Where is River? I close my eyes and try to think of a plan. What would Helmut do now? My mother? There was that boat once before, and I'd heard Helmut promise my mother it would go away on its own. *But I can't go back there*, my mother had said. *I won't.*

Petal, you don't have to. Helmut held her close to him. *This is our home.*

The boat never came that time. And anyway, a few days later, my mother and Helmut were gone.

"Sky." River's voice. Finally. Calling for me. "Skyblue," he yells. "Where are you?"

"I'm over here," I call, not wanting to peek around the edge of Falls, not wanting to yell too loudly. "River," I call back. "I'm by Falls."

He turns the corner, and then he's here again. Close to me. I wrap my arms around him, holding my ear against his heart. It beats slower now. "What took you so long?" My voice trembles in a way that makes me sound angry, but I'm not angry, just afraid.

"Skyblue," he whispers into the top of my hair. He kisses my forehead lightly and stands back. "You don't have to be afraid. They're not going to hurt us."

I realize what he's saying then. That he has talked to the not-quite-Helmut and maybe even the one called Jeremy. That he has not been running in the night, searching for me. He has been back there. With them.

"River?" I whisper.

"They're here to save us," he says.

"Save us?" My voice is trembling so much now I can barely speak, and tears burn, warm in my eyes. "We don't need saving." I try to blink back the tears because I don't want River to see them. But it's too late. He reaches his thumb up to brush a teardrop from my cheek.

"If we stay here, Sky, we're going to die." He says the words solidly, calmly, as if he is the practical one, not me.

I shake my head. "We've lived here forever," I say. "This is our home."

"Not forever," he says. He looks past me now, into the distance, as if he remembers something before this. His eyes find the water that shares his name, River: beautiful and calm and deep. He looks back to me and puts his hands on my shoulders. "They know Helmut," he says.

"They do? How?"

"I don't know. But they said his name to me. It was the first thing they said: *Helmut*. I didn't tell them that; they just knew."

I hear what he's saying, but I don't quite understand it. *How?* Helmut was here, with us, forever, and there was no one else. Just the four of us.

"They want us to leave Island with them," River is saying now. "Don't you think that's what Helmut would want? For us to leave with people who knew him?"

"No," I tell him. There's no way this is what Helmut would want. I think of how he held on to my mother, promising her that this was our home, that nothing would take them away. "Helmut loved Island. He'd want us to stay here forever."

River shakes his head. "We're running out of food. You know we are. The fish are harder and harder to catch. The traps are almost always empty." He pauses. "Island killed them. If we stay, it'll kill us, too," he says softly.

"That's ridiculous," I say, though his words thrum underneath my skin, deep in my chest. "And besides," I say, "Ocean still might bring them back." I imagine it, the way I've imagined it before, walking down to Beach one morning to find my mother and Helmut just sitting there, holding hands, by the edge of the water, healed and new.

He shakes his head. "It's been too long, Sky."

I turn away from him so he doesn't see the tears stinging my eyes, harder now than before. I know he's right—I do. But I don't want to admit it. When Tree of Days started marking weeks, then months, then nearly a year—I knew. But I never thought we'd leave Island. I always thought we'd be here. Just in case.

"We're going," River says now, putting his hand on my shoulder. "We have to."

"No, we don't," I say.

"We do," he says, softer. "Skyblue, come on. This is a good thing. These men who knew Helmut are here to take us on their boat. To take us back." But I'm not sure if he really believes this or if he just wants to disobey Helmut, even this long after Helmut has been gone.

"Where?" I ask him, and I can't believe I'm asking this. There is nowhere else, there is only here. I'm not leaving. He's not leaving. This is ridiculous.

"Where we came from."

California. I hear my mother's voice. *Where people are skeletons.*

He laces his fingers through mine and pulls me away from Falls, to the edge of Grassy Hill. But I pull my hand from his grip and shake my head. "We can't," I say again. His eyes are green, like the grass, and I watch as they fill with tears. He doesn't move for a moment, but then he nods slowly, understanding. River can't make me do something I don't want to do. And he doesn't say anything else as he begins to climb Grassy Hill. I watch his thick legs climb, his blond braid down his back, the arch of his strong shoulders. *If he goes without me, I will never see him again. I will be here all alone.*

"Riv, wait," I call after him. He stops and turns to look at me. "Don't leave me. Please."

He doesn't say anything, but he stares at me and holds out his hand, waiting, waiting, waiting for me to take it.

I do.

5

THERE ARE TWO MEN WHO came on the boat. The one whose voice we heard from Shelter, Roger, and the one he was calling for, Jeremy. Roger is tall, taller than River, and also bigger. He doesn't seem to have any hair, or if he does, it's covered with a funny round leaf he wears over his head. His cheeks are smooth, and I think that makes him look like a woman, although there is something about him that reminds me altogether more of Helmut than my mother. The other one, Jeremy, is smaller, my size. His beard is silver, and so is his hair, which is curly like mine but so short it reminds me of rabbit fur. His eyes are hidden by small black shells, and I don't like that I can't see them, that I don't know what color they are.

River holds my hand as we walk down to Beach toward their boat. The moment doesn't feel real, doesn't feel like something that is actually happening to us. It's morning now, and I remember that I need to check the traps, that I need to make a notch in

Tree of Days, that River and I need to catch a fish today or we might be stuck eating only flowers again tonight for dinner.

My toes curl against the sand, the way they have every morning. Ocean calls to me, wide and blue and green, and it's not until I notice the strange, large white thing—*the boat*—farther down Beach that it really hits me that we're leaving. That River and I are walking down Beach together in a different way than we ever have.

Still, I walk with River, as if in a dream, as if my legs know nothing else but sinking in the sand and following these strange men to this strange boat. When we reach the edge of Beach, just by the water and not too far from Fishing Cove, the boat looms large and white in front of us, like a sea monster, and my legs stop moving; my feet plant themselves in the sand.

"Come on," River says, tugging on my hand, but his voice falters a little. Maybe he's changed his mind.

"We could still stay," I say. But he shakes his head.

"Come on aboard, kids," Roger is calling. He moves the round leaf and wipes the top of his head with his hand, and I see he really doesn't have any hair.

We walk up a small, flat hill, and then we are on this thing, this boat. It's so large and so white, the space of it much bigger than Shelter. I put my hand against the side as I hear Roger say he's getting ready to "start the engine," and the boat side feels so hard. Harder than anything I have ever felt, even rocks.

I hear a giant roar, and the boat moves beneath my feet. I hold on tight to the side to steady myself, and I watch as suddenly Island moves away. River stands behind me, holding on tightly to my shoulders. I feel his breath against my neck as we both stare at the water, swirling out below us, Island moving quickly away from us. At first it looks just the way it did when we swam past Rocks yesterday. It's behind us, but I can still see Fishing Cove and the path back to Shelter. But then the water moves beneath the boat, faster and faster, and Island grows smaller and smaller. Beach starts to disappear, and I can't tell Fishing Cove from the rest of it. Island turns green, and becomes the size of a rock.

I watch the water swirl beneath the boat, and suddenly, I can't breathe. *What am I doing here?* I can't leave Island.

I shake River's arms off my shoulders, and I climb up the side of the boat and I jump.

I hit the water hard, and Ocean rushes in my ears, pulling me under, stinging my skin so that my entire body feels numb. I try to lift my head up, to swim back toward Island, but the current from the boat is strong and pulls me tightly, trying to force me underwater.

"Sky!" I hear River's voice, rising and falling against the pull of the waves. The noise of the boat suddenly quiets, and I hear what I think is Roger's voice saying, "Oh holy hell. She jumped."

Island bobs ahead of me as my head falls in and out of the waves. It's so small now, a green pebble. I'm not sure I can swim to it. But I want to. I have to.

If I just close my eyes, maybe the water will take me there, back, the way it must've once when my mother and Helmut first came here. Ocean is all powerful. It knows things and it does things. It takes and it gives. Once Helmut put the remains of a rotted fish into the water, and the next morning Ocean brought it back, ten-fold, with a pile of fresh fish left for us on Beach. It was as if Ocean knew we were starving, we needed something. And I think now, even as it's pulling me under, it will know where I need to go, where I belong.

But then I hear a splash, and I feel big arms around my shoulders, pulling me, holding on to me. "What are you doing?" River whispers in my ear.

"I don't want to go," I tell him, and I struggle to get out of his grip, to move toward Island. The water pulls me under again, but River pulls me up, harder. I'm crying, coughing, choking on water.

"I'm afraid, too, Sky," River says over the bob of the waves.

My rabbit pelt is drenched, and I'm shivering once River and I are back on the boat. Jeremy offers me a big yellow thing he calls *a poncho*. I don't answer him, but he throws it over my shoulders anyway. It sticks to my skin, but I'm too tired to protest now. Roger makes the boat roar again, and the water churns beneath us. I stare out in the distance, as Island grows smaller and smaller, and eventually all I can see, everywhere, is blue water meets blue sky.

"Hey, kids," Jeremy says after a little while. He comes up behind us, and I jump when I hear his voice. His eyes are still hidden by small black shells, and I get that same nervous feeling around him that I got when River swam out past Rocks yesterday. "We should be back at port by tomorrow morning, all right?"

River nods, as if he already knows this, and I wonder if it's something he and Jeremy and Roger discussed while I was hiding at Falls last night.

"Roger radioed the Coast Guard, and they're going to send someone to get you two back to the States."

"The States?" I ask.

"California," Jeremy says. "That's where you all were from before you got stranded here." River glances at me and shrugs guiltily, and I think that he knew about California, too, even though we've never really talked about it before.

"Why don't you get some rest below board?" Jeremy says. "You've got a big day ahead of you tomorrow." I shake my head, but River tugs on my arm. I'm so angry with him. I hate him. I really do, but I don't want to stand by the edge of the boat, all alone with only Jeremy and his strange, covered eyes.

I follow River, who follows Jeremy down a hill of smooth, sharp rocks. "There you go," Jeremy says when we reach the bottom, pointing to two large boxes. "Nothing fancy, but a bed for each of you." He pauses. "I'll be just up the stairs if you need anything. Oh, and there's food in the fridge if you get hungry." He points to a small black box in the corner. It buzzes and hums, as if it is full of insects, and I know I won't be hungry enough to eat what's inside, no matter how much my stomach rumbles. "You need anything else?" Jeremy asks.

"Bathroom Tree," I say because I feel the urge pressing there, in my belly, and I have no idea how people on boats do this sort of thing. *If* they do this sort of thing.

"Over there." Jeremy points next to the humming black thing. I don't see a tree or a hole, but Jeremy walks past us, pulls on something, and part of the boat tears away, revealing a tiny, dark cave. "Toilet's in here, all right?"

River nods, and I just stare. Jeremy frowns and lifts the shells from his eyes, and now I can see his eyes are silver gray, the color of the skin of the fish River caught for my birthday. I don't think you can trust eyes that color; there is something about them so animallike, so fishlike, skeleton-like, that my belly aches.

Jeremy walks back toward the coming-in place that brought us down here. "The American Official should be here first thing in the morning, all right?" We don't say anything, and he shakes his head, looking right at River. "Holy hell, kid," he says, "Helmut Almstedt. It's like you're a bloody ghost."

He climbs back up the rocks, and I wonder what he means, and who Almstedt is, but only for a second, because I now really, really need to pee. I stand and run to what Jeremy called Toilet, which is a large white circular hole coming up from the ground on top of some kind of tree stump. At Bathroom Tree there are two holes in the ground, well hidden from view and easy to squat over, but this hole seems too tall for me to squat. "River," I whisper, holding my legs together and twisting. "How do I use this?"

River examines it, lifting pieces, taking something from the top that looks like a thick white piece of rectangle wood. "I think you sit up here," River says, and now that the top is gone, I see water flows underneath, down and into the circle. "And you must put your feet on this circle part." He points to the rim around the circular hole.

I don't know if he's right or what the point is of peeing into water, but I have to go really bad, so I push him out of the way and do as he says. "Don't look," I whisper again as I sit on the high part of Toilet and rest my feet on the circle below. The sound of my pee hitting the water is so loud, I'm embarrassed that River can hear it, but he pretends not to notice, and when I'm finished he takes a turn, then replaces the rectangle piece where he found it.

It seems so dirty not to wash my hands in Falls when I'm finished, but Falls is very far away now, I remind myself, and the only water I see is inside this thing, *Toilet*, and I'm not about to touch that now.

River walks to the boxes Jeremy called Bed and pulls the rabbit pelts from the top. He hands one to me, and it is not nearly as soft as our rabbit pelts. River puts his on the ground, and I do the same. We lie there, back to back, and close our eyes, as the ground sways beneath us.

"You told them about California," I whisper.

"I told you, they knew my father," he answers. "They already knew."

For a quick second I wonder if Roger and Jeremy could be The Others Who We Never Met, who my mother and Helmut would sometimes speak of in hushed tones when they discussed The Accident. I always thought these were the people who came on the boat with my mother and Helmut in the beginning, but that they had drowned in Ocean on the way to Island. But every time I asked my mother, she just told me it didn't matter now. That they were gone. Dead. So they couldn't be Roger and Jeremy, unless Ocean had brought them back to Island after all this time.

"I think maybe Roger even thought that I was him, at first. That he was calling *me* Helmut," River says now, as if this is just occurring to him. "They said I look like him." He pauses. "Or him a long time ago, anyway." He clears his throat, and I understand that by a long time ago, he means before Island. And this is a weight, unspoken between us until now, this other life my mother and Helmut had, in California. I wonder if there are other people out there in California, aside from Roger and Jeremy, who once knew Helmut, my mother. And then for the first time I wonder whether there could be anyone else out there who knew me. But I remember nothing except my mother, Helmut, River, Island, and so I'm not sure I believe that anything else can be real.

"You do look like him," I say to River. But then I add, "Sort of." Because despite their similar looks, there's something about River that is so unmistakably different from Helmut. They have the same blond hair, wide cheeks, broad forehead and shoulders, but where Helmut's expression looked tough and worn, River's is soft, kind. Helmut was practical. River is a dreamer. And you can see this in the lines around their eyes: River's smile; Helmut's frown. "I don't like this," I say softly. "I really want to go back."

"We can't go back," he says.

"Why not?"

"Sky," he says my name. "Skyblue."

I don't say anything for a little while. I close my eyes, and I lean into the feel of his back against mine. The yellow poncho sticks to my skin, hard enough so it hurts. The ground is uncomfortable against my side, and my leg aches where I scraped it last night.

"What have you done?" I finally whisper.

I'm not sure if River is asleep now or if he's only pretending, but he doesn't answer.

6

I HEAR THE SOUND OF voices, and I open my eyes, expecting to see the familiar shapes of Shelter surrounding me, the voices of my mother and Helmut, but it is so dark, a darkness I have never known, and no matter how many times I blink, I can't get my eyes to see. "River," I yell, feeling around for him, my hand searching desperately in the darkness. "River."

"I'm here," River's voice comes across the black, and then his hand reaches around until he finds mine.

"Hard to believe they were living there all this time," an unfamiliar voice says from somewhere above us. *The voice of a skeleton*, I think, and I shiver.

"That must be The American Official," River says. And then I remember where we are: *Below Board, the boat*. River and I left Island with Roger and Jeremy.

I am shaking, the enormity of what we have done hitting me fresh all over again. River tries to steady my hand in his. But I am torn between being mad at him still and wanting to pull away, and being so afraid that I want to hold on to him for comfort.

I don't pull away. My tongue feels thick, and my head aches. "River," I whisper into the darkness. He squeezes my hand in response.

I didn't sleep well on the uncomfortable rabbit pelt. All night I tossed and turned and dreamed of skeletons.

I've seen skeletons before: the bones of fish, the bones of rabbits, the bones of the green birds that cry even in the night. But in my dream, the skeletons looked like Jeremy and Roger, bones the size of men, with black shells hiding their eyes.

"I couldn't believe it myself when I came face-to-face with the boy," I hear Roger saying now from just above us. I'm guessing now at the top of the rock hill. "I thought it was Helmut Almstedt at first, and it scared the bloody hell out of me." One of them laughs. Roger, I think.

"Are they agitated?" The American Official says.

"Aw, no, mate. They're just a couple of scared kids," Roger says. "The girl's a little wild, but the boy—he might look like Helmut, but he's not too bad."

"Unbelievable . . . ," The American Official says. "I wasn't sure what to expect when I got the call. But I came prepared."

We hear the sound of footsteps coming down the rocks, coming toward us. River pulls me closer to him, and I can hear his heart, so loud it's as if it's beating in my ear.

Suddenly there is a bright sun above us, and it is so bright I can't see anything for a moment. Then I see Roger. His no-hair is hidden again, and his face is red and shining with sweat.

"Hey there, kids," he says, his voice softening. "This here is Mr. Sawyer."

"Sergeant Sawyer," the man says as he steps around Roger. He is not too tall, but his entire body is covered in a green that reminds me of the trees shrouding Shelter. The only thing I can see is his face, and his skin is dark, darker than mine and River's, the color of the rocks in the deeper, cooler middle part of the body of water that shares River's name.

"He's come to take you kids home," Roger says.

"Home?" I ask, thinking again of Island, of my rabbit pelt mat back at Shelter and my bracelet. *My bracelet.* How could I have left it there when I went to the boat with River? I was so stunned I wasn't thinking clearly. My mother gave me that bracelet, and now it's the only thing left of her, the pale pink shells to decorate my wrist.

"California," Sergeant Sawyer is saying.

I let go of River's hand, and I stand up. I shake my head. *No.* That's not home. Island is home. My bracelet is there. I have to go back. I have to get it. "Take me back to Island." I look at Roger, asking him directly, pleading with him, because I think he's the one I trust the most. His eyes are blue, like my mother's were.

"Sky." River stands, too, and says my name softly. He tries to pull me close to him. But I shake him off.

"I need to go back," I say.

Roger shakes his head. "But you've been rescued now, sweetheart."

Sergeant Sawyer pushes Roger out of the way. "Let me handle this," he says. Then he turns to stare at me and River. "So you both understand and speak English?"

River nods, though I don't know whether we do or not.

I peer beyond Sergeant Sawyer, calculating the distance between here and the top of the boat, the water. There's enough space between the two men for me to push my way through, like the distance between the two palm trees where my favorite and most trusted rabbit trap lies. And maybe if I can make it past them, I can jump into the water and the water will know me; it will hold me close, take me to the place I belong. Or maybe I can even convince Jeremy to take me if I stare into his silver fish eyes and beg him to do it.

"And you do believe yourselves to be American citizens?"

"I . . . ," River stumbles, and though we are not as close together now, I can still hear his heart beating, loud and wild.

I edge away from him, and I know I need to run, to get back to Island somehow. I rush toward the men, the rock hill, holding my arms out to push past them. "Sky," River is shouting. "Stop. What are you doing?"

I make it up the rocks, and above me, the sky is close and Ocean seems far. Beach is in front of us but it is not like I have ever known it. It seems to be made of palm wood, like our traps, and there are people there. So many of them, and they are wearing strange things. Skeleton men and women everywhere. I can still hear River calling for me as my eyes search desperately for a way into Ocean that won't make me walk on this strange wood with all these skeletons. I feel tears running down my cheeks, but I don't stop to wipe them away.

Suddenly, Sergeant Sawyer catches my wrist with his hand. I struggle to pull away, but he holds on too tightly. Still, I fight him with everything I have, and I kick his legs until he stumbles a little back down the rocks. He catches his balance, and I notice he's holding a thin white stick between his teeth now, grabbing onto it with his other hand, and then he jabs it hard into my arm, through the flesh of the poncho.

I feel like I've been stung by the biggest and worst insect I have ever felt, but I am still trying to run. "Where the hell does she think she's going?" I hear Sergeant Sawyer say.

And then the entire world goes still.

7

I OPEN MY EYES AND the world is white.

Not white like the sand that danced just beyond the edge of Beach in tiny pure dunes. Or even white like the full, puffy clouds hanging low in the cool blue sky, filled with rain. No. Now the white is all wrong. Everything around me is that color, and the world is a square, the whiteness of it so bright it hurts my eyes. I blink, and then I notice there's the sound of something I don't recognize. A strange kind of bird, close and regular, chirping in my ear.

I sit up, and I realize I am in a box. Bed. Like the one that was in Below Board on the boat. *The boat? River?*

"River." I call his name softly at first, then louder. "River. River." He doesn't answer, and my voice sounds strange in this white place, different.

I hear a knocking sound, and then I see part of the white move. A green person steps in, and I remember the man from the boat, Sergeant Sawyer. I move to rub my arm where he stung me, and I realize my wrists are tied to Bed with heavy, thick leaves. I also see there is a long string coming out of my wrist. I lean in to tug on it with my teeth.

"Don't," the green man says, rushing toward me. I pull harder. His hand reaches across and gently pushes my head back. "Please," he says. "Don't do that. I'll take it out for you. But if you do it that way, it's going to hurt, all right?" He speaks slowly, his voice like the curl of a wave in Ocean. I let go of the string, and he squats next to Bed and sits on some strange sort of tree stump.

"Where's River?" I ask.

"River?" he says.

"River," I repeat.

"Oh . . . River, right. He's just next door." I don't know what that means, but before I can ask more, the green man's hand is on my arm, and he tugs gently, pulling on the string. "This is just an IV," he says. "It's hydrating you."

He looks at me as if he's waiting for me to say something in response, but I don't understand any of what he said. Still, he stares so hard I nod, just so he will stop staring like that. "I want to see River," I say.

He doesn't answer as he pulls the string out the rest of the way and places some kind of sticky leaf on my wrist. I struggle to get out of the other, thicker leaves that are tying me to Bed. "I'm going to have someone bring in some food and water, and she'll take those off," he says. "As long as you eat and drink, I won't need to put this back in, okay?" He stares at me again, and I nod again. "Good. First we'll get you something to eat, and then we'll talk about seeing people."

"People?" I ask, and though it seems impossible, I wonder if my mother and Helmut are here, too. If this is where Ocean brought them. But he doesn't answer my question.

He stops by the opening he walked in. "Do you know where you are?" he asks.

"California?" I whisper.

He nods. Then he smiles at me. "Welcome home," he says.

———•———

A few minutes later, the white moves again, and another green person enters in the coming-in place, this one carrying a long slab of wood. "I brought you some breakfast," the person says, her voice sweet and high like my mother's. Her hair is bright and blond like River's, though much shorter and pulled back in a small, tight ball at the nape of her neck.

She puts the wood slab over my stomach, and then sits down where the last green person sat. "I'm going to unfasten these," she says, tugging at the thick leaves wrapped around my wrists. "But we need you to behave. Do you understand what that means?"

Behave. It was a word my mother used when she wanted me to listen to her and follow Helmut's rules, to promise no swimming past Rocks, no fires on Beach, no lying, no running down Grassy Hill to Falls in the darkness.

I nod, and her fingers gently move against my wrists. She pulls at the leaves, and they make a loud sound as if very tiny rabbits are scattering across them, tearing the leaves away, and I jump. "Don't be alarmed," she says. "Just Velcro." I don't know that kind of animal, and I hope it isn't poisonous. But as suddenly as Velcro began scattering, it stops. The thick leaves are gone. My wrists are bare, my skin looking lighter than it did on Island but seemingly unharmed. I open and close my fingers a few times, stretching them. My arms, my wrists, my fingers are all sore.

"I'm sorry about that," she says. "But it was for your own safety." I don't know what she means by that, so I don't say anything. "Go ahead," she says. "Eat. You must be hungry."

On top of the slab of wood, on a big white circle, there are berries and something brown I don't recognize. On the side there is coconut milk in a tall container. I am hungry, but even more, I'm thirsty. So I pick up the coconut milk and throw it down my throat. It's so sour that I think I might throw it right back up, and I start to cough. I stare at the berries cautiously and pick at the blue ones, the most familiar. They are sweet, their juice melting against my tongue, and I pick them up by the handful and drop them down my throat.

"There's a spoon," the woman says, her eyes open wide, her fingers on a silver stick. She hands it to me, and I see the end is a circle. I turn it over, not sure what I'm supposed to do with it. "Here," the woman says. She uses the circle to scoop a few berries and then gently places them in my mouth. I understand what she wants me to do now, but it seems silly when I could just use my fingers and my hand more efficiently. Still, I don't want her to think I'm not behaving, to put the hard leaves and Velcro back on my wrists, so I do as she showed me and use a spoon.

"Good," she says, and she smiles. "I knew you would learn fast. It'll only be a matter of time before the island is just a distant memory." I drop the spoon, and it echoes, like stones being thrown into the body of water that shares River's name. "I'm sorry," she says. "I didn't mean . . ." She shakes her head.

"I want to see River," I say, trying to keep the tone of my voice even, the way Helmut's always was, even if we knew he was angry. He always got what he wanted, Helmut did. No matter what.

"You will," she says. "I promise you, you will."

"Now," I say, still even. "I want to see him now."

She frowns, looks toward the coming-in place, and then looks back at me. "First," she says, "there's someone else who really wants to see you."

———

My mother rarely talked about where she came from, who she was with before Island. It's not that I didn't ask, that I wasn't sometimes curious, like River, if there was anything else beyond the blue lilt of Ocean. The small tidbits she'd whispered to me about California and skeletons—these were always just before sleep in Shelter, on the brink of dreaming. During the day she ignored my questions or told me there was nothing worth saying. "This," she would say, holding out her arms to span the scope of Ocean, surrounding us, "is everything."

My mother told me once I had a real father—not Helmut—who had died before I was born. But when I asked her to tell me more, who he was, what he was like, what had happened to him, her entire face grew still, as if just the mention of him, the memory, shut something down inside her.

And so I have no understanding now of what the green

43

woman said to me. *There's someone else.* No. There is no one else, nothing else. Only me. Only River.

———·———

It doesn't take the green woman long to return to the coming-in place. She walks in, stands there for a moment, and stares at me, and then she turns to say something to someone else, behind her, someone I can't quite see. "Go ahead," I hear the green person say.

I am not at all prepared for what I see next. Stepping out from behind the green person is a woman: she is small with blond hair and sharp blue eyes, and she is wearing a strange-looking red pelt. She is familiar. Mine. It's as if Ocean really has healed her finally and brought her back to me, new and well. And she's here again, almost close enough for me to touch: my mother.

8

THE WOMAN STEPS FORWARD, CLOSER to me, tentatively, the way I would approach a trap if I noticed the animal inside was still alive, afraid, staring at me, pleading with me to let it go. "Megan?" the woman says, and her voice is all wrong. It's deeper than my mother's, and emptier, as if her throat is filled with wind as she speaks. As she gets closer, I see now that her face is different, too. Her skin is paler, with more lines. *This is a trick*, I think, and maybe she, whoever she is, is one of those skeletons my mother told me about.

"Megan," the woman says again, "do you remember me? Do you know who I am?"

Remember her? I shake my head and look past her to the green woman. "Where's River?" I say again.

But she doesn't answer me, and this fake woman's face turns into a frown. She bites her lip and quickly turns into her pretend skeleton smile again. I notice her lips are a bright, unnatural purple, so similar to the color of our flowers. "Megan," she tries again.

"Sky," I finally correct her. "My name is Sky."

She reaches for my hand and squeezes it, but I quickly pull away. Her fingers are hard and sharp, as if I am touching directly to her bones. "Oh, honey, I'm just so glad you're here. I can't even tell you. After all this time . . ." She shakes her head. "It's been so long I didn't think I'd ever see you again."

"I don't know you," I say with a startling vehemence, so the words come out as if I am spitting them at her.

"You probably don't remember," she says. She looks down at this strangely shaped—and what seems to be rabbit pelt—container she has hooked over her shoulder, sticks her hand in, and pulls something out. "Here," she says. "This was taken on your first birthday."

She hands the thing to me, and it has the texture of a thin leaf, only there are people drawn on top of it. River and I used to draw in the sand with sticks when we were younger, but never anything like this, with sharp colors and with perfect lines that make the people look entirely real, similar to the way our reflections sometimes stared back at us as we stood on the edge of River in the high sunlight.

"Here." She points to a tiny person, what I guess to be a baby human, though I have never actually seen one before. "This is you." The baby human she points to has brown curls, similar in color to mine but much, much shorter, and her face is covered with some kind of pink sand, as if she'd been stuffing it in her mouth. "This is me. And this is your mother." She points to the other two people on the leaf, and I take it from her, twirling it up, closer to the sun. Then I bring it back down, closer to my eyes. Is it? My mother? She looks different here. Her skin is paler, her hair darker and shorter. I stroke her face with my thumb, and I want it to become warm and real, the way it was on Island, even as I lay beside her sleeping that last night. Her skin didn't grow pale and cold until I awoke the next morning and caught her on her side, blue lips agape, as if in surprise.

"Who are you?" I whisper to the woman now.

She smiles at me. "I'm your grandmother, honey." I shake my head because I don't understand; I don't even know what that is. "I'm your mother's mother," she says.

"Oh." The word catches in my throat, like a sob. *My mother had a mother. Has* a mother. Of course she did; I knew that my mother had to come from somewhere. My mother explained it to River and me when we were younger, where people came from, how they came to be, how someday new people would come to Island through River and me. It was just that I always thought my mother's mother must be dead, the way my father was, or she would've been on Island with us. I try to remember if my mother had even told me that her mother was dead, which would make me feel certain that this woman, here, is lying. But I can't remember what my mother said about her mother.

"I don't believe you," I say now, though I'm not sure whether I believe her or not.

"Okay," she says, and she takes the leaf back from me. She casts her eyes downward, as if I've wounded her.

The green woman has stepped closer, and she puts her hand on the other woman's shoulder. "Maybe we should let her rest, Alice. This has all been very traumatic for her."

The woman who says she's my grandmother nods and stands. "I'll be back, honey," she says to me. She touches her bone-fingers to my cheek, and for a second, I don't pull away. "You look just like her, you know. Just the way she looked when she was sixteen." Tears well up in her eyes and then run down her cheeks, making brown streaks like tracks of raindrops through mud.

I pull away and turn over so I don't have to look at her anymore as she leaves. And then I close my eyes and try to make her disappear, make this all disappear. But no matter how hard I try, I can't forget the sound of her voice, the echo of it in my head now, new but strangely familiar: *I'm your mother's mother.*

9

MY MOTHER WAS A FLOWER.

Her skin was smooth and shimmering like a petal, for which she was named. Her voice was soft, and her face looked kissed by the sun, a milky deep-coconut brown, not an angry red like Helmut's. Her delicate hands fed me and pulled the strands of my unruly hair into a gentle braid. They held me at night in Shelter, stroking my cheek if I had my bad dream about the fish. They taught me things: how to draw circles in the sand, how to make and count the notches in Tree of Days, and how to turn a rabbit's pelt into something that would cover our womanly parts. She taught me how to cook a fish, and how to hold my breath underwater without drowning.

She taught me that the land and the water, the trees and the animals, they were all necessary, all useful. And she showed me how. *This world of ours is a paradise, a paradise found,* she told me over and over again, whenever I would complain that I was hungry, tired, sore.

The only imperfection in my mother's soft brown skin, in my mother at all, was a round and ugly pale purple circle on her left shoulder. When I asked her what it was, where it had come from, she would always shake her head and say it meant nothing. It had come from nothing. Some days, though, she would complain it was growing hot again, and then she would shrivel, the way flowers do when the rains don't come and the sun burns them. She would stay in Shelter and refuse to come out, even if Helmut and I brought back a bounty from the traps. And then Helmut would tell River and me to go wait at Beach until he came for us.

Sometimes we would wait so long, the sun would lower across Ocean. The moon and Venus would come, and River and I would sit there hungry and scared in the darkness before Helmut came to get us.

But then the next morning, the world would be new again. My mother would be smiling, laughing, her purple imperfection cooled and forgotten. Her face bright and full of happiness again, and opening to the sunlight.

———

"Hello." The sound of a voice startles me, and I sit up, feeling full and confused. I realize I must've fallen asleep after the grandmother woman left, and that I have been dreaming: first, of my mother, that she was here. That Ocean brought her back to me, and her purple circle was gone. And then also of River, that he was here, too, in this box with me, his back lying against mine, holding on to me as I slept. I feel around for him now, then turn to look for him, but he's not here. Neither is my mother.

The air is darker now, and I squint to make out where the voice came from. There is a shadow by the coming-in place, and a hand that moves up. Then the sun alights above me, but a strangely shaped square one, bursting yellow light into my eyes.

"May I come in?" the voice asks. In the light of the sun, I see it is the green woman again, and I sigh. She doesn't wait for me to answer before walking in and sitting down next to Bed. "Hello," she says, smiling at me. Why do all these people smile so much when it seems they have nothing happy to say? "I should've introduced myself before. I'm sorry. I'm Dr. Cabot, and now that you've had a chance to rest, to . . . take some of this in, I'd like to explain everything to you. Would that be okay?"

"I need to see River," I say again, tears of frustration building behind my eyes. It's like I'm shouting his name into great, wide Ocean, and there's no one around to hear me, least of all him.

"I know," she says. "And you will. But I'd like to go over everything with you first." She pauses. "Some of this is going to be confusing to you and probably hard to hear. But I think it's important that you know the truth, that you know what's going on." I don't say anything in response, so she clears her throat. "All right, then. You and, um . . . River, you were living on an island in the South Pacific. About a hundred and fifty nautical miles east of the American territory of Samoa." She looks at me as if waiting for me to say something, but I don't know what. I have no idea what Samoa is, but I recognize *Pacific*, which is where my mother always said we were. "We believe that you were on a boat, and that the boat crashed onto the island in a storm approximately fourteen years ago." *The Accident. The Others Who We Never Met.* "I'm sorry, is this all too much?"

I shake my head. "Okay," she says. "Well, from what we can piece together, you and your mother, Helmut and his son—you were the only four survivors." I nod. "But your mother and Helmut are deceased now?"

"Deceased?"

"No longer living."

"Yes," I whisper.

"But you and Helmut's son lived on the island until now." Her voice is cold like Falls in the early morning. But also precise, like River's stone, slicing the head off a fish. *River*.

"I really need to see him," I say, with all the bravery I can muster, though something about this woman, her talking, the preciseness of it, is making it very hard for me to breathe.

She simply nods. "We didn't know about the island until about a year ago. There are so many little islands in that part of the Pacific. We're always discovering new ones. Plates shift, tectonics and all that. Oh . . . I'm losing you. Well, never mind. That's not the important part." She pauses and licks her lips, which are strangely red, as if they are stained with berry juice, but I am thinking about what she said . . . *so many little Islands*? She must be wrong; there is only Island, in Ocean, only us. "About a year ago, some Australian explorers found what they thought to be some wreckage from your boat and that led them close to your island. But from their observations, we thought it to be uninhabited. It was assumed that you had all been killed in the boat crash. But we were all wrong, weren't we?" She pauses again and stares at me funny for a moment, until I nod again. "I'm sorry about all that back in Samoa. Sergeant Sawyer, he can be a little . . . well, you were frightened, and I can understand that. But you've been rescued now. There's no need to be frightened anymore."

But I am frightened. I try to judge whether Dr. Cabot can be trusted, but her face is as blank and pure as untouched sand, giving away nothing about what she's thinking or feeling. So I don't tell her that we didn't need to be rescued from Island. That River and I, we were just fine. That Sergeant Sawyer and the insect he put in my arm, Velcro running under the leaves on my wrists, this strange white room, the strange grandmother woman, the idea that there are many Islands in Ocean, not just ours . . . these feel like things I need rescuing from now.

If only I could talk to River. He would know what to do.

"Everyone here wants to help you," she adds.

"Here?" I ask, glancing at all the white, white, white surrounding me.

"I'm sorry. I should've told you all this right away. It's just I hoped seeing your grandmother might . . ." She shakes her head. "But you want to know where you are. Of course you do. That's perfectly reasonable. This is a military hospital, in Camp Solanas, California, just outside San Diego," she says. "We're keeping you here while we verify your identity, and then we can clear you through customs." I have no idea what she's saying, or how it all seems to make perfect sense to her when it means nothing to me. "But we're fairly certain that you are Megan Anna Baynes," she says.

"My name is Sky," I say, but my voice is a whisper now, filled with uncertainty. "Sky," I repeat. "Sky." A little louder.

She ignores me. "You're sixteen years old, and you were born right down the road in San Diego."

"I am Sky," I say again.

She nods. "We think most likely your mother decided to change your name after she left. But not legally, of course, which for our purposes would still make you Megan Anna Baynes." She pauses. "But just to be sure, we're verifying your identity with a DNA test."

"A what?" I ask her.

"D-N-A." She says each sound sharply and slowly. "We've taken your grandmother's blood and some of your blood, and we'll basically see if they're a match. If you two are family."

"My blood?" I recoil in horror at the awfulness of these people for taking my blood. *Skeletons.* I shiver.

"It's a very standard test. And very accurate," she says. "We should have the results back tomorrow, and if they come back as we believe they should, then we'll be able to clear you through customs, and you can leave the military base and . . ." Her voice drops off.

"And what?" I ask.

"And go home," she says.

10

THE NIGHT MY MOTHER AND Helmut ate the mushrooms it was raining. A few times a year we would get a storm that would last longer than a few hours, sometimes for a week. It was going to be one of those—I could tell just by the heaviness of the air, the persistent smell of moisture stinging my nose. Our traps had already been empty for days, and we were starving.

Helmut brought the mushrooms back, two large handfuls of them. They had been growing by River, just on the other side of Falls, such a treat, Helmut said. We'd had mushrooms before, but these looked different. The other ones had been tiny and white, and these were larger, with thick black stems.

Helmut handed one to each of us and pulled some purple flowers from the wooden box. My mother stared at it for a moment and then looked to Helmut. He took her hand and pulled her out of Shelter, into the rain.

"Oh, Petal," I heard him say from outside. Then he lowered

his voice to a whisper, so I couldn't make out what else he was saying.

I sniffed my mushroom, and it smelled like dirt, like the mud at the bottom of River that would sometimes stick between my toes.

Before I could take a bite, River grabbed my hand. "Come on," he said. "I have to show you something."

"Now? I'm starving." He nodded, and he tugged my hand and pulled me into the rain.

Helmut and my mother stood there, outside Shelter, their faces wet and slick with water. My mother was smiling, and Helmut held his hand on her cheek while he whispered in her ear.

"Where are you going?" Helmut asked as we walked past them.

"Bathroom Tree," River said quickly, and pulled me with him.

"Hurry back," Helmut said.

River nodded, and we started through the rain. I followed him, even though I wasn't sure why, what he was doing, what he needed to show me at Bathroom Tree. My feet sank into the wet ground, the water tumbling through my hair, splashing across my cheeks.

River walked down Grassy Hill, sliding a little, past Bathroom Tree, nearly tumbling into the water that shares his name. I followed, mud splashing up my legs to my knees, and as we slid, the mushroom fell from my hands into the mud and my stomach ached with hunger.

"What are we doing?" I asked River as he rinsed the mud

off himself in Falls. "I'm hungry. And I don't even need to use Bathroom Tree."

He didn't answer but walked to the other side of Falls, and so did I. Then he pointed. I saw rows and rows of purple flowers, their delicate petals breaking in the weight of the rain.

"What?" I asked him.

"This is where Helmut said he found the mushrooms," River said.

"So?"

"So he lied," River shouted into the rain, his words breaking as drops spilled down his cheeks, onto his tongue.

"Maybe he just made a mistake," I said.

River shook his head. "There are no mushrooms here. I come here all the time to collect the flowers. I came here this morning." That was always River's job, collecting, as Helmut always said, the things without teeth, the things even a dreamer could catch: flowers, leaves, coconuts.

"So?" I said again. "You just lied about us going to Bathroom Tree."

"That's different," River said.

"How?"

He shrugged. "I don't know," he said. "It just is."

I was uncomfortable with the notion of lying. I knew what it was. I'd done it once, when I was younger and I told my mother I hadn't swum past Rocks, only for Helmut to tell her that I had, that he'd seen me. "There is no lying here," my mother had reprimanded me. "We aren't going to survive unless we tell each other the truth. Always. Do you understand?" She'd shaken me a little. I'd understood. I'd never lied to her again, and didn't think she'd ever lied. Or that River or Helmut had, either. And I felt uneasy then, thinking that suddenly everyone seemed to be lying.

"Besides," River said, picking some wet purple flowers. "You know how they like to be alone in Shelter when they start whispering like that." He handed me some flowers, and I nodded.

I knew he was right, and that even though Helmut said hurry back, he probably wouldn't be mad now if we didn't. I took the flowers from him and chewed on a wet, slick petal. And we sat there for a while in Cove By Falls, listening to the sound of the rain.

It was dusk by the time we walked back to Shelter, and Helmut and my mother were already asleep, his thick arm wrapped tightly around her.

I leaned down to kiss her on the cheek before lying on the other side of her, and she murmured a little bit and smiled. "Good night, Mom," I whispered.

"Good night, Megan," she whispered back.

That was the last thing she ever said to me.

———

The square sun comes and goes when green people tap the coming-in place. Someone brings me more food and a silver stick called a fork that looks like a smaller kind of fish spear.

The woman who says she is my grandmother does not come in, but neither does River, though I ask for him again and again.

"Tomorrow," the last green woman says. "I promise. First thing in the morning."

The square sun hurts my eyes, and I'm relieved when she makes it go away and it's dark again. After she is gone, in the dark, I can trick myself into a false sense of comfort and sleep. In the dark, I could be anywhere.

I imagine River that night of my birthday, when he rolled over on his other side and wrapped his arm around me, his warm breath whispering in my hair.

I imagine he is here with me now.

In my hazy half sleep, I hear him whispering to me. "Helmut lied," he's saying.

11

I AWAKE TO THE SOUND of a noise, like a bird pecking a tree, and a different green woman is here, again, with more food. "Good morning," she says as she walks in the coming-in place and turns on the square sun.

"How do you do that?" I ask. My head feels thick with sleep, warm from the pretend River, and then suddenly cold when I realize his presence was nothing more than a dream, again.

"Do what?" she asks.

"Turn the sun off and on like that." I point to the yellow square above me.

"Oh." She wrinkles up her face. "That's a light," she says. She puts the food on top of my stomach and then walks back to the coming-in place. "Look, here's the switch. I press it, and the light goes off." She does, and the sun disappears. "Then I press it again, and it goes back on."

"How?" I ask.

"Electricity," she says. I shake my head. "It's ... it's just a system of wires and energy that gives us power." I shake my head again. "Oh, man," she says. "Maybe I should get Dr. Cabot."

"That's okay," I say, not quite ready to see her again, knowing that now it is tomorrow and she will have news of the D-N-A. Then I realize that I suddenly have to pee, and I think it has been days since I've gone, which I don't understand, but now I have to go. A lot. "Where is Bathroom Tree?" I ask, trying to remember the word that Jeremy used on the boat, but now it escapes me.

"Oh," she says. "They removed your catheter, so that makes sense. It's right through here." She pulls and another coming-in place appears. "Do you need help getting out of bed?" I shake my head, and she nods. "I'll give you some privacy," she says. "And I'll get Dr. Cabot."

After she leaves, I get out of Bed, and my legs feel unsteady. I nearly fall, and I grab onto the side of Bed to catch myself. Then I go and use their strange Bathroom Tree the way River showed me on the boat, and when I'm finished I wipe my hands on the sides of what I'm wearing—which I see now is a white thing that covers most of my body. It's thinner than my rabbit pelt, even though it covers more of my body, and it's cold in here, colder even than Falls first thing in the morning. I shiver.

I walk tentatively to the coming-in place, wondering what lies just beyond. Dr. Cabot called this place Military Hospital, and the green man from yesterday told me River was at Next Door. I sense that means he's close, but also that me walking through the coming-in place now might not be considered behaving, and that if I do, Dr. Cabot might tie me back to Bed and Velcro might run on my wrists. I wonder if next time they will bite, and I shiver.

But I need to see River, and so I push on the coming-in place, the way I've watched all the green people do. The tall square moves a little, and out in the beyond, there is more white, a narrower space, like a pathway between the trees. Only there are no trees and barely any light, and the pathway is narrow. "River," I whisper out into the beyond. "River." I say his name a little louder.

I walk down the pathway until I notice a separation in the white, where a bit of yellow light pours out to where I'm standing, glowing against my bare, cold feet. It's another coming-in place, I realize, and I push on it lightly. "River," I whisper. "Are you in there?"

"Sky?"

I push harder, and beyond the coming-in place, the space looks identical to mine. White, white, white, with Bed in the center. River sits on the end of it now, wearing something strange. Like what the green people wear, only it is not green. The bottom half is blue like the sky, the top part white like sand. It's weird to see him like that, the flesh of his chest and his back and his shoulders hidden. But I don't care. I'm so happy to see him right now.

"River!" I practically jump on him, wrapping him in a giant hug.

"Skyblue," he whispers into my hair, and he strokes my messy braid back, twirling it between his fingers.

"I've been asking and asking for you. But they wouldn't let me see you." It's hard to speak because suddenly I'm choking on tears. River wipes at my cheeks with his thumbs, pushing them away.

"How's your leg?" River asks.

"My leg?" He points, and I look down to my calf, which I notice now is covered with a large white leaf, with a little bit of red—blood—seeping through. That must've been from when I fell that last night on Island. It hurts a little, I realize now. Although I haven't noticed it until this moment.

"They said it was infected," River says.

"Infected?"

"They said you might've died without their help."

"Oh, Riv, come on. It's just a little scrape. The aloe would've fixed it."

He shrugs, and then I notice what it is that's so different about him. Not just what he's wearing but other things, too. The blond hair on his face is gone, and so is his braid. His hair is short and tied back in a small point at the nape of his neck. "They cut your braid," I gasp.

"I did it," he says, pulling back, looking away.

"Why?" He shakes his head, but he doesn't answer. He sits back on the edge of Bed. "We need to find a way to get out of here," I tell him. "I don't trust these people. There's a woman here who says she's my grandmother." My words fall out in a tumble, my voice sounding small, the way it used to when I was very young still, just a child.

"Sky, stop." He takes my arms in his hands. "She is your grandmother."

I shake my head. "How do you know that?"

"I just do," he says.

"You can't possibly remember her." I put my hands on my hips. "You were what, three, when you left here?"

"Four," River says. "And I don't remember . . . her." His voice trails off as if there is more he should tell me.

"But you remember," I say. "Something? Someone?"

He shrugs, but he doesn't say anything else. He holds his lips together, firmly, in a line, and I know he doesn't want to tell me. Whatever it is he knows, he isn't going to let me in on it. Which stings worse than when Sergeant Sawyer poked my arm through the poncho back on the boat. River and I tell each other everything, or we used to.

It occurs to me that everything is different, that River is already different. And not just the way he looks, either, but the way he seems. He stares at me now, as if we haven't shared hundreds of nights and days together, as if here in this strange place he's not even sure he knows me anymore. And it's the first time I understand it, that Island is lost to us now, maybe forever. The thought sinks in my chest like a rock in the water that shared River's name, hard and heavy, and for a moment I'm not sure I can breathe.

"Sky," he says, reaching for my arms, but I shrug him off. "You're going to go with her, and you're going to have a good life here."

"And what about you? You'll come with me?" I ask, my voice still small.

"I can't," he says.

"Why not?"

"Because. I just can't, all right?" He runs his fingers through his shorter hair, and I can tell that he's still not used to it, that he still misses what we've lost, too, even if he isn't going to admit it.

"Riv." I reach for him, but now he's the one who pulls back.

"Listen," he says. "Everything is different now. And we need to figure things out here on our own, okay?"

"Our own?"

"You'll be with your grandmother. You'll love it."

"And you?" He shrugs. "River," I say, "I'm not going anywhere without you. I've been with you forever, and I'm not going to let these green people keep me from seeing you."

He shakes his head. "They didn't," he says softly.

"Yes, they did. I've been asking for you since I woke up."

"I know," he says, and then he looks down and lowers his voice. "I told them I thought it was better if we didn't see each other. I told them I didn't want to see you."

His words are so sharp, like that stone cutting through the belly of the fish, and now he's cutting through me, ripping out my guts, throwing them away carelessly. Red entrails twisting in the wind, staining all this awful whiteness.

"I don't understand," I whisper.

He reaches out and twirls the end of my braid one last time. "You take care of yourself." His voice trembles, and I think maybe he wants to cry, except his face is solidly emotionless, his skin smooth the way I remember it as a child. He's running next to me on Beach, sitting in the sand, drawing with me.

"River," I say one last time.

"No," he says. "Not River." He pauses. "Lucas."

———

Back in my own space, I find myself crying. On Island the only time I remember feeling this way was after I dragged my mother's limp body into Ocean. But now there are tears I don't even know I had, and they come and they come, until my chest rattles like a trap that has snapped its kill, and suddenly the entire world is dead, silent.

"I've got good news," Dr. Cabot says, stepping in through the coming-in place. She stares at me for a moment, raising her thick blond eyebrows, as if she thinks about asking me what's wrong, but then she seems to change her mind. "DNA is back, and you are who we thought you are. We're clearing you with customs as we speak, and then we'll be able to release you into your grandmother's custody." She pauses. "Of course, I will be happy to assist you with whatever you need after that, but your grandmother insisted she's bringing in her own private psychiatrist to work with you in her home."

"And what if I don't want to go?" I whisper.

"You're a minor in the state of California," she says. "And so by law we have to . . ."

I don't understand what she's saying, and though she is still talking, I stop listening because I do understand I'm going to have to go . . . somewhere, that I can't stay here, in Military Hospital, the whiteness, forever. I wouldn't even want to. I can't go back to Island, and even if I could, I would be alone, and I wouldn't want to be there alone. River—no, *Lucas*—doesn't want to be with me here, now that he has a choice. On Island, I never questioned my place in the world, where I belonged, where I'm supposed to be. Now I am a girl without a place. It's worse than hunger—it's the saddest, most lonely thing I've ever felt.

Dr. Cabot sits down next to Bed, and she picks up my hand. Her fingers are fleshier than the woman who called herself my grandmother, thick and full, and if they were covered in blond hair, they might remind me of Helmut's. "Now, I know all this must be very scary for you." I shake my head. How can she know anything? "And this is all going to take some getting used to after everything you've been through. But I promise you"— she squeezes my hand—"you're going to love it here once you adjust." I pull my hand away from her and turn on my side, facing away. "Why don't you relax for a bit," she says. "Your grandmother should be allowed to take you home within the hour."

12

I DO NOT UNDERSTAND BEGINNINGS, that things happened to me once, before I could remember them. There are beginnings on Island I can't remember, either. Getting there, for one. The origins of Shelter or the wooden traps. The beginning of Tree of Days and Cooler. I know the stories, the things my mother told me about The Others Who We Never Met, The Accident, that Helmut was so good at surviving, that we were so lucky to have him. I know that every 365 days, counting from the thirty-second notch on Tree of Days, I turned another year older, and that every 365 days from the fifty-sixth notch on Tree of Days, River did.

But now my memory is like Ocean. It moves in and out, back and forth. Sometimes it brings me gifts and sometimes it takes them away just as quickly.

Helmut always told us that memories are things that never happened, stories we make up in our mind to make ourselves feel better. River tried to argue with him about this once.

"That's not true," River said, shaking his head hard. He was younger then, stupid enough to think he actually had a chance at winning an argument with Helmut. "I remember my mother," River told him once, "and she loved me."

"That's ridiculous." Helmut laughed. "You didn't even know your mother. She died before you were born. Petal is the only mother you've ever known."

My mother nodded and murmured in agreement, though she was frowning, her forehead dewy and shining with sweat the way it always got when the sun was too high in the sky, too bright, too hot.

"I knew her," River insisted to me later as we sat in Cove By Falls together, leaving my mother and Helmut to have their alone time in Shelter, which they asked us for at least once every seven notches, sometimes more.

River dangled his feet in the water. He was smaller than me then. Shorter and thinner. Sometimes I thought I might be strong enough to pick him up and hang him over my shoulders. Helmut said I could, before he laughed, like he was joking.

"I knew my mother," River told me. "Helmut is wrong."

"You're an idiot," I told him, skimming the water with my feet so it splashed up at him. "Memories are just stories you tell yourself."

<hr>

Helmut did not believe in stories. Not memories. Not anything. My mother told River and me the story once of two animals in a boat, going out to sea. The owl and the pussycat.

They sailed away for a year and a day, and they danced by the light of the moon.

She smiled as she said it, as if maybe this was her memory. Her story. I tried to imagine her and Helmut out in Ocean, dancing together.

"Who am I in this stupid scenario?" Helmut growled. "The owl or the cat?"

"What's a cat?" River asked.

"It's kind of like a rabbit," my mother answered.

The owl. Helmut was the owl. Of course.

———

I think about all this now as I sit at the edge of Bed, waiting for the grandmother woman to come back for me. I think about River's memories, his stories, his insistence once that his mother was real, that he could honestly remember her, as something he could touch, a real person. Not just a story.

Maybe he's already forgotten everything else. All the nights in Shelter where we slept back to back. The fish he caught me as a present. The pictures he drew me in the sand, the wet flowers he handed me on the night of the mushrooms.

The way he just pushed me away in his space, as if he didn't care about me, as if he never even cared at all, makes it feel like all the things we did together on Island, they are memories, too. Untrue stories I am telling myself. Things that never even happened. Things that meant nothing.

And then I wonder if River is leaving this place with this woman he thinks he remembers: his *mother*. If suddenly she means more to him than I ever did. If River loves her more than he loves me.

And then it feels like I know nothing now. I am nothing.

13

THE GRANDMOTHER WOMAN ARRIVES TOO soon. Without a view of the sun overhead, I don't know how much time has actually passed since Dr. Cabot left, but I do know I'm not ready to see the grandmother woman again, to go somewhere with her.

She walks in, and today she is wearing night, black. Her hair is down, and short, I notice now, just at her shoulders. Her strange purple lips twitch and then form a smile as she hands me a pile of things.

"What's this?" I ask her.

"Blue jeans, T-shirt, panties, bra, and flip-flops."

I stare at her, unsure what she expects me to do with this stuff or if she expects me to thank her. I sniff it and it smells sweet, like flowers. "I don't understand," I finally say.

She smiles in that strange way that makes her seem more nervous than happy. The same look my mother got when Helmut was gone too long or his voice got too loud. "Clothes, what we wear here," she says. "Let me help you get this stuff on."

She tugs at my thin white pelt until I stand there before her, cold and naked, and embarrassed that this woman I don't know is seeing me like this.

But then she averts her eyes, as if she is embarrassed, too, and she holds the pieces out to me one by one:

Panties. "Pull them over your legs."

Bra. "Here, let me," and she hooks it around my ribs.

Blue jeans. "Over the legs again"—which I don't understand, since panties already cover my womanly parts.

T-shirt. "Over the head; pull your arms through."

And then last—flip-flops on my feet.

I feel strange in all this . . . stuff. Everything is too tight, and it's hard to breathe. But the grandmother woman doesn't seem to notice. As soon as all her clothes are on my body, she takes my arms and pulls me out the coming-in place.

"You're going to love the house," she says. And we walk back into the long pathway where I walked earlier and found River. "We're walking distance to the Pacific Ocean, so you'll feel right at home."

She holds tightly to my arm, pulling me, and I feel light like a bird. I glide along next to her, skimming the water, as if I can walk on it. She talks, and her words feel very far away and empty. I'm dressed just like River now, I think, in these strange, uncomfortable things that tug at my stomach and my chest. *River.* His coming-in place is open, and as we walk by his space, I see that it is already empty. River is gone, without me. I'm not sure if I will ever see him again, and I bite my lip to keep from crying.

"Do you know where he went?" I ask the grandmother woman now.

"Who?" she says.

"River."

"Who?"

"Lucas," I say, the word feeling funny on my tongue.

"Oh." She stops walking for a moment and looks at me. "Don't worry about him," she says. "He'll be fine. Okay? I promise you. And besides, we have so much else to talk about." Her voice goes on and on, like the bright green birds that would chatter all night just before the rains. Helmut got so mad at their squawking that he swore if he ever saw one, he'd climb the tree and wring its neck. They were smart birds; they never showed themselves when they were that loud. "Now, I know you have a lot to learn," she is saying now, "so anything you don't know, you can ask me. Don't be afraid. And I have a team of professionals coming to the house. You'll be so much more comfortable there than in some sort of . . . establishment."

I nod, though I don't really understand what she's saying. Except it seems she is right about one thing. I have a lot to learn. When we reach the end of the pathway, then turn, then walk down another, and then finally go out a coming-in place and into real sunlight, everything is unfamiliar.

The ground is black like the night sky and hard beneath my feet, which already feel strange in these terrible flip-flops. They flap and make weird squawking noises as I walk, and my toes slip away. I don't understand why I have them on, and I reach down to take them off.

"Don't do that, honey." The grandmother woman stops me with her hand. "The ground is dirty." I wonder if that means there is nothing like Falls here, that there is no way to get clean

74

in California, and the thought makes my heart pound. *Everything is different. Everything is wrong. River is gone.*

I look up to catch the sky. I feel like it's been forever since I've seen it, and I want it to comfort me now, to show me that something here is as it always was. But even that looks different. Less blue and more white gray. The air is cold against my skin, and I shiver.

"I should've brought you a sweatshirt," she says, and she looks up to the sky, too. "It isn't always like this. This is just June gloom, the marine layer hanging around a little longer than it should. Give it a month and the sky will blue up again in the afternoons. The air will warm up a little, too."

I don't answer her but I look around. In the distance there are pale brown hills, higher than anything I have ever seen. They are blank, like the sand, missing green trees. A few palms dot the far side of this blackness we are standing on, but they are different from the palms I know, thinner, flimsier. And between us and them, there are rows and rows of strange, oddly shaped . . . bushes? All different colors and sizes, but very shiny like sea glass, dotting the blackness.

The grandmother woman takes my arm and pulls me toward one of them, a red one, the color of what she was wearing when she first came to see me. She pulls something out of the rabbit pelt container over her shoulder and then reaches in front of me to pull the strange bush—(or maybe it's a cave?)—apart. "Go ahead," she says. "Get in."

I shake my head. I have no idea what this is or what it will do to me. The inside looks like a small black cave, and I'm afraid I might become trapped.

"Oh, good lord," she says. "I didn't even think . . ." She puts her hand on my arm. "Honey, this is a car. This is how people get from place to place. I turn it on with my key." She holds up the thing in her hand. "And then I power the engine on, and it takes us where we want to go."

I think of the engine on the boat, the way it moved so far and so fast once Roger turned it on, Island becoming like a tiny shell behind us. "Like the boat?" I ask her now.

"Yes, sort of. Only it takes us places on land."

"Why can't we walk?"

"Oh." She laughs. "Honey, think of it this way: this island where you've been all this time, it's the size of this freckle." She points to a tiny brown spot on her wrist. "And, California, well, it's the size of this." She gestures to show the length of her body. "It would take us two days to walk home from here. "We're not all that close. Even in the car, it'll take a good thirty minutes or more. Freeway traffic this time of day, well, it could take even longer."

Nothing she says makes sense. *Freeway? Traffic? California is the size of her body? Island the size of a brown spot on her arm?* But I understand that I need to do what she's asking or stand here in this strange blackness forever. So I get into Car Cave, and I let her tie a rope around me, which she promises will keep me safe. I don't argue with her, because, really, what other choice do I have now?

And this, I begin to realize, might be the worst feeling of all. Even worse than being here without River. On Island, especially this past year, every decision I made was my own. But here, I'm so lost. I know nothing. *I am nothing.* All I can do, for now, is listen to her and do as she says.

I watch as she moves her key, turning it funny as if she was going to roast it like a fish over Fire Pit.

Suddenly I hear a loud noise, like the rush of Ocean in my ears, only harder, louder, the way Ocean would sound if it pulled me under and I would have to struggle for a moment to find my way back to the surface to breathe.

But then I understand Car Cave is moving, pulling my body, not gently, along with it.

Black whirs around us. To my side, Military Hospital slowly grows smaller, just the way Island did as the boat moved across Ocean. And soon we have whirred so much I can no longer see Military Hospital at all.

I put my hand up to try to stop everything from moving so fast, to hold on and catch a fistful of the air, but my hand slams into something hard. I push and I push, grasping to feel the air against my skin.

"Oh, honey, don't do that," the grandmother woman says. "You'll hurt yourself on the window."

We are still for a moment, and I stop pushing. There is a small red sun in front of us, and I sigh, thinking this is over. But then the sun turns green, and we are flying, as if Car Cave is a bird and we're riding its wings.

Suddenly there are these strange cars everywhere, all around us, so close, moving so fast. So many colors, a swirl of water and sand, sky and rocks, birds and trees, and one that is red, like blood, that moves so close to us, I think I could touch it, or that it might touch me—and crush me—and I push my hand harder now to try to push myself out, to save myself.

I clutch my stomach with my hand that is not pushing to get out. I start gagging and I know it, that all the strange food I ate at Military Hospital is going to come back up.

As suddenly as it began, the motion stops, the grandmother woman escapes, runs to my side, and is pulling the rope off me to let me out of Car Cave and into the cool rush of noisy air.

Just in time for all the food to come back up, swirling in strange colors against the black ground.

"Oh, honey," she says, rubbing my back. "I wasn't thinking. I'm sorry. The freeway is a lot sometimes, even for me."

She keeps rubbing my back, until the food stops coming, until I sigh and wish all the strange whirring cars away. I wish for Ocean, the starry sky, the sounds green birds make at night.

"I'll get off at the next exit," she says, "and we'll take the side streets back. Fewer cars, a little slower going." She pauses. "You tell me if you need to be sick again, and I'll pull over."

I nod, because I sense she is trying to help me now, even though I don't understand most of what she just said. And besides, I don't think there is anything left in me. My stomach is empty; I am empty.

She helps me back behind the rope in Car Cave, but before she walks back to her place and moves her key again, she says, "Why don't you try to close your eyes. It might help a little bit." She pauses. And then she says softly, "That's what I used to tell your mother, when she was a little girl and she'd get carsick."

My mother, in Car Cave? I shake my head because it doesn't feel real. But I do as she says and close my eyes.

A woman begins singing softly in my ear, and I have no idea who she is or why she's here. I hadn't noticed anyone else in Car Cave, and her voice sounds different from the grandmother woman's, higher, more pure. I like it. It reminds me of my mother, the way she'd sing me to sleep in Shelter when I was little, holding on to me tightly, singing about the sunshine.

I can't go back there, she pleaded with Helmut.

Skeletons, she told me. *Everyone is broken there.*

I squeeze my eyes shut tightly, picturing the lull of Ocean, the great expanse of nothingness lying beyond it, River's fingers tangling in my braid, my belly full with my birthday fish. Just a memory now. And if Helmut was right about memory, then that means nothing about my life on Island was real. As if my whole life up until now has been nothing but a dream.

14

EVENTUALLY THE MOTION OF CAR Cave stops again, and there is quiet. "We're here," the grandmother woman says, and I open my eyes, at last. *Here?* "Home, sweet home."

In front of me is something large, what I'm guessing is her shelter. It's unlike anything I have ever seen or imagined up until now. A very tall, high multicolored square reaching for the sky.

She unties her rope, gets out, and opens up Car Cave for me. She tugs on my hand to pull me out, and I keep myself limp, holding on to her, following her, allowing her to pull me.

Suddenly I hear the flutter of a flock of noisy birds, then the flashing of a hundred suns. I turn, and there are people rushing up behind us. So many of them, all at once, that I can't remember how to breathe.

"Mrs. Henderson, how does it feel to have your granddaughter back after all this time?"

"No comment," the grandmother woman says, holding up her hands to block away the man's sun.

"Megan," another voice calls, a woman. "How did it feel to be Helmut Almstedt's captive all these years?"

I turn, and she stands behind me, waving a stick in my face. Her sun, her electricity, is so bright, I can barely see in the wash of yellow.

"Come on." The grandmother woman grabs my shoulders tightly and spins me toward her shelter. "Just ignore them." She turns back. "Get off my property, or I'll call the police," she yells.

Then she pulls something from her rabbit pelt, presses a tiny square, and a large, wide coming-in place begins to open in front of us. "This is the garage," she says. "Come on in. Don't be nervous, honey. Don't look behind you." She pulls me into the large, dark square, hits the tiny square in her hand again, and the coming-in place closes behind us. We stand there in the darkness for a moment.

"What did she mean, Helmut's captive?" I ask. I can still hear the flock of them squawking behind the closed coming-in place. *Captive*. It sounds like "capture," which makes me think of the rabbits and birds in our traps.

"Oh, Megan, honey . . ." She sighs, but she doesn't answer my question. She twirls the end of my braid with her fingers, almost like River always did, except it doesn't feel the same from her, and I pull away, out of her reach. "We'll need to get your hair taken care of, won't we?" she says. "But first things first, I guess. Come on, let's go inside."

She pulls my hand, and I follow, wondering what she means about getting my hair taken care of and why she didn't answer my question about Helmut. I think of River's short hair, the way he looks so different now. *River*. Helmut's son, looking so much like him that Roger thought he was him. How does the grandmother woman know Helmut? How did Roger and Jeremy know him? How did that woman holding the stick in my face know him?

Then I think, none of them knew him. How could they? I am the only one. River and I, we're the only two left who knew him.

—————·—————

My first memory of Helmut is watching as he snapped a rabbit's neck, quickly, precisely, so its head fell limp, ready for us to skin it. This is truth; this happened. I know it did, no matter what Helmut always said about memory, and as I think about it now, I wonder if Helmut's insistence about memory was only right for things that happened *away from* Island. Everything seems so different here; maybe memory is different, too?

That morning, with the rabbit, I felt my mother flinch as she wrapped her arm around me. She had one arm around me, one around River. She always held us to her like that, as if we were both her children, not just me. River hid his eyes in my mother's hip then, but I watched, eyes wide open. Fascinated? Horrified? I don't know.

"Come on, Sky," Helmut said, looking at me, smiling. "You can be my helper."

"Oh, Helmut." My mother shook her head. "Really, she's too young."

"Are you? Too young?" he said, staring straight into my eyes. His eyes were the color of palm bark. When they held you, you

82

did not dare look away. I was four, maybe five. But I shook my head. He laughed. "She's a tough one, Petal," he said to my mother, whose arm pulled around me tighter. "Come on, Sky. Show my boy how it's done, why don't you?" River still had his eyes turned into my mother's pelt, and I felt bad for him. But the dead animal seemed appealing to me in a way, too. I wanted to know. What to do with it, how to, as Helmut always put it, make it useful.

Helmut handed me the sharp stone. "We'll bleed it, then cut away the fur for a pelt. Then we'll clean it in Falls and roast the meat for dinner." I nodded. "Right here," he said, pointing to the rabbit's neck. "You make the first cut."

I took a deep breath and gripped tightly to the stone, and then I did as he asked. Helmut smiled over me to my mother. "What a good girl you have here, Petal." He tousled my hair with his large, wide palm. "Now," he said, "you'll have the honor of cooking us dinner tonight." He paused. "Why don't you watch her, River? You might actually learn something."

15

I FOLLOW THE GRANDMOTHER WOMAN into her shelter through a place she calls Laundry Room. There are tall, square boxes on one side that she tells me she uses to wash and dry clothes. I'm relieved that there is some way to get clean here, but it seems strange to put your clothes in a box to wash them rather than Falls, and to dry them in a box, too? Does the California air not dry things as the air on Island did?

I follow behind her, letting my hands graze everything, while the grandmother woman spouts off new and unfamiliar words: *Wall. Door. Handle. Mirror. Floor. Railing.* So many words I don't know, so many things I have never seen. I don't think I'll be able to remember them all exactly as she's told them to me. And it makes me feel so tired now to think that I will have to.

Then I follow her up what she calls *Steps*. And they are, I realize, like the rock hill on the boat, only they are softer, and she says it's okay to take the flip-flops off in here, so I do. Steps sink beneath my toes like soft, warm sand, but the grains do not stick to the bottom of my feet. I follow behind her slowly, basking in the feel of my bare feet on something other than flip-flops.

At the top of Steps, there is another pathway, *Hallway*. I follow her down it and then through a coming-in place, no, *Door*.

"Here you have it, honey," she says. "This will be your bedroom. I hope you like it. It used to be your mother's once upon a time."

"My mother's?" I whisper, and I try to imagine her here, in this space, among all this, wearing the strange sorts of things I'm wearing, feeling the strange sorts of things I'm feeling. But when I close my eyes and try to picture her, all I can see is the way she looked lying there in Shelter, that last morning, her lips parted slightly and as blue as Ocean.

I open my eyes again and take in *Bedroom*. It's a square, like the space in Military Hospital, only it's pink like the shells on my bracelet were, with Pink Bed in the middle, and square drawings of Ocean on all the walls. The grandmother woman seems to notice me staring at them. "I just hung these pictures up this morning," she says. "To make you feel at home."

Pictures. I think of the picture she showed me of the baby human and my mother, and how it seems pictures can be all things. I reach out and touch one, and it's cool and smooth, nothing at all like the real thing. Just like the picture of my mother.

"You said it was close," I whisper, running my hand against the pretend water.

"What is, honey?"

"Ocean."

She nods. "Yes, the ocean's just two blocks from here."

"I want to go there," I say.

"Of course," she tells me. "But why don't you get some rest first. The doctor said your leg is still healing, and we need to make sure you take it easy and keep up with your antibiotics."

"I've already rested," I tell her. "I want to see Ocean."

She walks over to the thing I think she called *Window*, then quickly pulls a stick to, as she says it, *close the blinds*. It makes Pink Bedroom turn dark, and I wish she hadn't. "They're like vultures." She shakes her head.

"Vultures?" Vultures, I know. Giant birds that would swoop in on the remains of dead animals. It was why we always put anything dead we didn't eat back into Ocean, the place Helmut told us the dead would become whole again and come back to us anew, as fresh food. But still, the vultures came and circled sometimes when we could not eat the meat fast enough. They would frighten me, with their giant wingspan, their yellow eyes, the way they would circle, hovering, waiting for just the right time to drop.

"When it quiets down out there, we'll go to the ocean, okay? The safest place for you to be now is here."

I don't understand why there's safety in Pink Bedroom, with Fake Ocean surrounding me. But I nod because I don't know what else to do.

"What do you like to eat, honey?" she asks me. "Whatever it is, you tell me, and I'll cook it for you for dinner."

"Fish," I say tentatively, thinking of River's face on the afternoon of my birthday, the way he grinned as he let his catch span the length of his arms.

"Fish," the grandmother woman says. "What kind of fish. Like sushi?"

"What's sushi?" I ask.

"Raw fish."

"Yuck." I shake my head. "You eat fish raw?" I think about the pink bloody flesh of the fish River caught me, and the thought turns my stomach.

"Sometimes, yes. But I can cook it, if that's how you like it." She pauses. "Is that how you ate it . . . there?"

I nod. "You have Fire Pit to cook it here?" I ask her, feeling hopeful that something here is the same, that there will be one thing I know, I understand.

"Sort of," she says. "I have a grill in the backyard." She reaches into her rabbit pelt container and pulls out a small, flat square. She presses on it, then holds it up to her ear and starts talking. "Hi, Ben," she says. "Can you do me a huge favor? Did your mom leave you the car today? She did. Okay, yes. Good. Can you run to Sandy's and bring me back some salmon. Or maybe halibut. You know what? Get both."

I'm not sure if she's talking to me or not, but her voice moves so fast, and she's not looking at me now, so I sit on the edge of Pink Bed and breathe deeply. I think of the way River looked sitting this way, when I saw him earlier. The way he wrapped his arms around me and whispered *Skyblue* into my hair. And the way he told me that we had to make our own way here, that he wanted to be without me.

I think of that morning again, my birthday. *Do you feel any different today, Sky?* My mother had told me that it would happen. *One day*, she would always say, *when you and River are older, you'll see each other differently. And that will be okay. That will be good. You'll be the ones to keep life on Island going.*

I think about River's hands on my bare back, the next morning, as we swam past Fishing Cove, the way I felt something as he pulled me close—warmth.

The way I felt about River, I realize now, might have been changing ever-so-slowly, creeping up on me, the way Helmut used to track a boar, slowly, patiently, with stealth.

But what about River? Did he feel anything that morning in the water, too, or was it just like any other time we swam together and our bare skin touched?

I understand that he feels different now, though I don't understand why. That morning was not that long ago, I realize, though now that I haven't made notches on Tree of Days each morning, I'm not really sure exactly how long it's been. Still, I know it hasn't been that long, and yet it feels like a lifetime.

I feel different now. Older. Younger. Confused. But I still wish River were here so I could tell him. So I could hold on to him next to Fake Ocean and ask him to go with me to the real thing, vultures or no.

I lean back into Pink Bed and close my eyes, and it's almost as if I can imagine myself there again, on Island, with River. And even with my mother and Helmut.

Though I told the grandmother woman I didn't need to rest, that I had already rested, as soon as I close my eyes and bask in the warm glow of the sand and Ocean, Falls and Shelter, I feel myself getting sleepy, just the way I did that night after I ate all the fish and River and I fell together on the rabbit pelt mats. I want to sleep so he can be with me again.

But just on the edge of dreaming, River and my mother so close, I hear the voice of the strange woman waving the stick in my face: *How did it feel to be Helmut Almstedt's captive all these years?*

16

IT'S DARK WHEN I OPEN my eyes again, and it takes me a moment to remember where I am, how I got here. I can't make out the pictures of Fake Ocean in the darkness, and though the grandmother woman says it's close, I can't smell or hear Ocean the way I always could on Island.

I stand up, and my leg is sore now. I walk carefully in the darkness, not sure if Pink Bedroom has light electricity or not. Door is slightly open, and Hallway is glowing.

"Hello," I call out, frightened for a moment that there could be vultures here, inside the grandmother woman's shelter. "Hello," I call again.

"Oh, Megan, you're awake." The grandmother woman stands beyond Steps. And though she has been very kind to me today, when she calls me Megan, I suddenly hate her, and I have the urge to run. Though where I'd go, I'm not sure. "I was just about to wake you," she says. "Come on down. Your fish is cooked. Careful on the steps. Use the railing."

She's pointing as she talks, and I remember *the railing* is the long, thin stick. I'm not sure how she wants me to use it, so I test its sturdiness with the foot on my good leg.

"No, no, no." She waves her arms in the air. "Not like that. Just hold on to it with your hand as you walk, so you don't fall. Like this, see?" She climbs Steps, then back down, touching *the railing* to show me.

I nod and do as she says, though *the railing* seems strange to me. All those times I climbed the twenty paces down Grassy Hill to Falls, and I never had anything to hold on to.

When I get to the bottom of Steps, I realize I have to pee, so I ask her where Bathroom Tree is. She frowns, but then she says, "Right through here." I follow her down Small Hallway until she opens White Door. "Make sure to wash your hands when you're done, okay? You know how to do that, right?" I shake my head slowly, and she shows me what she calls *the sink* and *the faucet*. When she lifts the faucet up, water pours out into the sink like a very small, clear Falls washing into a container. "And use soap," she says, going through the motions, showing me what she wants me to do.

I'm getting impatient because I really have to pee, so I start taking the rectangle off while she's rubbing her hands together, creating white sea foam. She pushes the faucet down, and the water disappears.

"Megan," she says, "what are you doing?" She pulls the rectangle from me and places it back.

"I really have to pee," I say.

"But leave that there. Have you been going in the toilet tank?" She sounds angry, and I'm not sure, so I shrug. "Oh dear lord," she says. "Here. You sit here." She points to the circle rim where I'd been resting my feet. "And then when you're done, you flush." She pushes something, and all the water begins to swirl down, down, away.

"Where does the water go?" I ask.

"Oh, I don't know. The sewer, I suppose."

That means nothing to me. "I really have to go," I say.

"Oh, okay. I'm sorry, honey." She puts her hand on my shoulder and walks out, closing Door behind her. "Don't forget to pull your pants and underwear down first!" she yells. "And pull them back up when you're finished."

It's seems like so much to remember, so much effort, all just to pee. Pants down. Pants up. Flush. The faucet. Soap.

Everything is so much harder here.

———— ·—·— ————

The grandmother woman is waiting for me in Small Hallway when I'm finished. "I heard you flush and turn the sink on and off," she says, patting me on the shoulder. "Good." It's embarrassing that she has been listening for my noises, and I wonder if she also listened for the strange sound of my pee hitting the water. On Island, everyone knew that if you were at Bathroom Tree you were to be left alone, that it was a place for privacy.

"Now, come on into the kitchen," she's saying. I follow her into a large open space with a lot of square wood boxes everywhere. "Have a seat at the table." She points to a large, round wood, and I begin to climb up on it. "No, no. On a chair," she says, pulling on another, smaller wood and showing me how she wants me to sit on it. I do, and that's when I notice we're not alone, that there is a boy here, standing across the space, holding on to a container like the one that brought me the disgusting coconut milk at Military Hospital.

"Hi." He waves and puts the container down in front of me.

"Oh, Megan," the grandmother woman says. "This is Ben. He lives next door. He went out and got the fish for us."

"Some coconut milk," he says, putting the container down in front of me. I notice that he's tall, like River, but his hair is brown and curly like mine, and short, very short, just below his ears. He has brown eyes, and his voice shakes a little when he talks.

"Ben is your age," the grandmother woman says. "His mom works a lot, so he spends a lot of time here. Keeps an old woman company, don't you, doll?" She puts an arm around his shoulders and hugs him to her.

I sniff the container and remember the sour taste of coconut milk at Military Hospital. "I don't think I like the coconut milk here," I say.

"Oh." The grandmother woman frowns. "How do you know?"

"I had some yesterday."

"Oh." She laughs. "That was probably cow's milk. This is actually coconut milk. I made a special trip to Trader Joe's this morning to pick some up for you."

She pushes the container closer to me, so that I feel I have no choice but to drink it. I hold the container to my lips and pour a small amount down my throat. It's not awful, like the other milk. But it's not exactly the same as real coconut milk, either. It's too sweet, and too cold. It sticks in my throat.

"It's good, right?" she asks. I nod because she sounds so eager to please me. She puts some fish meat on the circle in front of me she calls *a plate*, and it smells good, almost familiar, like my birthday fish. I scoop the meat up with my fingers, and she hands me a fork spear. But I put it back down and keep eating with my fingers. I realize she and Ben are just standing there, watching me eat, but I don't even care. I'm so hungry now, and the fish tastes so good. Even on *a plate*, in this strange faraway place.

I fill my belly, and for a little while, it is like filling myself with hope, that maybe everything here will be okay.

———•———

After I have eaten an entire fish and my belly is full, I tell the grandmother woman again that I want to see Ocean.

She sighs, walks away, and then walks back. "They're still out there," she says. "It'll die down in a few days."

"I could take her," Ben says softly. "We'll go out the back, climb the fence into my yard, and then take the back path there."

"I don't know." The grandmother woman frowns.

"Yes," I say, though I am not sure about Ben and whether I can trust him. But he is offering to take me to Ocean, and that is all that I care about now.

"I don't know," she says again, but her voice breaks, so I think that means yes. My mother used to do the same thing, when Helmut would ask her to do something she didn't really want to, and it surprises me that they can seem so much the same, even though they are not the same at all.

"Come on," Ben says. "Follow me." Then he turns to the grandmother woman and says, "We'll be back in twenty minutes, Alice. I promise."

17

THE AIR OUTSIDE THE GRANDMOTHER woman's shelter is cool and damp, and I shiver a little as I follow Ben into the night. The sky is black and gray, with barely any yellow stars. I spot the half-moon hugging a gray streak of cloud, but I can't find Venus where it should be, resting just below it.

I'm wearing flip-flops again, and I find it hard to walk quietly, as Ben said we must so that we don't "tip off the press."

"Come on," Ben whispers, and he climbs over what he calls *Fence*, then reaches out his hand to help me. But I am good at climbing, having climbed trees on Island to get coconuts since I was very young, and I do it without his help now, though I take the flip-flops off first.

On the other side of Fence, there are trees, tall and thick and different looking from palms. But trees nonetheless. I inhale their sharp smell and reach my hand out to touch one. It's sharp, and I pull back. "Pine trees," Ben whispers. "Much nicer to look at than to touch."

We walk for a few minutes in the darkness, through pine trees. Ben tries to hold on to my hand, he says so he won't lose me. His hand is large and damp, and unfamiliar feeling. I think about River, as we went that last morning together, hand in hand, toward Fishing Cove, the boat. And I pull my hand away from Ben. "I don't get lost," I tell him, and he nods and watches me so carefully that it makes me feel nervous to be walking next to him.

But it's not long before I can smell Ocean, hear it, and then I run past Ben toward Beach. I couldn't get lost here, by Ocean. I pull the flip-flops off again and let my toes sink into the sand.

The sand is colder and harder here than it ever was on Island, but still the grains are familiar, sticking between my toes. The rush of Ocean sounds the same, too. And in the small glow of the half-moon, the water is black. I run toward it, and as the tide rushes against my toes I jump and howl a little bit. "It's so cold," I say to Ben.

He nods. "Welcome to California," he says. He's breathing hard, having run to catch up to me.

"But this is the Pacific?"

"Yep."

I shake my head. I don't understand it, how this could be the same great warm Ocean that I've known my entire life. And then I realize just how far away I am, just how different this California world is. Even Ocean isn't *really* the same.

"Is this where you came to catch the fish?" I ask Ben now, trying to console myself with the thought that fish are here, too, as on Island. That despite all the distance, the cold water, the fish still swim here.

"No." Ben laughs. "I didn't catch the fish. I bought it. At the fish market." I don't know what that is, and he seems to understand that, so he explains. "There are people here who catch fish, and then they take it to this place where people like me go to buy it. That's the fish market."

"How do you buy it?" I ask.

"I gave them some money, and they gave me the fish."

"Oh," I say. "Okay." Though I'm still confused.

I step back from the water's edge and look at him. His face looks very small in the glow of the moon, and even though the grandmother woman said he was my age, there's something about him that seems so much younger.

I sit down on the sand, and he sits next to me. I don't sink as much as I'd expect—this sand is much harder than the sand I'm used to, especially this close to the water. "It must've been kind of cool to live on an island like that," Ben says softly. "I mean, you probably didn't have to deal with all the crap we have here. Like curfews and homework and school."

I don't know what any of that is, either, but I don't ask. I just say, "Yeah. I guess not."

"I've been thinking about it all day. Trying to see this place as you must see it now. Guess it kind of sucks here, doesn't it?"

On Island we would suck the moist meat off the bones of fish, but I don't understand what that has to do with being here, in this strange place, as Ben says it. But from his voice, *sucks here* sounds like something bad. I don't answer him; I lace my fingers through the sand, digging until the grains grind under my nails and seep between my fingers. "Can I ask you something?" I say.

"Sure."

"Do you know who Helmut is?"

"Of course." He nods. "Everyone knows who he is."

"But how?" I ask. "He was on Island for . . ." I try to remember what Dr. Cabot told me. "Fourteen years." I pause. "If you're my age, then you would've been, what, two, when he was here?"

"Yeah." Ben nods. "I didn't *know* him know him. But I know of him. Everyone does. Urban legend."

"But how do you know Urban Legend?" I ask, not at all sure what he means. Though I wonder if this is the same way Roger and Jeremy knew Helmut, too.

"Google." He pauses. "That probably doesn't mean anything to you, does it?" I shake my head. "Well, before he left California he, um . . . well. Maybe I shouldn't be the one to tell you this." He stands, but I tug on his arm until he sits back down.

"Tell me. Please," I say, though I'm not sure if I want to hear what he's going to say or not.

"Okay, well, when he lived here, he had this group of people who lived with him, and he was kind of their leader. Some bad things happened. I mean, he did them, I guess. And then he got in a boat and took his people with him, and they, like, basically fell off the face of the earth."

"I don't know what that means," I say, though I suddenly have this awful, sick feeling in my chest, and I'm worried all that delicious fish is about to come back up, into Cold Ocean.

"You should ask your grandmother. She'll be able to explain it to you better. She actually knew him, I think." I nod, though I have a feeling that even if I ask her, she won't tell me. That she will just start talking about something else the way she did when

I asked her if she knew where River went. But also I don't believe what Ben just told me, that Helmut did something really bad before he left. I don't know if Ben is lying or maybe the person, Google, who told him about Helmut, might've been.

"Come on," Ben says now, standing again. "We better get back before Alice gets worried."

I stand up and follow him, inhaling the salty smell. Cold Ocean smells just as Ocean always did, and I calm myself with this thought. There is something here, something familiar.

And on the walk back, I watch carefully where Ben steps, memorizing the pathway back through the pine trees, so when I need to I can escape from the grandmother woman's shelter and come back to Cold Ocean all on my own.

18

I AWAKE THE NEXT MORNING with the smell of Ocean still in my nose, and it takes me a little time to realize it was either a dream or a memory. That you cannot really smell Ocean from here, Pink Bedroom. I check, and Fake Ocean does not have a smell.

"Megan, honey." The grandmother woman opens Door, and there she is, standing in Pink Bedroom, looking almost as strange and unfamiliar as she did yesterday as she handed me clothes in Military Hospital.

My stomach rumbles, and I wish I'd saved some of the fish from last night to eat now. But before I can even ask her, she says, "Come on downstairs and eat some breakfast, and then I have someone coming over to meet you."

"Someone?" I ask, hopeful that it could be River, that he has changed his mind and he has found me this quickly.

"Her name is Missusfairfield," she says. "We've been friends for a long time, and she is very good with teaching special-needs children. She's retired now, but she has agreed to meet you and possibly take you on as a private study."

I sigh, not understanding any of what she said, hearing only that this person with the very strange long name is not River, and that she is re-tired. I feel re-tired myself, as if all this is just too much, as if it would be easier to sleep and sleep and sleep and make it all go away. But I am also hungry, and the grand-mother woman promised breakfast. So I allow her to take my hand and pull me gently from Bed.

"How's that leg feeling?" she asks as I put my feet on the soft ground.

I shrug and follow her down Steps, holding on to the railing as she reminds me to. Nothing hurts, not even my leg. But there is an emptiness in me now, here, without River, in this strange place. And I wonder if this is what it feels like to be dead, if this is what my mother was feeling that morning when her lips were blue.

The grandmother woman asks me if I need to use the toilet, and I realize I do and that this means I cannot be dead. So I nod, and she reminds me about flushing and washing my hands the way my mother used to remind me to clean my hands in Falls after I used Bathroom Tree when I was a very small child. But I am not a small child now, no matter what she might think, and it is annoying that she treats me that way.

After I am finished, she tells me to sit down where I sat to eat my fish last night. She puts a plate on the table, with a strange-looking, thick yellow leaf on it. She hands me a fork spear and points to the plate.

"What's this?" I ask.

"An omelet," she says. I stare at her. "Eggs, cheese . . ." I hesitate, then touch *an omelet* with the fork spear, and then push hard to spear it and pick it up. It hangs there, large and strange, shell shaped and stinky. I'm not quite sure what I'm supposed to do with it, because from the way it smells, I really don't want to put it in my mouth.

"Oh," she says. "You know what? Maybe I should get you some fruit instead."

She grabs the plate and omelet away, walks over to all her strange boxes, and then comes back with a different plate with blue and red berries, like the ones I ate at Military Hospital with a spoon. Now I pick them up and eat them quickly with my fingers, and she doesn't tell me not to.

As I'm eating, a high bird chirps, and then the grandmother woman murmurs something softly to herself and runs away. When she comes back, there is another woman with her— *Missusfairfield*, I guess. She is small, smaller than the grandmother woman, with bright orange-coral hair. Her skin is loose and wrinkled, but even more than the grandmother woman's, and I wonder if that's because she's re-tired and hasn't slept enough. But I don't ask. She looks at the grandmother woman, leans in close to me, and then smiles so wide that I can see all her teeth, even the strange silvery ones in the back.

"Well, hello there, Megan," she says. "Do you mind if I take a seat?" She points to *the chair* next to me, and I'm not sure where she wants to take it, but since the grandmother woman doesn't argue, I guess it's okay, and I nod.

But she seems to change her mind about taking it, because all she does is sit on it. "Now," she says, still smiling. "I'd just like for us to get acquainted today. Most children your age would have already been in school for ten or eleven years, so you'll have a lot to catch up on, and Alice has asked me here to see if I might be able to help you with that. Today, I'd just like to assess where you're at. How far behind in school you might be."

I don't know what school is, but I remember Ben mentioned it last night, when he talked about things that suck here, so I imagine it is a place where you go to eat, and she said something about catch, so maybe also learn to catch food? I will be good at this, I think, and I hope this can go quickly so I can make my way back to Cold Ocean in the daylight, where I hope it will suddenly be warmer.

"Now," she says, "do you know what this is?"

She hands me a small, thin wooden spear, and I think this must be another eating tool. This would be perfect for eating the blue berries. There is one left on the plate, and I use the thin wooden spear to stab it, then pick it up, and suck it off. It tastes funny, and I make a face, wondering if this is why "suck" sounded like a bad thing when Ben said it.

"Oh, no, no!" She pulls the spear quickly from my hand. The grandmother woman makes a startled noise and puts her hand over her mouth, reminding me of the way the green birds sound at night. "This is a pen-cil," Missusfairfield says. "We don't put this in our mouths." Her voice is very slow and high, the way I remember my mother's sounding when River and I were very small, and I am embarrassed that I have done something wrong and that she is talking to me like I am a child. "We use this to write and draw," she is saying now. "Do you know what that is?"

"River and I would draw in the sand," I say quietly.

"Okay, yes. Very good." She claps her hands together. "But here we use a pen-cil to write on paper." She holds up something else, very white, like Military Hospital, but very fine and fluttery like feathers, only square. She puts it down on the table and then presses it in with a pen-cil, moving a pen-cil to make a black shape, the way River and I would use our fingers in the sand. "Now," she says, handing me back a pen-cil, "you try."

I hold on to a pen-cil, just the way she did, and press against paper. A small black notch appears.

"Did you used to write in the sand, too?" she asks me. I nod. "Well, go ahead and show me, then; show me what you know. Can you write your name?"

The feel of a pen-cil in my hand is very strange, and I grip it hard and tight like a fishing spear. I move it slowly and watch a thin black line moving around, until I have made a circle. I want to draw another one, just like we used to draw in the sand. Two interconnected circles, me and River. River and me. But as I move a pen-cil, I hear a noise, like a trap snapping, and then it makes no more black.

Missusfairfield takes it from my hand. "You just pressed a little too hard and broke the point," she says. "Don't worry. You'll get the hang of it." She pauses and puts her finger on my circle. "Now, tell me what this is?"

"Me," I say. Because isn't that what she asked me for?

She nods slowly and then turns and looks at the grandmother woman.

"Honey, why don't you go lie down in the living room for a

bit, rest your leg on the couch, while Missusfairfield and I have a little chat."

She walks me into a new space that I haven't seen yet, *Living Room*. I expect for animals to be in here, something living, and I cautiously tiptoe around, listening for their sounds. But I hear and see nothing but strange-shaped caves and boxes and rocks, kind of like Bed, but not exactly. The grandmother woman walks back out, and I don't know what *the couch* is, but there is a very bright multicolored rabbit pelt on the ground, so I lie on that.

I close my eyes, squeeze them shut tightly, wishing, wishing I could find it again, that feeling of lying on the rabbit pelt with River in Shelter. But this rabbit pelt is too thin, and it scratches my cheek. And River is somewhere else. Maybe with his mother. I wonder if she lives in a strange shelter like the grandmother woman does, if he is near Beach, if he understands or even remembers things about this world that I do not and I'm not sure I ever will. If he misses me the way I am missing him, an ache, an emptiness, a hunger that I feel will never go away no matter how much food I eat. Or if his mother has filled this space for him, if with her, he has already forgotten about me.

I hear a piece of what the grandmother woman and Missusfairfield are saying, and I open my eyes. "Very special case," Missusfairfield (I think) is saying.

"Like a two-year-old trapped in a sixteen-year-old's body." (The grandmother woman.)

"But she survived all those years on an island . . . I can't even imagine . . ." Their voices drop, and I don't hear anything for a while, and then I hear the sound of footsteps and Missusfairfield again. "She doesn't know anything . . ."

I feel my face turning hot, that they think I know nothing. On Island, I knew everything. I was the practical one. River, the dreamer.

And then again there are tears burning hot in my eyes, rolling down my cheeks. I am not only a girl without a place but also a girl without knowledge. I imagine Helmut would've said that is the worst thing that could ever happen to me, and I understand I can never live here, among these strange things, with these strange people. I will find River, and I will convince him that we have to go back. That what we had there together on Island, it has to mean more than this new woman, *this mother*, he has found here.

"So much to learn . . . ," I hear Missusfairfield say.

I think about Helmut, the way he talked about tracking animals, about capturing them, knowing them.

The way you have to do it is to outsmart them, he said. *Blend into their surroundings. Make them think you're one of them, and then they never even see you coming.*

19

I GUESS THAT MISSUSFAIRFIELD HAS agreed to teach me, because she comes back the next morning as I am eating breakfast and thinking about Ocean. I never got to go back there yesterday. Ben wasn't here, and the grandmother woman said the vultures worried her too much. I am determined to get there today. But then the high bird chirps, and Missusfairfield is back.

"Now," she says to me after the grandmother woman has led her in. She places a small hand gently on my shoulder. "First things first. We need to teach you how to navigate this world."

I put one last blue berry in my mouth with my fingers and nod. *Navigate.* There was much to navigate on Island, and knowing it, all of it, was what kept us alive. But now I understand that once I can navigate this new, strange world of California, I will be able to figure out a way to navigate my way back to River, to

Island. And so, for now, I forget about Ocean, and I stand up and follow Missusfairfield's lead.

We spend a long time practicing the names and uses for every-thing in the grandmother woman's shelter, *the house*. I learn that it is normal to sit on *the couch* (not lie on *the rug*). That only *a spoon*, *a fork*, and *a knife* are used for eating. That Cooler here is *the fridge*, and that there is a box in the Living Room (where things are not actually *living*) called *a television* where you can watch pretend people doing real things. She also teaches me that *Mrs.* is a nice way to refer to a woman, and that *Fairfield* is her second name. Her first name, she says, is Elizabeth. But since we are practicing for school, she thinks it is better that I call her Mrs. Fairfield. I don't really understand why she has two names, and why she is telling me I have to call her by one, but I just nod and agree to call her whatever she wants.

After a while I am tired, and it is hard to remember and understand so much. I also start to wonder if all this is silly because I can't see how understanding *the couch* or her name will help me find my way back. But then Mrs. Fairfield shows me *the blinds*, *the window*, *the screen*, how they open, letting the outside in, and I realize she has given me something real, some-thing I can use.

I wait until darkness, until the grandmother woman is quiet and sleeping, and then I open the blinds and the window in Pink Bedroom. I push on the screen until it moves, until the air is open and cool and entirely against my skin, and then I climb out and down the tree, just as I always did on Island when I went for coconuts. I follow the path Ben and I took the other night, through the rough pines until finally, at last, I am there again. *Ocean.* No, *the ocean*, as Mrs. Fairfield called it.

I run to its edge, letting my feet soak in the cold, cold water.

"River," I yell his name again and again, hoping he will hear me, that he has come to find the water, too, and that he is close by.

But the only thing I hear is the sound of the cold waves crashing upon the sand.

The next morning, Mrs. Fairfield announces that she wants to teach me to read. The grandmother woman nods and makes bird noises with her tongue. I am tired, having barely slept after making my way back from the ocean, and not really sure what they're talking about or why I need to know it.

"Your mother loved books," the grandmother woman tells me, shaking her tiny head. "She was an English major in college."

That doesn't mean anything to me, so I just shrug.

But then the grandmother woman leads me back up the steps and shows me *books*, what she calls my mother's *collection.* There are piles and piles of them, looking similar to the pieces of wood we'd throw in Fire Pit. They sit inside *the closet* in Pink Bedroom. I can't imagine them meaning anything to my mother, though from the way the grandmother woman talks, it sounds as if they were important to her once.

"I couldn't bear to get rid of them, not even after all this time," she says.

It seems like such a waste to just leave them here rather than using them to fuel her Fire Pit, or *the grill*, as she called it. But I don't say anything.

And Mrs. Fairfield just smiles, pats the grandmother woman on the shoulder, and then tells me she wants to start with something "simpler."

Back at the table, Mrs. Fairfield introduces me to *the newspaper*, and I listen now because I notice right away that the newspaper has pictures. They are real-looking, like the one the grandmother woman showed me at Military Hospital. And even better, the pictures in the newspaper are of me. Us.

There are pictures of my mother and Helmut, looking much younger than I remember them. Then below them, me, being carried on a long white bed into Military Hospital, River beside me, looking worried and holding tightly to my hand. I don't remember this happening, and it's strange to see and understand that these pictures can hold memories that I do not.

Mrs. Fairfield shows me *the words* and tells me she is going to read them to me. She asks me to follow along, as she talks and points, but I don't even listen. I'm just staring so hard at the picture of me and River.

"Can I keep this?" I ask her when she finally stops talking.

"Oh," she says. "You want to practice?" I nod even though I don't think that's what I want to do. "Well, of course, then. It's all yours."

After she leaves that day, I put the newspaper under the pillow in Pink Bed.

I don't read or learn the words. But every night, for many

nights after, I take it out and touch the sandy texture of River's face. He looks so worried about me here, not at all like someone who would want to leave me behind the moment we got to California.

I go over and over it again in my mind, that last time I saw him, the things he said to me, the way his fingers held my braid and he whispered, *Skyblue*.

One day I finally ask the grandmother woman if she knows what happened to him, where he is now. "I need to see him," I say.

"Oh, honey." She shakes her head. "Everything is different now. That boy is no good. You can't be with him. Besides . . ." Her voice trails off. "He could be anywhere by now." I remember what she told me, that morning when I first got in her car. Island was a freckle; California, the length of her body. Even though I ask her and I ask her again, her answer is always the same. Empty. And it's hard to like her, the way I feel she wants me to, when she won't even help me find River.

So all I have of him now is the newspaper. Every night, I hold on to the thinning, brittle picture of him, wondering where he is, what his life with his mother is like. I touch his grainy face again and again, until the picture starts to fade, the lines of his face wear away.

After I tiptoe down the hallway to listen for the grandmother woman's snore, I put the picture back under the pillow and I remove the screen from the window. I slide down the tree and I run through the pines to the ocean because I know this is where I'll find him again. The real him. Not the fake, fading picture.

I make sure I'm always back before morning, climbing up

the way I went out. I don't think the grandmother woman knows I do this, but she hasn't exactly said I can't, either. She has not explained the rules to me, as Helmut always did. And so I go almost every night.

I call for River in the depths of the ocean, the waves often swallowing my voice. Sometimes I hear a rustle in the pines, and I wonder if he can hear me, but if he can, he doesn't answer back.

20

THE SUN RISES AND SETS in the sky in California, just as it did on Island. June gloom, gray skies, and all. Every morning, the world grows lighter outside the window, and I make a black notch on the wall behind the bed with the pencil I took from Mrs. Fairfield. Every night the sky falls black. I track the pattern of the moon, half to three-quarters to full to the smallest silver feather in the sky, and by the time it is a half-moon again, the day sky grows bluer, the air a little warmer. One day, the sun rises, a flaming orange ball over the tall brown hills. There are twenty-two black notches on the wall behind the bed. My grandmother informs me that it is July, that in California there are months that change, just like the cycle of the moon.

By this time, the vultures have mostly disappeared, except for the occasional one that might block my grandmother's car as she tries to back up, which will cause her to get out and yell and scream so loud that I worry she might shake the earth in one of those earthquakes Mrs. Fairfield has told me about.

Each morning now, not too long after I watch the sun come up through my window, I start with what my grandmother calls her "team of professionals": Mrs. Fairfield; then a psychiatrist, Dr. Banks; and finally Ben. Mrs. Fairfield, who insists she is catching me up so I might go to school someday, though I know I never will. Dr. Banks to help me work through "issues." And Ben to make me, as my grandmother says, a normal sixteen-year-old girl.

Mrs. Fairfield explains the word *normal* to me by telling me that it's what's usual, expected. She says being normal would mean I think and act and feel the same as all the other people in California, and I know I will never be that. And anyway, I don't want to. What I want, in the small crevices of night, when I'm alone again, in silence and darkness, is to find my way back to Island, to a life that made sense to me, that did not require a "team of professionals." To River.

The only thing that makes me feel even close to *normal* is the ocean, though I don't tell that to my grandmother or Mrs. Fairfield because I know that this is not what they mean, that they wouldn't even understand.

———•———

Dr. Banks, the psychiatrist on my grandmother's "team of professionals," is a very tall woman, her body like the trunk of a palm, thin and flat, her back arching into her large, wide head overcome by masses of gray hair.

She comes to the house at different times of the day, depending on what my grandmother calls her *schedule*. "But she's the best," my grandmother says. "The very best." I would not want to see the worst in California if that is true.

She sits on the couch while I sit across from her on the love seat, and on her first few visits all she does is stare at me and say, "Now, what would you like to talk about, Megan?"

"My name is not Megan," I remind her, the way I've reminded everyone, again and again. She ignores me, the way they all do. I hate it when she calls me Megan, when anyone calls me Megan, but they all insist. *That's your name*, my grandmother always says, her face turning an awful red.

After a few days, Dr. Banks starts asking me about Helmut, whether he ever hurt me and whether I felt afraid. I think about what Ben told me, about the word *captive*. But still, I really can't understand what she's asking me, what she wants me to say. If I did, I probably would just say it, just to get her to stop talking to me, and unlike my lessons with Mrs. Fairfield and Ben, I don't see how anything Dr. Banks is doing or saying will help me really learn this world, help me get back to Island.

She asks again and again, though, about Helmut, and my answer is always the same.

"No," I say. "And no. Helmut loved me. My mother loved me."

Dr. Banks frowns and says things like, "This is a safe space, Megan. You don't have to lie here."

"I'm not lying." I grit my teeth.

When she leaves, I tell my grandmother that I don't think she's helping, that I don't think I need her, but my grandmother just frowns and shakes her head. "Oh, honey," she says. "Just give it time."

———◆———

The only one who doesn't call me Megan is Ben, but only when my grandmother can't hear him. Sometimes, I think he's nervous around her in the same strange way that River sometimes seemed nervous around Helmut.

"Sky is a pretty name," Ben tells me one afternoon as we walk along the edge of the ocean. It's the time of day we usually go to the beach together. "It's different. I see why you like it so much."

"I thought you were supposed to make me normal," I say. "Doesn't different mean not normal?"

He laughs. We trail the edge of the ocean walking next to each other, our bare feet, tangled with ugly green seaweed, moving together, skimming the cool water. "Yeah, well, Alice probably didn't pick the best person for that."

"So you're not normal?" I ask him.

He shakes his head, and I think I like him more. "But don't tell," he whispers, and he laughs again. I like that now it feels as if we're keeping a secret together, something my grandmother doesn't know, that I do. Ben is always nice to me, and I sometimes think about asking him to tell me more about Helmut, except then I worry that whatever he says might make me hate him, as I do all the others.

"Come on, Island Girl," he says, stopping our walk and turning back. "It's almost time for dinner."

"Island Girl?" I ask him.

"That can be my nickname for you," he says. "I've been thinking it over, and I like that one way better than my other choice,
'Not-Megan.'" He pauses. "I mean, that's practically already your
name, you say it to everyone so much."

I think he's laughing at me now, and that makes me angry.
Everyone wants to call me something that I'm not, even him.
Why can't I just be Sky? The person I am. The person I always
have been? "How would you like it if suddenly your name wasn't
Ben anymore and everyone started calling you something you
didn't even know?"

He reaches down for my hand, and I pull away. But then he
reaches again and squeezes my hand gently, so I think that
maybe he wasn't laughing at me. Maybe he was trying to be nice
by calling me *Island Girl*? "I get it, Sky," he says. "It totally sucks."

And for the first time, I think I understand exactly what he
means by that.

21

THE NEXT AFTERNOON, AFTER THE "team of professionals" has left for the day and Ben's mom (who I haven't met yet) is home from work and he's spending time with her, my grandmother announces she's taking me somewhere.

"Let's do a girls' day," she says. "Live it up a little . . . We'll go get our nails done and our makeup, and do some shopping and get our hair . . . shaped." She tugs on the end of my braid, but not in a nice way, the way River would do when he was teasing me or comforting me. My grandmother's hands on my braid annoy me, and I shrug her off.

I've already learned a lot here, but not everything—not even close—and I don't understand where she wants me to go with her.

"Come on," she says, as if I have a choice. "It'll be fun." She picks up her purse and pulls my elbow toward the door. "Everyone has been teaching you things, helping you, but me. You've been here for weeks, and I feel like we've barely spent any time together."

She's right. I do eat dinner with her every night, and some nights with Ben, too. She cooks things and asks me to taste them, even when I think they look and smell strange. "You don't have to eat all of it," she says, staring at me, pushing me with her eyes. "Just a little taste and I'll leave you alone."

But each night, right after I've eaten some of her food, or pushed it around on my plate, I always say I'm tired and go upstairs to the pink bedroom. I wait for her to turn off the television box, close the door to her bedroom, and go to sleep before I take out the window screen and find my way down to the ocean again. Or if I'm really tired, I go straight to sleep and I find Island again in my dreams.

I think it disappoints her that I refuse to watch the television box with her after dinner. But the few times I've sat there with her, all I've seen are pretend faraway people talking to each other about things that have nothing to do with me. I don't understand why she's interested in them if they're not even here, if they're not even real.

She leads me into the garage now and opens the car door for me. "Your mother and I used to do this when she was your age, you know?" I don't know, of course, so I don't answer. When I think of my mother, I think of her singing softly in my ear, pulling her fingers through my braid, holding on to me on the rabbit pelt mat in Shelter. I can't imagine her here, in this place. I think it's too big, too loud, too much. It would swallow her whole.

My grandmother starts the car and backs down the driveway,

and I think about the fact that we haven't talked much about my mother, neither one of us. There is so much she must know about my mother from before Island, and all she's told me about are her books. It's this thing that sits between us, as wide as the Pacific Ocean, and maybe that's part of the reason why I've been avoiding her. Whenever my grandmother starts to talk about my mother, it's like she's telling me a story about this person she made up, this girl who never even existed, and I can't listen without feeling sad and upset.

Suddenly, the car stops hard and I fly forward, then back. My grandmother gets out and storms down the driveway screaming: "You idiot . . . I nearly killed you . . . I'll tell you where you can put your camera . . ."

She's tough, I think. And I imagine she could skin a rabbit with a stone if she needed to. For some reason, this thought makes me uncomfortable now, that the two of us might have something in common, that if I were really trying to learn to fit in here—not just to find a way to get back to Island—then I might understand that she is the practical one, like me.

But that thought quickly falls away as she gets back into the car and says, "Sorry about that, Megan. Those vultures . . ."

I don't hear the rest. I hear only the awful sound of my fake name in her voice. *I am not Megan. I am Sky.*

But I'm so tired of saying it. Of talking and talking and having her not listen, so I say nothing now. I just clench my hands at my sides.

She doesn't say anything else, either, as she turns down the street, but I hear her breath in her chest, rattling a little. She turns onto what I now know is the Coastal Highway, and her breathing evens. Outside my window, the Pacific spans wide and gray and white. A bird swoops down into the waves, and I put my hand to the glass, wishing I could get out and touch the ocean, feel the spray of the salt water against my skin. The ocean lulls me, teases me. So close, and so far.

After a few minutes, she drives away from the ocean and pulls into what I know now is a parking lot. Then she stops the car and turns to me and smiles. "Okay," she says. "We're here. Your mother used to love the salon when she was your age. She was such a girlie-girl, always worrying about her hair and makeup and nails. Oh, heaven forbid her polish wouldn't look perfect or she would have a hair out of place."

"I don't know what that means," I say. None of it. Makeup. Polish. Worrying about your nails? Nails are for digging and scratching, pulling scales from fish skin.

"Megan, honey." She puts her hand on my knee. "I loved your mother very much. Everything that's happened, well . . . I got through it by hanging on to the good times we had. And now that you're here, I want to share some of that with you, okay?" She smiles. "Let's go get ourselves all gussied up in there."

Gussied up? It sounds like something I would do with a large bird killed in our traps, when I would remove its feathers, one by one, letting them twist in the wind. My mother hated birds. She called them messy creatures, and she wanted nothing to do with them until they were cleaned and ready for roasting.

"Come on, Megan. We'll start with this." My grandmother tugs on my braid, and again, I pull away.

I clench my hands at my sides, the word *Megan* hurting my ears. "What did you mean before, when you said shape my hair?" I ask.

"We'll just have them cut it, maybe get some layers, make it look pretty so you don't have to have it in this ratty braid all the time."

I think of River, the way he looked that last morning, sitting on the edge of the bed, his hair short, his face so different. My hair, my braid, is just like my mother's was. She taught me to comb it with my fingers, to knot it at the end. So many mornings she did it for me, just after I came out of Falls, and she'd sit on Drying Rock with me, her fingers twisting delicately through the strands down my back. *My hair.* It feels like all I have left now of my life on Island, of her. I'm not going to let the salon cut it. I will learn things, eat things, pretend to be Megan, if it means it will all make me know enough to figure out a way back to Island, but I will not cut my hair. I can't.

"I don't want it shaped." I shake my head, my braid whipping hard against my lower back.

"When your mother was your age, she loved getting her hair done." She reaches out and touches my braid and smiles, as if thinking of another time, another person, my mother. *My mother.* Her hair was long and thick, like mine. She'd almost always be humming after she went to Falls to get clean, and back at Shelter, I'd watch her twirl her long strands of hair through her fingers, quickly tying it into a neat braid. "Your mother loved the salon, Megan." My grandmother's thin fingers twirl through the end of my braid, and she frowns with distaste.

Skeletons, my mother said.

"No!" I shout, and I yank myself out of her grasp. Every bit of hatred I feel for this new world bursts right out of my skin—all the times she has called me Megan, her stupid team of professionals. It seeps over me, an anger I have never felt before, like seaweed clinging to my skin, suffocating me. "My mother hated it here!" I yell at her. My words echo in the car, and then they stop, and the air is very, very silent.

My grandmother sits there for a moment, her fingers shaking in the stillness of the air. Her mouth is open, arched, the wide shape of a seashell. "Maybe," she eventually says. "Just before she left, she might have hated it here." She pauses. "But she didn't always."

"She said the people were cold here," I spit at her. "Skeletons." I see my grandmother's face turn, everything shifting down. She bites her purple bottom lip, and her eyes—my mother's blue eyes—brim with tears. Then I feel a little bad. "She didn't mean you," I say. Though maybe she did. I don't know.

My grandmother nods and then shakes her head a little, gripping tightly to the wheel, even though the car is stopped. She doesn't say anything for another long moment. Then she speaks softly, her voice shaking just like her hands. "How did she die?" she asks me.

Her question seems so important, like something she may have wanted to ask me the whole time, and yet it takes me by surprise, that she is saying it here, now, out loud, just after she was talking about things like shaping hair and getting gussied.

"Did he kill her?" she whispers.

"Who?" I ask, though that horrible, sick feeling is back, and my stomach churns uneasily.

"Helmut," she says as if she has bitten into something rotten. It is the first time I have heard her say his name, and it sounds so much different in her voice than it ever sounded in my mother's.

"No." I shake my head. "Of course not. He would never do that. He loved her." I think of all the times her lips would touch his, and he would wrap her tiny body in his large arms, holding her tight to his chest. I think of the time she was bleeding and how he healed her, in Ocean.

"Okay," she says now, but the word sounds funny, as if she's choking on it, as if she doesn't believe me.

"He did. He loved her," I say again. "He loved us." And then I hate my grandmother a little more for not understanding anything real about me, about my life until now.

"Okay," she says again. "But just tell me something. Did she suffer?"

I close my eyes, thinking about that morning, her lips cold and blue. "I don't think so. She ate some mushrooms, and then she went to sleep." I pause. "And she never woke up."

A funny cry starts in my grandmother's throat, like the noise of a trapped animal that has recognized that this is it, the end— there is no way out. I'm not sure what she's thinking or why she is reacting this way, but then she reaches up and quickly wipes away a tear that has escaped her eye and onto her cheek. Then another one. And I remember the way I felt that morning, when I saw my mother there, her lips cold and blue. The way I felt when I gave her back to Ocean and the water swallowed her up, took her away.

My grandmother's tears keep coming, and then I understand

something: my grandmother must have loved my mother once, even if my mother might not have felt the same.

"I'm sorry," I whisper, suddenly wishing I hadn't yelled.

"Oh, honey." She reaches across for my hand, and her fingers are white now and grip onto me tightly. "You have nothing to be sorry for."

She gives my hand a squeeze, and then she wipes her face dry. She clears her throat. "You know what, I changed my mind. I think your hair looks just right the way it is for now." She pauses for a moment and looks down at the wheel. "I'm very tired," she says. "Would you mind if we just went back to the house and did our girls' day another time?"

Before I have a chance to answer her, she starts the car and turns us around, driving back toward her house.

22

MRS. FAIRFIELD BRINGS THE NEWSPAPER with her every morning, and as the days go by, I begin to notice the way my picture moves from the first page to the second page, to the third page, and finally, one day, just a few days after the strange conversation with my grandmother in the parking lot of the salon, I am not in the newspaper at all. That day, too, even the last vulture seems to have disappeared from the street outside my grandmother's house.

As Mrs. Fairfield and I start our morning routine at the kitchen table, my grandmother glances over our shoulders at the pictures and the words on the front page of the newspaper. Her cheeks turn a gray white, and she quickly turns away. "You'll be fine down here today without me, won't you, Elizabeth?" she says to Mrs. Fairfield, her voice shaking a little.

"Of course, Alice." Mrs. Fairfield turns to me and smiles too wide, revealing her silvery back teeth. "We'll do just fine, won't we, Megan?" She pats my hand, and I sigh and nod, annoyed with the way she talks to me as if I am a small child. And the way she says *Megan*, like it is a sweet bite of coconut she is savoring in her silver teeth.

"I need to go back to bed," my grandmother says. "Rest my eyes for a while."

It was the same thing she said to me that afternoon when we got back from the salon, and I understand that this is what people say here when they are sad or when they need to be alone. I am not sure why she is feeling this way now, but I don't ask.

"Now." Mrs. Fairfield turns back to me after my grandmother walks up the steps. "I want to talk to you about our newspaper today."

"That I'm not on it?" I ask. But what I'm really thinking is that River's not. And that I would do anything to see a picture of him real enough to feel he was really here, with me.

"Yes," she says. "But also about what *is* in it."

She reads the front article out loud, asking me to follow along, and I do not understand so many of the words that are in it: *gun, murder, shot, shooting*. Though I do understand the word *dead*, and the number of people who seem to be: *sixteen*. Which I also understand is a lot. Many more people than I ever knew on Island.

"Do you understand?" she asks when she's finished reading. "There was a shooting in Iowa. Sixteen people murdered."

"Murdered?" I ask.

"Murder is when people die in a bad way," she says. "When someone else takes their life on purpose." She shows me the picture of a *gun*, which she says was used for murder

127

in this case, but I cannot understand how it was used exactly. Or why.

I ask her, and I ask her again. But all she keeps saying is, "It's such a senseless tragedy. Murder is a terrible thing."

And nothing about any of that makes me understand it.

———•———

"People forget," Dr. Banks says a few hours later, when she asks me what I learned with Mrs. Fairfield that morning and I tell her how River and I were gone from the newspaper. "Everyone fixates on these things for a while, and then life just goes on. Gets back to normal. Something else happens." There's that word again: *normal*.

But this something else—*shooting, murder*—it does not seem *normal* to me at all.

"I don't understand," I tell Dr. Banks, thinking about how my grandmother called her the very best and thinking she should be able to explain this to me better than Mrs. Fairfield.

"What don't you understand?" Dr. Banks says in that annoying way she has of always repeating my questions right back to me.

"Why would someone murder people with a gun?"

Dr. Banks nods. "In many ways your island life was filled with innocence." I nod, but I don't really know if it was or not. "But bad things happen in the real world, Megan. They just do. Nobody has all the answers." She pauses. "Even on the island bad things happened, didn't they?" She pokes at me with her words, the way my mother used to poke at me with her finger to sometimes hurry me along in Falls or back to Shelter if it looked like it was about to rain.

I think about the morning I found my mother, lips parted, blue, cold, and I nod, looking back at Dr. Banks. "My mother and Helmut died," I say.

"And that's all?" she asks me.

I think about the animal noise my grandmother made when I told her about how my mother died, her white fingers clutching tightly onto mine. I have this feeling that she and Dr. Banks think they know something about my life on Island that I do not. But I also know that that is impossible.

Dr. Banks raises her eyebrows, waiting for me to say something else. But I shrug. I really don't understand what she's waiting for.

———•———

That afternoon, Ben wants me to drive with him to the fish market to pick up dinner. We've walked together almost every afternoon along the beach, but so far, the only car I've been in is my grandmother's. And only a few times. The last one, our failed trip to the salon, after which my grandmother spent the rest of the afternoon in her bedroom, just as she has done today. *Resting her eyes.*

She's still up there when Ben walks through the front door without knocking, as he always does, and asks if I want to go with him. Ben has already told me that turning sixteen in California means that you are finally old enough to drive, and that he has had his license for six months now. I'd rather walk along the beach than drive anywhere because the car still frightens me a little. But I also know the fish market isn't far and we don't have to use the freeway to get there. And I am so tired of being trapped in my grandmother's house.

"She's in her bedroom," I tell Ben. And he nods, as if he's not surprised, and he climbs up the steps, two at time, calling her name.

A few minutes later, he is back downstairs again, smiling. "She's cool with it," he says. "As long as I promise to drive carefully." He pauses. "Which I always do, by the way." He laughs when he says it, which I think means maybe he actually doesn't, but I don't know the first thing about driving.

I've already learned that Ben spent a lot of time with my grandmother when he was younger. She said that his mom paid her to watch him. *But really,* she told me, *he was watching me.* She smiled when she said it, as if that all made perfect sense. I think that, in a way, Ben is what I would've been if I'd lived here my whole life. That she thinks of herself as his grandmother, and I guess that's why she is okay with me going with him. She trusts him. And he seems to like her—a lot.

I am starting to trust him, too, I think now. Not the way I trust River, the way I trusted him as I stood by Falls that morning and he pleaded with me to leave Island. The way he offered me his hand, and I took it. *It'll be okay,* he told me. And I wish I had convinced him then that it wouldn't be. A part of me is angry with him now, for promising me, and then leaving me. Here. All alone. But even more, I am angry with myself. River is the dreamer; I am the practical one. I should've known better.

And I'm not alone here, I guess. I have my grandmother, and I have Ben. A team of professionals. Hundreds and hundreds of strangers in California, driving closely to one another on the I-5. When I open the window in my bedroom to climb out at night, I can hear the distant whir of all those cars, but strangely enough, I can't hear the ocean from there.

It's funny, though, how my insides feel so empty now. How I feel more alone surrounded by all these people than I ever did on Island.

Ben's car is blue and much longer than my grandmother's. It's higher off the ground, too, and that's because Ben says it's an SUV, and it's his mother's car. "If I had my choice," he says as he helps me in, "I'd drive something way cooler. A Jag or a Porsche."

"Then why don't you?" I ask.

He laughs. "Dude, maybe someday. When I've got tons of money."

I don't understand this money thing. Mrs. Fairfield has explained it to me, showing me dollar bills and coins, credit cards, and checks as I've repeatedly asked her where the money comes from. How people get it. Why they need it. I imagine this big, wide pool surrounded by rocks, like Fishing Cove, where money floats and people spear it with spears.

Mrs. Fairfield shakes her pointy coral head and laughs. *That's not the way the world works, Megan.*

I do understand that money seems to be necessary to do anything here, and that I am going to have to figure out how to get some if I'm ever going to figure out how to get back to Island.

This is also why I like going places with Ben. The more I go, the more I leave my grandmother's house, the more I learn about this world, for real.

On the ride to the fish market, Ben drives his SUV a little faster than my grandmother drives her red car, and the movement makes me feel sick again. The omelet my grandmother made for breakfast sloshes around in my stomach, threatening to come back up even though that was a long time ago. I hold on to the window, and I don't breathe again until he stops and we are there.

We get out of the car, and the salt water curls deliciously in my nose, calming my stomach. I can't see it from here, but I know we're by the ocean, and that makes me happy.

"Wait," Ben says as I start to walk without him. He runs around to my side and puts his arm around me. Then he turns and looks back quickly.

"Oh," I say, realizing he is trying to shield me from the vultures. "They're gone now. Didn't you read about what happened in the newspaper?"

"The shooting, you mean?" I nod. "Well, at least they're leaving you alone now, right?"

"I guess so," I say. "But what do you think of it? The shooting. Everyone tried to explain it to me this morning. But I couldn't really understand it."

He shrugs. "It's sad to say, but I guess I'm kind of used to it. That stuff happens all the time. I mean it happened to . . ." He looks at me hard for a moment and then shakes his head.

"To what?" I ask.

"Never mind." He pauses. "It sucks. It really does. The world is a crazy, stupid place."

The world, I've come to learn now that Mrs. Fairfield has taught me about *maps*, includes so much. The great wide Pacific Ocean. And the Atlantic, Indian, Arctic, and Southern Oceans, too. California. The United States. Samoa. And even Island, which, as hard as Mrs. Fairfield and I tried, we couldn't locate on any maps she showed me. In the space where Mrs. Fairfield said Island should be, there is only blue, blue water. "Well," Mrs. Fairfield had said. "I guess they're going to have to redo this map now, aren't they?" I didn't tell her, but that upset me. I don't think I want the rest of the great wide world to know about it. Island was mine and River's, my mother's and Helmut's. And I would not consider it crazy, stupid, or *sucks*, like Ben considers his world. But deep down, I also worried about how hard it will be to find it again, if it isn't even on Mrs. Fairfield's maps.

"Check this out," Ben says now, opening the door to the tiny building in front of us. There are red letters on the door glass. I try to read them, but I don't recognize the words. "Sandy's Fish Market," Ben says, helping me out.

"Thanks," I say.

"Every fish you could imagine," Ben says as we step inside. "Brought right off the boat." *The boat.* I think of River and me lying there on the boat's floor, our last night together, him holding on to me, promising me everything was going to be fine.

"They wheel them inside in these giant trash cans," Ben is saying, and I realize he's still talking about the fish. "These huge black bins piled up with fresh-caught fish. It's kind of awesome to see."

"Yeah, awesome," I repeat back, doing as Mrs. Fairfield has asked me to—to echo Ben.

Awesome. It sounds like a silly, empty word. The words we used on Island had meaning. *Fish. Water. Shelter. Falls. Spears. Fire.* Everything meant something. Everything in our world was useful.

The door shuts behind us, chirping like a bird, and the smell of the ocean, dead fish, is strong in this small space. In front of me, there's a large window filled with fish of all colors and sizes, already scaled, trimmed, cleaned, and filleted. Which is kind of disappointing. They don't really even look like fish still.

"Come on," Ben says, slipping a bill into my hand. "Twenty dollars. Pick whatever you want and pay yourself."

"Did Mrs. Fairfield tell you to do this?" I ask.

He shrugs, and I laugh. Because it's funny. Kind of. I take the twenty dollars and walk up to the window, trying to read the choices. The letters jumble and the words aren't familiar, or maybe they are and I just don't how to read them yet. Mrs. Fairfield talks a lot about letters and sounds, and sounding things out, but that seems like a lot of effort now, so I don't even try it.

The man behind the window asks if he can help me. And instead of reading anything, I point to what looks the best to me, the fish that are most familiar to the ones I know. Silvery skin. Pink fleshy insides.

"Do you have any wahoo?" I ask, because according to Mrs. Fairfield, this is most likely the kind of fish we caught and ate on Island. She showed me a picture of one, and I nodded, telling her that yes, she was right. Maybe she was, maybe she wasn't. She also showed me pictures of rabbits and wallabies, and tried to convince me that I had them confused, that it was not rabbit we always ate and wore on Island, but wallaby. I don't know.

"Wahoo?" the man repeats. I nod. "Let me check in the back." He opens a wide door and yells, "Hey, Lucas, any wahoo come in today?"

Not River. Lucas.

All this time, he's been so close? Not at the ocean. At the fish market? Of course.

Mrs. Fairfield showed me the words in the newspaper, too. *Lucas. Megan.* And my mother, who they and my grandmother referred to as *Angela*, not Petal. Only Helmut seemed to be Helmut both in California and on Island.

"Lucas," the man yells again.

I feel a cry rising in my throat, and I think I hold it back, except I must not, because Ben reaches for my shoulder. "Sky," he whispers. "You okay?"

I shake my head.

"Hey, Lucas," the man calls one more time. I hold my ear tight for the answer, the sound of his voice. If I could just hear it. *Skyblue.*

"He's still out on the boat," another voice calls, a man. Not River.

"Any wahoo back there?"

I don't hear what the man says. My entire body feels tight, soaking in the still fish air. I can't move. I can't breathe.

"If you try back in the morning, we might have some," the man behind the window is saying now.

Ben steps forward and takes the twenty dollars from my hand. "We'll just take what you have, then," I hear him say. "The halibut, and maybe some of the mahi."

"She all right?" the man asks.

"Yeah, sure," Ben says. "She's fine."

I feel the fish man's eyes on me, cold and still. I squirm a little, uncomfortable with him staring so closely. "She that girl from the paper?" he asks Ben.

"No," Ben says quickly. He stands up a little straighter and shoves the twenty dollars across the window. "Can you just hurry up with the fish? Please." His voice trembles.

Finally the man hands the brown package across the window, and Ben grabs it, then grabs me, wrapping his arm around my shoulders, pulling me tightly to him, as if he's trying to hide me in his side.

We get into the SUV quickly, and then we sit there for a moment, not saying anything. Ben puts his hands on the wheel, and I notice they're shaking.

Hey, Lucas. He's here. So close.

"Shit," Ben says now.

"Shit," I echo back.

"Oh no, don't. Don't say that one in front of Alice. It's not a good word."

"Okay," I say. But how am I supposed to know the difference? How are there good words and bad ones, useful ones and empty ones? I'm supposed to echo. But I'm not. I'm Sky but I'm Megan. I'm neither one. Or I'm both.

River is here. Or Lucas is. I've found him. Even if he didn't want to be found.

And now that I know where he is, all I have to do is come back and talk to him, and convince him to go back to Island with me.

23

INSTEAD OF GOING RIGHT BACK to my grandmother's house, Ben pulls into the garage at the next house over, his house, first. "You wanna come in for a little bit?" he asks as he turns off the car.

I nod because I'm not ready to go back to my grandmother's house yet. But as I follow him inside, I am not really paying much attention to what he's saying to me. I am still imagining him, *my River*, inside the fish market, on a boat, catching fish, almost as he always was. So close to here.

"My mom's at work," I realize Ben is saying now as I follow him into his kitchen. "That's why it's so quiet." His mom is almost always at work, this place where Mrs. Fairfield tells me people get money. My grandmother doesn't work, but somehow she still seems to have money. Ben's mother works a lot, and yet he mentioned in the car how he'd drive a different one if he had more money. It really is confusing. But I get tired of asking questions. And besides, it is hard to concentrate on worrying about this world now when my mind is flooding with my old one. *River.*

I haven't been in Ben's house before now, and as he puts the fish in his silver fridge to keep it good, I notice the inside of his house is nearly the same as my grandmother's in the shapes and placement of the rooms, but everything else about the house seems different. In my grandmother's house, every room has its color, mostly a very bright one, and most of the rooms have carpet. In Ben's house, the walls are white, and the floors are tile, like my grandmother's kitchen and bathrooms.

I follow Ben up the tiled stairs, which are smooth and cool against the bottoms of my feet, and I notice his bedroom is the same one as mine, second door past the stairs, only inside his room, his walls are white and covered with pictures. Not fake oceans, like in my room, but people—drawings, like the ones River and I used to make in the sand, only Ben's are much better, more detailed, more real-looking, almost like the pictures in the newspaper but not quite.

"Did you make these?" I ask. He nods. "They're really nice," I say. "Especially this one." I run my finger across one that looks a lot like me. And by that, I mean Sky-me, the girl in the rabbit pelt who lived on Island and smiled and knew everything there was to know, not Megan-me, the girl with the jeans and flip-flops who doesn't know much. The girl in this drawing is smiling. I'm not sure if I've smiled since coming to California.

"They're all right," Ben says, shrugging and sitting down on his bed. But I stare at the picture a minute longer, noticing two words underneath.

"What does this say?" I ask him.

"Island Girl," he says, and he shrugs. I remember how I got mad at him that day when he called me that, how, at first, I thought he was laughing at me. But now I can see from the picture that he wasn't. That by *nickname*, he really did mean something nice. Ben sees me, I think. He actually sees *me*. I don't understand why it's so much different for him than for my grandmother or Mrs. Fairfield, or even Dr. Banks. But it is, and he's my favorite one in California, the only one I really find myself liking, wanting to talk to and spend time with. And maybe it's because he draws me the way I am, rather than trying to change me. To make me *normal*. I have the sudden sense that I might miss him when River and I go back to Island, but then I quickly push the thought away because it makes me feel uncomfortable. I don't need anyone else, I remind myself. River and me. Me and River. Shelter and Falls. The sky and the stars. Ocean and Fishing Cove. That is all I need. All I am.

Ben sits down on his bed and pats the space next to him, so I sit down, too. He lies back against a pillow, and I echo him and do the same. The white ceiling above us is covered with fake, too-large yellow stars. And suddenly I feel sad for him. It does not seem like any kind of life, sleeping this way, with fake stars shining up above your head.

Ben has a big bed and there's space between us now, not like the way River and I always lay so close on the rabbit pelt mats. But suddenly I'm aware that Ben and I are sharing a space and that we could be closer if we each moved just a little bit. Though we don't.

Maybe Ben notices, too, because he rolls over, away from

me, to pick up his iPod from the table, and he turns on music. This is part of making me *normal*, him teaching me about this stuff. I like music, the way it sounds, the way it can change from one moment to the next, the way you can just push a button and make the way you're feeling surround you, without even having to say anything at all. I wonder if there would be a way for me to take an iPod with me back to Island, to listen to music there still, but then I realize that thought is ridiculous.

"You'll like this song," Ben says now. "It's a blues song. Nina Simone." He grins, and a thick low voice fills the room, singing about birds and sun and feeling good. I felt that once not so long ago, didn't I? All of that. On Island, my birthday, the sun on my face as River held out his catch, spanning the width of his arms. I'll feel that again soon. Once I find River at the fish market and we figure out our way back.

"All this nature stuff—you like this, right?" Ben asks.

I nod, but I like the sound of her voice more than what she's saying to me. It is clear and deep and sweet, like my mother's. "So this is what *normal* people our age listen to in California?" I ask Ben.

"Nope." He laughs. "Total throwback song from probably Alice's teenage years." He shrugs. "I told you I suck at this normal stuff."

"But how do you know so much about this not-normal music?" I ask.

He grins again. "My father is a jazz drummer in a band—a drummer, you know that, right?" I shake my head, and he taps with his fingers against the table. "The person in the band who keeps the beat. At least, he was. I mean, I guess he still is." He pauses. "Anyway, when I was younger, he used to play me records, teach me about all this stuff."

"And now?" I ask, and I think it's strange no one around me has mentioned Ben's father up until this moment.

"Now . . . I don't know. He left for a gig one night when I was seven, and I haven't seen him since."

"My father died before I was born," I tell Ben, and he nods as if maybe he already knows this. "Where did your father go?"

Ben shrugs. "I dunno," he says. "But he's sure as hell not here."

"Maybe he's on an island," I say.

"Are you making a joke?" he says. I shrug because I'm not sure what I'm doing. I don't really think his father is on an island, though maybe. Mrs. Fairfield showed me many other islands on her maps, but they all had strange names I'd never heard of or would've never imagined existing before now. I never understood before that Island was not the only one, that we were not the only ones. And I'm still not sure I understand or believe it. Maps are just drawings on paper. Nothing more. I looked out over Ocean nearly my entire life, and the only thing I saw was blue water meets blue sky.

"Dude, I don't know how it happened, but you are totally becoming normal," Ben says now. "And so not funny, by the way." Still, he laughs a little as he reaches across the bed and pokes me in the ribs.

"Ow!" I protest, but it doesn't hurt, and I realize I'm smiling, actually smiling, the way I did when River would tease me sometimes, when he would chase me around Beach threatening to pull me under into Ocean if I wouldn't go wash my rabbit pelt in Falls, already. I think that's what Ben is doing now, poking me in the ribs, and then I remember how close River is, just out on a boat and soon back at the fish market, and something a little uneasy twists in my stomach.

"I'm sorry," I say, not smiling anymore. Because his father is lost, and so am I.

"You don't need to be sorry for making a joke," Ben says. "That's what people do."

"No," I say. "I mean about your father."

He nods, but he doesn't say anything else, and we listen to Nina for a few more minutes, not saying anything.

Just as Nina seems to be making a big finish, Ben sits up and looks at me. "Can I ask you something?" he says. "What happened back there at the fish market? Why did you freak out?"

"Freak out?" I echo him. "I don't know." I feel strange talking to Ben about River. The spot where Ben poked me in the ribs doesn't hurt, but it feels a little warm, as if my body, my senses, are more awake now.

"Yeah, you do," he says softly. "You just don't want to tell me."

I realize he's right. That I've lied to him. That in my short time in California, I've already become a liar. And maybe it's only a matter of time before I'm cold and broken. A skeleton. "Lucas," I say. "The man asked for Lucas."

"And you thought of your Lucas?"

I nod, though I wonder if there is any way he is mine anymore. River was mine. *Lucas*, this strange person he might have become here in California—he doesn't even feel like mine at all.

"What happened between the two of you, anyway?" Ben

143

asks. "You were together all that time on your island, right?" I nod. "And you were friends?"

I nod again, though I don't know if *friends* is the right word. In California, there's so much to learn and watch and understand. But on Island, it was simple, River and I ending every day in Shelter, back to back. River was everything to me, and I was everything to him. At least, I thought I was.

"So what happened?" Ben pushes.

"I don't know," I say. "He didn't want to be friends with me here, I guess." I don't say it out loud, but I think if I could just talk to him again . . . see him again, I could change his mind. I would, I know it. Or maybe I would tell him he could bring his mother with us, that if she is as good and perfect as he remembered her, then she will love Island, as we do.

"That sucks," Ben says. "He kind of sounds like a dick."

"He's not," I say, though I don't really know what that is. It just doesn't sound nice, and there's nothing about River that wasn't nice. Lucas, maybe. River, no.

I feel tears in my eyes. I want to stop them from coming, but I can't, and Ben sits up and puts his hand to my cheek, the way River once did, to wipe them away. "Well, I say you're better off without him," he says. "Alice hates him. And she's a pretty good judge of character."

The thought that my grandmother feels that much, that she has *hate* for River, makes me mad. "That's ridiculous," I say. "She's never even met him. You can't hate someone you've never met."

"I don't know," he says, but he looks away from me as he says it, so I can't see in his eyes what he might be thinking.

He picks up the iPod and turns on a new song. "R.E.M.," he tells me. " 'It's the End of the World as We Know It.' "

I listen to the words, and it's like they're talking to me, like Ben is talking to me through them. The world has ended, and the R.E.M.'s are still feeling fine. I don't feel fine at all, and Ben's words still echo uneasily in my head. *Alice hates him*, he said of River. *And she's a pretty good judge of character.* But that doesn't even make any sense. Is Ben lying? Is he a skeleton, just like all the rest of them?

I stand up quickly. The bed shakes, and Ben startles and turns the music off.

"I think I should go back now," I say. Maybe I have been wrong to trust him, to come here with him, and I want to get back to Pink Bedroom, to come up with a plan to get back to the fish market, to River.

Ben opens his mouth as if he wants to say something, but then he seems to change his mind because he says nothing. He nods and stands up, and then we walk back to my grand-mother's house in silence.

24

"I HAVE A QUESTION FOR you," I tell Dr. Banks a few nights later. She has come after dinner tonight, and darkness floods past the window, the moon bloated again, nearly full. From the next room, I hear the noises of the television box, unfamiliar voices, shouting.

"Yes, Megan," Dr. Banks says. "What's that?" She smiles her silly this-is-your-safe-space smile, and a part of me wants to reach across her face and hit her now just to make the smile go away. I wouldn't have hit anyone on Island, ever. My mother, Helmut, they wouldn't have allowed it. And besides that, I never wanted to. But Dr. Banks's lips are a terrible shade of pink—lipstick—I know, because my grandmother showed me how to put it on and asked me if I wanted to try some of hers. But honestly, I just don't see the point.

"Well," I say now, looking away from her so I don't have to see that awful pink smile. I hear the sound of tiny footsteps in the other room—my grandmother's—and I guess she's listening to us while trying to pretend that she's watching the television box. "We all had different names on Island," I say. "I am Sky. Lucas was River. My mother, Angela"—the name still feels funny on my tongue—"was Petal. But Helmut was Helmut." I remember what Ben told me that first night, that he'd learned about Helmut from the Google, that Helmut had done some bad things. But all the newspapers Mrs. Fairfield has shown me have made little, if any, mention of Helmut, and I don't know if that's because the stuff Ben told me was wrong or if it was that Mrs. Fairfield has been leaving pieces out.

"That's an interesting question, Megan." Dr. Banks draws her pink lips together in a line. "But first let's address something else. You said, 'I am Sky.' Not 'I was Sky.'"

"So?" I say, suddenly wishing I hadn't asked anything at all.

"So you have trouble being called Megan, don't you?"

I sigh. "Maybe."

"And why is that?"

"I don't know," I say because I am not going to tell her the truth, that soon I will be back on Island, with River, and I will be Sky again, always. That I *am* Sky. No matter what.

Dr. Banks does that annoying thing where she just stares at me. She stares and stares and stares until I say something else. "My mother called me Sky," I say. "That's what she told me my name was."

"She called you Megan once, too."

"I don't remember that," I say, though I think about the last moment my mother spoke to me, when she might have said Megan.

147

She nods. "But why do you think you get so angry when people who do remember that call you Megan?"

"I don't," I say, but even as I say it I realize that, actually, I do.

"All right." She holds up her hands. "But you don't like it, do you?"

"Not really," I admit. "Everything is different here. I don't know anything anymore." I have not meant to be honest with her, but the words have escaped me before I can stop them. And it feels good to say them out loud. *I know nothing here. I am nothing here.*

"Not even your name," she says softly. I nod. "So what if I call you Sky? Would you like me more?"

"I don't think so," I say.

She laughs. "Your brutal honesty is refreshing." She smiles more openly now, and maybe if I think about it, I would like her a little better if she called me Sky. I'm not sure why, though, but I can't tell her that. "So back to your question," she says. "Why Helmut never changed his name." She leans over and rubs her forehead. "It's a very good question, Megan—Sky," she quickly corrects herself. I can't help it—I smile a little. "I don't know that I can give you the answer. From what we know of Helmut, he was a narcissist, which means he was very much in love with himself, his image. He held himself above others. People like him usually do."

"People like him?" I say softly.

"It's complicated," she says, and that's when I understand that Mrs. Fairfield has been hiding things from me, not reading me all of the newspaper, leaving the most important pieces out. I think about how my grandmother asked if he'd killed my mother, and I wonder why she would think that, what it is that everyone in this world thinks they know about that I don't.

"It's complicated," I echo after her. "You mean, you don't want to tell me?" Outside, I watch the bloated moon move behind a pale gray cloud. I listen hard, wishing I could hear the ocean from here. But I can't. There's so much noise in this house. Machinery. The television box. The dishwasher. The fan whirring above my head. The refrigerator buzzing in the next room. My head hurts.

"It's not that I don't want to . . . it's just that . . . I want to wait until you're strong enough here. Until you have the tools to process it all."

That's ridiculous. I am strong already. Stronger than her, than anyone I have met in this California world. "You think Helmut was a bad man," I say. "Everyone thinks he was. But he wasn't. He loved us. He loved me." I hear my voice rising in my throat, my face turning red in frustration.

"It is just all very complicated," she says again, pressing her pink lips together.

She is such a dick, I think, Ben's word echoing in my head. I'm still not sure what the word means, but I'm pretty sure that she is one, whatever it is. "He was like my father." I am yelling now. "And there was nothing complicated about it. Not there, anyway. Everything was simple. He loved me. He loved us. He took care of us."

She nods slowly. "Why don't you calm down and tell me what you know about your real father."

"I don't want to calm down!" I yell, and I am breathing heavily. I want to reach across and grab her palm tree neck and shake it until she tells me everything I want to know. I resist the urge and twist my fingers together.

"Do you know how he died?" she asks. I shake my head, and suddenly I'm uncomfortable again. My stomach hurts. My head aches. I should probably feel sadness, for this man, this real father who is dead. But I never knew him, so I don't. "You want me to tell you the truth?"

"Yes!" I say, and I am yelling louder now. The noise from the television box in the other room quiets, and I know my grandmother has heard me yelling and is now listening in. But why is it so hard here for people just to tell the truth? Why does everything have to be so *complicated*?

"Your father didn't just happen to die. He was murdered," she says. Her voice is calm, quiet. "You know what that is, right?"

I nod, thinking of the article I'd read with Mrs. Fairfield about the shooting. *Murdered*. It wasn't a word I ever needed on Island, and yet here in California, it suddenly feels so necessary, so important to understand. "My father was murdered?" I repeat back, in a whisper now, trying to make it mean something in my mind. But it doesn't.

"Yes," she says. "He was murdered. And I'm sorry that I have to tell you this, but you said you want the truth." She pauses. "Helmut was the one who did it. Helmut murdered your father."

No. I shake my head. I shake it and I shake it.

"You asked for the truth," she's saying, "and I did as you asked. Now you need to do as I ask and talk to me. How does this make you feel?"

I shake my head. Again.

I can't listen to her anymore or talk to her anymore. She is cold and broken. A skeleton.

I stand up and run past Dr. Banks, past the worried red face of my grandmother peeking around the corner from the next room, as if she felt the disturbance in me the way I would once feel the coming of a rainstorm.

"Honey," she calls after me. "What are you doing?" My hand reaches for the back door. "It's dark out there. Where are you going?" She won't follow me, because she told me her eyes are bad, that it's hard for her to see at night. Even if she wanted to come after me, she couldn't see to catch me in the darkness.

The door slams behind me, and I hear her yelling, "Wait, at least let's call Ben to go with you." But I run fast; I don't stop. I climb the fence and make my way to the path, and then I run faster through the pine trees. The loose pine needles sting the bottoms of my feet, as I run too fast and my flip-flops slide, but I don't care. I reach down and take them off. I'm done with this place. With California, filled with skeletons and liars. I'm done with my grandmother's team of professionals, with all the things she and they think I need to learn. I'm done with Dr. Banks. With Megan. With all of it.

The cool sand hits my toes, and it's a relief. The pads of my feet still sting from the pine needles, but I don't stop until I reach the edge of the water, until I feel it roaring in my ears and in my heart. This is what I know. This is what I know is true. The great, wide mouth of the Pacific, calling to me.

I walk in the water, and it's freezing, cold enough to burn my skin, but I don't care. I want to swim in it, to fall in it, under the waves to let them carry me away, home. I want the tide to pull me out and far south until the water is warmer and bluer. Until the sky is familiar and the air clings to my skin.

In the sting of the water, I think of Helmut, of all the nights he brought me food and things to keep me warm in Shelter. Of the way he taught me things: to fish, to trap, to track, to cook. Of the way his giant palm would cap my head lightly when I made him proud. My mother explained things to me and River, things like family and love and counting seconds into minutes into hours into days, which became notches. River knew Helmut was his, and Petal was mine. But Petal loved him like a son and Helmut loved me like a daughter.

Now nothing can be true. None of it. And I hate Dr. Banks, and I hate my real father, who I never met, who I never knew. And I hate myself for hating him.

I am in the cold ocean up to my waist now, and my wet jeans feel awful sticking to my skin, but I keep walking. Hate is heavy, and it tugs me under, hard. I go in to my chest. I bob in a wave that breaks over my head, and then I'm sputtering, shivering. But I need to be in the ocean. It will heal me, make me whole again.

I think of the time when my mother's monthly blood did not come, according to Tree of Days. We made notches and notches, and still it did not come. My mother's face opened, like a flower, and so did Helmut's with the width of a smile I never saw from him. And then notches and notches and notches later, the monthly blood did come. My mother's face grew clammy, cold and pale, and there was so much blood that she couldn't stop it with a palm leaf, like she normally did. Helmut picked her up and carried her, running her body down to Beach, running with her into Ocean, holding on to her there until the waves healed her, until the blood stopped coming. The water heals, and it washes away.

My head aches with so much new knowledge that I do not want, that I did not ask for. I let the waves tug me and pull me, take me and hold me under. Until suddenly I feel a hand on my shoulder, an arm around my chest, pulling me back, pulling me to the sand.

"Skyblue," he whispers into my hair. "What are you doing?"

25

I'M STILL SHIVERING BACK ON the sand. The California night air and water are too cold to do what I just did, and my teeth chatter, and it's hard to catch my breath. River puts his arms around me and rubs my skin, trying to warm me, and I'm crying, but I'm not sure if it's because I'm happy or angry or confused. None of them. Or all of them.

"Where have you been?" I whisper to him, and the words are hard to get out. He doesn't answer, but he pulls me close to his chest and holds me there until my crying stops and I begin to hiccup. His heart beats quickly in my ear, even through the fabric of his sweatshirt, such a familiar sound that it dulls the cold and the water, and for a moment I hold on to just the sound of him, living, next to me.

"What were you doing, Sky? Running in Ocean like that. The current is strong here. It'll pull you under."

"I was fine," I tell him. "I'm a good swimmer." I wasn't

swimming, exactly, but I don't know what I was doing, so I don't tell him.

"That's not the point," he says. "You shouldn't take chances like that."

"Right, like you weren't the one who swam past Rocks to catch a fish?"

"That was different," he says. "Everything is different now."

"Yeah." I pull away from him, and I shiver again, but I wrap my own arms around my knees, curling myself into a tight ball.

"Skyblue," he whispers, kissing the top of my head, the way he always did before we went to sleep on Island. He takes off his sweatshirt and pulls it over my head. I close my eyes, breathe deeply. It smells faintly of fish and salt water. Home.

"River," I whisper when he sits back, "did Helmut kill my real father?"

He doesn't answer for a moment, and then he says simply: "Yes."

"Are you sure?"

"Yes." He sighs.

I think of what Dr. Banks called my *brutal honesty*, and I think River's is worse. With one word, he makes me feel like I need to throw up, and I clutch my stomach tightly. "How come you never told me?"

"I didn't know," he says. "At least, I didn't know for sure." He pauses. "It wasn't just your father, Sky." His voice falters a little, and I reach across the sand for his hand. Our fingers lace together, interlocking perfectly. "It was my mother, too."

That doesn't make any sense. If River did not leave me at the hospital to be with his mother, then where did he go, and why? He can't live at the fish market or on the market's boat. People live in houses here.

"Megan," a voice calls from the blackness, loudly. Then a little softer: "Island Girl, are you out here? Sky?"

"It's Ben," I whisper.

"Who?" River asks.

"He's . . ." and I'm not sure how to explain it. I want to say that he's my friend, but I remember that's the way Ben described River, and it doesn't seem right to use the same word to describe both of them.

"That boy that you're always with," he says softly, and I wonder how he knows.

"Sky," Ben calls again. "Where are you? Alice is freaking out . . ."

"I have to go." River pulls his hand away quickly, and then leans over and tangles his finger in my braid.

"Don't go." I reach up and hold on to his arm. "I've wanted to find you this whole time. We have to figure out a way to go back to Island, Riv. Together."

But he tugs it away. "I have to go," he says again, pulling farther away from me.

"Sky," Ben calls, his voice floating closer.

"Ben's nice—you'll like him," I say to River, grabbing for his arm, but he slips through my fingers. And even as I say it, I'm not sure. I think of what Ben said the other day, about my grandmother hating River and how he trusts her.

"Don't do anything stupid," River whispers behind him. "And whatever you do, don't tell your grandmother you saw me."

"River," I plead. "Please. Don't leave . . ."

The night wind whispers against my cheek, and in a second, his body has disappeared into the darkness, down the same pine path I ran here on. And Ben is there, putting his hand on my shoulder.

"There you are," he says. "What the hell? Alice said you just ran away."

"I . . ." I look around for any trace of River. But the only shapes I can make out in the darkness and the hazy glow of moonlight are the tall pines, arching in the wind. *Don't tell your grandmother you saw me*, he said, and I'm not sure how much I can trust Ben now. I don't think he'd keep secrets from my grandmother, his beloved Alice who has spent his entire life taking care of him almost as if he is her own. The way Helmut did for me. And I swallow hard, unable still to believe it. Helmut *murdered* my father, River's mother. "I just wanted to go for a swim," I finally say to Ben.

"Now?" he asks. "Dude, it's, like, sixty degrees out and pitch black."

I shrug. "I just wanted to be with Ocean . . . the ocean for a little bit. All right?"

He sits down next to me, in the spot where River just was. "Yeah, I get it," he says, and his voice sounds so kind and understanding that I feel a little bad that I'm keeping something from him now. I'm not lying, exactly, I know. But I'm not being *brutally honest*, either. "You miss it a lot, don't you?" he says after a few minutes. "Your island, I mean." I know what he means, and I nod.

"Did you know that Helmut killed my father?" I ask him. Even as I say it, as I know River believes it, it still doesn't sound right or true. Or possible. Why would Helmut do that? How could he do that?

"Yeah."

"Why didn't you tell me?"

He shrugs. "Alice said not to talk about all the bad stuff that happened in the past. That it might upset you, keep you from adjusting or something."

"All the bad stuff?" I say. "There's more?"

"I don't know," he says. "It was all a long time ago. I wasn't there."

"But there is more?"

"Yeah." He sighs. "I guess so."

"Then you need to tell me."

"I don't know . . . ," he says. "You should ask Alice. Or your weirdo therapist lady."

"No. I want you to tell me. You're my . . . friend, right?" Though I am still not sure whether he is or not.

He stands up, holding out his hand for me to take. "Come on, Alice is back at her house totally freaking out. And I ran out of my house so fast to come look for you that I left my phone there, so I can't call her. Let me just walk you home now. Okay? And we can talk about this more another time."

"Home?" I whisper. I look out ahead of me. The water rushes against the sand. River called it Ocean, but it's not. It's *the* ocean. Everything in California is more distant, more removed, not belonging to anyone at all.

And the water here didn't heal me; it chilled me, and I can't make myself feel warm now, even in River's sweatshirt.

"I don't even have Ocean anymore," I tell Ben.

"Sure you do," Ben says. "It's right here. Right in front of us."

I ignore his hand and stand up on my own. "But it's not mine anymore."

———————

Later, in my bed, I lie there wrapped tightly in River's sweatshirt. I pull the hood over my head and inhale deeply, and then I close my eyes and breathe in his new, California scent. It's different than it was on Island. But there's still something about it that reminds me distinctly of him.

The sweatshirt is warm, a little damp, and holds on to me tightly, like the feel of River's back hugging mine as we lay there together on our rabbit pelt mats.

26

THAT NIGHT, I DREAM OF HELMUT.

We walk along the edge of Ocean together, and Helmut holds his spear tightly in one hand, my hand tightly in his other. I am small again—five, maybe—and when I get tired of walking, Helmut picks me up and places me on his thick shoulders. I wrap my arms around his neck, getting tangled up in his blond hair and beard, the same yellow color as River's. I'm laughing, until I look down and see the circle of blood around his neck, a sharp, fatal cut, like the one River made with the stone to take the head off my birthday fish.

He deserved it, River says to me from somewhere behind me on the beach. *He killed them.*

———•———

I wake up sweating, my arms tangled in River's too-big sweatshirt. It was a memory, my dream, until it got to the awful part. Helmut would often carry me on his shoulders down on Beach when my feet got sore and tired, when it was too hot or too hard for me to walk. He would bounce me a little and teach me things, telling me about the tides and the moons, and the best way to catch and prepare a fish. I was six when he let me try it with his spear for the first time. I shot it into the water and pulled it back, squealing with delight to see a slippery silver fish on the point.

"Shhh." Helmut put his large hand over my mouth. "You'll scare the rest of them away." Then he smiled at me. "Let's go show Petal what you did. Only six and already catching dinner."

Back on the sand, Helmut lifted me up and hung me on his shoulders. They shook when he laughed, great big booms of laughter. In his hand he held out the spear, my first dead fish, dangling and bloody, on the end.

———◦———

If my grandmother overheard my conversation with Dr. Banks, or if Dr. Banks told her what happened last night, she doesn't mention it when I walk downstairs this morning. When Ben walked me back in last night, she'd only clutched me tightly to her, so tightly it was almost hard to breathe, and whispered into my hair, "Don't run off like that again, Megan. You scared me. I already lost you once, you know. I can't lose you again."

But instead of feeling her joy, I'd felt annoyed. What about what I've lost? No one seems to care.

At the table in her kitchen this morning, she sits there in her pink bathrobe, her blond hair uncombed, holding on tightly to a steaming cup of coffee. At my place she's already put out a glass of coconut milk and something new today I don't recognize.

"Blueberry muffin," she says as I eye it skeptically. It looks nothing like a blue berry.

I'm still in River's sweatshirt, and though she puckers her lips when she seems to notice this, she doesn't ask me about it. I've seen Ben wearing a similar one, and she probably just thinks it's his. I know she has known Ben for a long time and doesn't know River at all, but still, it doesn't make sense to me why she hates River so much. And why River seemed worried about me telling her I saw him last night.

"Can I ask you something?" I say as I take a bite of her muffin. It feels strange in my mouth. Too soft and too sweet. I force myself to swallow some and wash it down with some of her coconut milk. Better than the oatmeal she gave me yesterday. Worse than the fruit salad she gave me the day before that.

"What is it, honey?" She sips her coffee, and her voice sounds strained, as if she spent the night crying, the way my mother's sounded once after she and Helmut got in a fight and Helmut didn't come back to Shelter until the next morning.

"Why do you hate River?"

She puts the coffee down a little too hard, and some brown liquid jumps over the side and onto the table. She wipes at it with her thumb. "That man," she says. And instinctively I know she means Helmut. "Nothing good can come from that man."

"River and Helmut are very different," I say.

"Well, you wouldn't know that to look at him. He's the spitting image."

"That's really not fair," I tell her.

"You know what's not fair?" she says. Her voice is low, and

her jaw is clenched. "He took my daughter away. He took *you* away. Fifteen years," she says. "Look what he did to you."

"What he did to me?" It sounds awful, as if I am some sort of sea monster, the kind my mother would tell me about as we walked through the skim of Ocean when I was little.

The doorbell chirps in the distance, and my grandmother stands quickly, taking her coffee with her. "Finish your breakfast," she says. "Mrs. Fairfield will be ready to get to work."

I watch her walk away, and then I stand up and throw the muffin in the trash can. It feels good. To do something I feel like doing in her house. Something I choose. However small.

My grandmother doesn't look like a skeleton in her bathrobe, with her uncombed hair and her coffee. But Mrs. Fairfield taught me about metaphors the other day, and now I think I understand what my mother had meant. My grandmother doesn't care, really, that she lost me or my mother to Island. Or what happened to us there. Or that maybe we weren't really lost. That we were happy. That we were alive, and Island was simple. That we all loved one another. She cares only about what was taken from her, what was done to her. Underneath her robe and her clothes and her flesh, I'm not sure I believe her heart is beating, as mine always has. As my mother's did. As River's does.

———————

"So tell me," Mrs. Fairfield says, sitting across the table from me. Her coral hair is in a pile on top of her head today, which makes her cheekbones appear higher, her face more slanted and bright red. She smiles too wide, and I am already annoyed by her, though we haven't even begun our lesson yet. "What do you know about religion?" she asks me, still smiling.

"Religion?" I ask.

"Your mother was raised Catholic. Do you know what that is?" I shake my head. "Okay, then. On the island, did you ever talk about things like a god or a church? Did you pray?"

"I don't know," I say, all those words unfamiliar to me. "I don't think so."

"Were there rituals you performed?"

"Rituals?"

"Things you repeated day after day or week after week for luck or good measure?"

I nod. "Yeah, I guess so. We had things we did every day."

"Such as?"

"Well, first thing in the morning, I would use Bathroom Tree. Then I made a notch in Tree of Days. I checked the traps—"

She smiles again and puts her hand on my arm so I stop talking. "The things you did there, the way you survived every day, it's amazing. It really is. But that's not what I mean. Not the chores you did, not your routine." She hesitates for a moment. "But what did you believe in?"

"I don't know," I say. She nods and raises her eyebrows a little but doesn't say anything. Which is what she does when she's expecting me to think, or try, harder. So I put my head down, to make it look like I'm thinking. "We believed in Island, I guess," I finally say, "and Ocean. That the land and the water would feed us and keep us safe."

"Well, okay," she says. "But think, Megan. What did Helmut teach you to believe in?"

He taught me a lot of things. To fish and to trap. To skin a rabbit and to start a fire, that Ocean saves and heals us, but I press my lips tightly together because I don't think this is what she's asking me. "Helmut had a lot of rules," I say. "Is this what you mean?"

"What kind of rules?" she asks, folding her hands in front of her on the kitchen table, as if she is ready and waiting to listen, should I find the right thing to say.

"Well, things to keep us safe. We couldn't swim out past Rocks, in Fishing Cove. We couldn't build fires on Beach . . ." She shakes her head, and I don't understand it, why she's pushing me so hard on this subject we've never talked about before. "Aren't we going to read today?" I ask her. I'm feeling anxious now to get through the lesson and suffer through what I plan on being a quiet half an hour with Dr. Banks so I can see Ben again and try to get him to tell me the truth. All of it. And to take me back to the fish market.

"Do you know what a cult is?" Mrs. Fairfield asks now. I shake my head. "Well, most of us here have organized religion. Your mother and your grandmother are Catholic, like I said. A lot of people are. They all believe the same things, celebrate the same holidays, go to the same place to pray, and pray to the same God. It's normal to be religious, to believe in one of the common religions."

Normal. There's that stupid word again. In telling me how normal she wants me to be, she's pointing out how normal I'm not. "Do you believe in Common Religions?" I ask her.

She nods. "I'm Lutheran," she says, "which is kind of like Catholic. But not exactly. Close. We celebrate the same holidays, pray to the same God, that sort of thing."

"Okay," I say, though I only understand the smallest bit of what she said. And now I'm starting to get bored, so I pick at the loose piece of skin by the corner of my thumb.

"A cult is an unusual form of religion—not normal. It's smaller. More extreme. It's run by a person with strange beliefs, and his followers go along with them, even if it's bad for them."

"Why are you telling me all this?" I ask.

"There was a man named Charles Manson back in the 1960s, right here in California. He started a cult he called the Manson Family. Anyway, he was the leader of this cult, and all the women in his 'family' were in love with him, or they thought they were, so they listened to him, they believed in him, even when he told them to do crazy things. Manson convinced them the end of the world was coming, and that they needed to start it by committing murders."

She says the word *murders*, and it thuds, hard, the way her dictionary does when she drops it on the kitchen table in front of me. I think of Dr. Banks as she told me that Helmut was a murderer, that he'd killed my father. So what is Mrs. Fairfield trying to tell me now? We were a cult on Island? A Manson Family? No way.

"Heaven's Gate was another one," she's saying now. "Also right here in California, just a little while after . . . you were born. Marshall Applewhite was their leader, and he persuaded about forty people to kill themselves. They took the religious book that the Catholics and the Lutherans use—the Bible—and they twisted it. They made themselves believe the world was ending. So they ended it first."

Ben's song about the end of the world echoes in my head,

and I wonder if R.E.M. is also a cult, and if Ben believes in them. But I don't ask her. Instead, I say again, "Why are you telling me all this?"

"Because," she says, "your grandmother asked me to teach you about Helmut Almstedt today." I realize that Dr. Banks must've told my grandmother everything, and I don't understand why my grandmother couldn't just tell me about Helmut herself. "And I want you to understand exactly what that man was. Who that man was." She pauses. "Charles Manson. Marshall Applewhite. Helmut Almstedt. They were the same," she says. "Helmut Almstedt"—she repeats his name, and now it sounds like she bit into something sour—"was an evil man."

27

HELMUT STOOD BY THE EDGE of Ocean, his face angled up, staring far ahead, watching the pale blue line that sat between the edge of the water and the edge of the sky, the edge of the world.

"What are you looking for?" I asked him once. I was young, but not too young. Old enough to catch a fish, skin a rabbit. Old enough to doubt sea monsters and to understand that my mother loved Helmut even though he sometimes made her cry.

"I'm looking for the end," he said.

"What does the end look like?" I asked him.

He sat in the sand, at the edge of the water, the way he did every morning just after using Bathroom Tree. He let his feet touch the surf. I sat next to him and did the same. "I don't know yet," he said.

"Well, then how will you know when you see it?"

"I just will," he told me. "You know everything on Island is perfect. We have everything we need. We have each other, without all the evil."

"What's evil?" I asked him.

He shook his head. "You don't need to know that word here. You're lucky, you know? Everyone isn't so lucky as you and River. Growing up here."

"Everyone?" I asked, not sure who he meant; who else was there besides the four of us?

"Me and your mother weren't that lucky."

I sat there for a little while with him in silence, staring, staring. I saw only blue water meeting blue sky. "It's not coming today, is it?" I asked him.

"I don't think so." He stood and I did the same. "But one day it will," he said. "Goodness doesn't live forever."

"And what will happen then?" I asked him.

"You don't worry about that," he told me. "I'll take care of you. You and your mother and River. You never have to worry. I'll always take care of you."

———————

After Mrs. Fairfield leaves for the morning, my grandmother walks into the kitchen, slowly, quietly. She holds on to a book, which she puts on top of the table, and then she sits down across from me. "Do you understand?" she asks, her voice breaking a little on the word *understand*, as if it's a hard question for her to ask me, as if maybe she doesn't quite understand herself.

"No," I tell her. Everything Mrs. Fairfield said about Helmut having a strange cult religion and being an evil man still makes no sense to me. Mrs. Fairfield didn't give details past that. She moved on to reading practice while my mind wandered to thoughts of Helmut there, on Beach. "Helmut loved me," I say again now to my grandmother. "He loved my mother. I know everyone thinks they knew him. But they didn't." And still, I can hear the echo of River's quiet *yes*, of his confession that Helmut killed his mother, too. But it has to be a mistake. River must be wrong. They all must be wrong.

"Okay," my grandmother says, pushing the book toward me across the table. "Then I'm going to give you this."

"What is it?"

"Articles from newspapers and magazines that I cut out. Every written word that I could find about you and your mother back then. If you don't or can't understand or believe me or Mrs. Fairfield or Dr. Banks, well, then you can read what's in here. See for yourself."

I can't read well enough yet to be able to understand any of this, and even if I could, I don't want to. Words on paper, they don't mean anything to me. I'm not even sure where they come from, who put them there. And if you don't know where words come from, how can you even know they're real? I shake my head and push the book back across the table toward her. "I don't need this," I say. "I know what I know."

"But, honey . . ." Her voice falters. She pushes the book back to me. I push it back to her. She sighs, opens the book, and flips through the pages until she pulls something out and hands it across the table to me.

"I don't want it," I say.

"It's just a picture," she says. "Take it." And without

meaning to, my eyes fall on it and they catch on my mother, the strange, younger version of her that my grandmother showed me in the picture that day at Military Hospital. She's holding a small baby human wrapped in pink. Me, I guess. And next to her, there's a man I don't recognize. He looks tall and slim, with curly brown hair and bright green eyes. His jaw is set, determined, the way River's looked when he wanted to swim for fish past Rocks. But still, the man is smiling. His teeth are white and shaped like tiny, perfect fish eggs.

My grandmother stares hard at my face and opens her mouth, as if trying to figure out what she wants to say next, what she thinks I might understand. "Do you know him?" she finally says, pointing to the man. I shake my head. "This man was Brad Baynes," she says. "Your father."

"No," I say. "You're lying." But my voice trembles because something inside me jolts, the feeling of an insect sting, so sharp and sudden and surprising and instantly painful. There's something about this man that looks familiar. There's a mirror in my bedroom here, and my reflection is more defined in it than it ever was standing at the edge of Falls, watching myself staring back at me from the water that shares River's name. I think it's the man's eyes. They're the same color as mine, the same slant and shape as mine when they look back at me from the mirror in my bedroom.

"I'm not lying, honey," she says softly. "I promise you, I'm not."

"But my father never knew me," I protest, thinking if I say what I know out loud, then I'll understand it again, the way I always have. "He died before I was born." This is what my mother always told me, and Helmut always confirmed with a nod of his thick blond head. My father never knew me and I never knew him, and so, like a boat, like a planet named Venus, he was something too far removed to be real.

"No." She shakes her head. "Your father did know you. He loved you." She pauses. "He died just after you turned one, just before you all left on the boat. Here"—she pushes the picture closer—"take it. Hold on to it. And when you're ready to talk or read the rest of this, it'll be here. I'll be here." Her voice trembles a little, and so, I notice now, does her hand as she picks up the picture, opens my palm, and lays it flat in there.

I look at it again. I can't help myself. The smiling man. His arm around my mother, and his other hand brushing the top of my head as if he's about to lean down and kiss me there. It is so strange to see my mother—to see us—with someone other than Helmut.

"I canceled Dr. Banks for today," my grandmother says, and I look back up. "Maybe this has all been too much for you, too fast. I don't know. I don't know how to do this, honey. I'm sorry. I wish I did." She shakes her head and bites her lip, getting purple lipstick on the cusp of her front tooth. "There's no rulebook for this sort of thing. I'm just trying the best I can to help you."

Her tiny face is red, and her blue eyes water with tears. Her front tooth is stained with purple lipstick, and it makes her seem sad and small and old. She wants to love me, I think, and I suddenly feel bad for hating her so much. For the first time, I wonder how everything would be different now if this man, my supposed real father, had lived, and if my mother and Helmut hadn't gotten on a boat and left California. If I'd known my grandmother, this strange woman named Alice, my whole life.

The people in California are cold and broken, my mother said. There had to be more to it than this. She must've had a good reason for leaving this man behind, for getting on the boat with Helmut. She loved me; they both did. I still feel so certain of that. Even now.

"I'm sorry," my grandmother says again. "I can't even imagine what this all must be like for you. I really can't. I know you're hurting here, and I want to take that away for you. I want to fix it for you."

"I'm not broken," I say quickly.

She nods. "I know," she says. "I didn't mean that you were." She smiles and reaches for my hand across the table. She squeezes it. "So tell me, honey, what would you like to do today?"

I want to find River again. I want to show him this picture of my supposed father. To ask him what else he knows about our life. What is true and what is not. I want to find him and hold on to him tightly and not let go. I open my mouth to tell her that, and then I remember the way River whispered so frantically last night not to tell her that I'd seen him. The way she'd spat at me this morning that nothing good could come from Helmut. So instead I say, "I want to go back to the fish market with Ben."

"Oh?" She smiles again, seeming happy that I have asked for something I guess she would consider so *normal*. "Well, absolutely. I'll give him a call."

28

"WHY DON'T YOU EVER HAVE anything else to do?" I ask Ben as we sit in his blue SUV and he turns on the engine and speeds down the street toward the Pacific. I lurch forward and back, and his car seems to tumble down the hill to the ocean, too fast. He has the windows open, and the cool salt air flows in, thick enough that I can taste the ocean on my tongue.

Ben laughs. "What do you mean?"

"Well, I don't really understand what people our age *do* here. It seems like you're always at your house, just waiting for when my grandmother calls you and asks you to do something with me." I picture him sitting in his room drawing pictures, listening to R.E.M. and Nina Simone and maybe even his lost father.

"I'm not always at my house," he says. "Alice calls me on my cell, so she can call me anywhere." He points to the square, his *cell*. I nod. Mrs. Fairfield has told me about this and shown me hers. She has even tried to get me to tap the square numbers and then talk to my grandmother with it as my grandmother holds her cell upstairs in her bedroom, but it frightens me, the way her voice comes through it, broken and distant from her body.

"So what are you doing when she calls you?" I say. "If you're not at your house."

He shrugs. "It's summer, so I go to the beach or go hang out with my friends . . ."

I wonder what he does at the beach, and it's strange to picture him there, without me, with other friends who are not me and who I don't even know. I don't know what *hang out* means, exactly, and I imagine Ben and his friends climbing the spiky pine trees and hanging from the low branches, but I don't want to ask Ben now. Though Ben is supposed to be my teacher, like Mrs. Fairfield, I don't want him to think I'm a silly, stupid child, the way Mrs. Fairfield seems to think of me.

"Maybe you could come with us sometime," Ben is saying, but the way his voice sounds, kind of strange and far away, I don't really think he means it.

"Yeah," I say, knowing that I never will, that soon I'll find River again, and this time I will not let him run from me, no matter what. "Maybe."

Ben shrugs. "Anyway, in a few weeks school will start again. And then I'll go to school during the day." I know what school is, spending the entire day with people like Mrs. Fairfield who try to teach you things—and it sounds awful. I'm relieved that my grandmother and Mrs. Fairfield have decided that I won't be ready for that yet, whatever that means.

"But you don't have any jobs?" I ask Ben. There was always something to *do* on Island. We had an order to every day, for survival. *Rituals*, like Mrs. Fairfield said. Food to gather or catch or clean. "River and I always had jobs," I tell him. "For as long as I can remember."

Ben gives a funny laugh and then says, "Well, not exactly . . ." He pauses. "I used to bag groceries at Vons for six bucks an hour, but then . . . you came."

I don't know what one thing has to do with the other, but we're approaching the fish market now and I feel excitement at the thought of seeing River again, at the possibility that he might be here today.

Ben pulls his SUV into the parking lot and turns it off. I hold the twenty dollars my grandmother gave me tightly in my hand. The picture rests in the large middle pocket of River's sweatshirt. "I want to go in by myself today," I tell Ben.

"Um . . . I don't know if Alice would like that."

"I'll be right back," I promise. "And we won't even have to tell her." Listen to me, a lying, lying liar. Ben frowns. "Come on, you're supposed to help me get normal. Don't normal people our age buy fish themselves?"

He hesitates for another moment, and then he nods. "If you're not back in five minutes, I'm coming in for you." He laughs when he says it, but I don't think he's kidding.

———•———

Inside, the fish market looks exactly as it did the other day, the big glass window filled with slabs, so gutted and cleaned that they don't even look like fish at all anymore.

"Hey," the man behind the window says as soon as he sees me, a flicker of recognition crossing his face, and I feel my body tensing up, remembering how he asked Ben if I was that girl, from Island. But he doesn't mention that. Instead, he says, "We got your wahoo in this morning. How much do you want?"

"I don't know," I say, and show him my twenty dollars. "What this buys." He nods, and I lean in closer, across the glass. "Is Lucas here?" I ask. This is the real reason I'm in here, of course, why I'm lying to Ben and my grandmother. I pull the sleeves of River's sweatshirt down, clutching them tightly between my fingers, suddenly nervous.

"Lucas?" he yells toward the back. "Hey, Lucas, come out here, would ya?"

I hold my breath as the man packages my wahoo in brown paper, and the back door swings open gently. A short man with no hair and a thick white beard walks out. I look past him, wanting to catch just the slightest glimpse of River.

"Can I help you with something?" the white-bearded man asks me.

I shake my head. "I'm looking for Lucas," I say.

"Yeah," he tells me. "I'm Lucas. What do you need?"

"You're not Lucas."

He laughs, a great big roar in his belly that reminds me of Helmut's laugh. "The hell I'm not," he says. "I'm Lucas. Lucas Sandy, owner of this place. Now, what can I do you for?"

I don't know what he's asking, but I feel my cheeks turning red and my legs wanting to collapse beneath me. There is more than one Lucas? How can that be possible?

The other man hands over the fish, and I hand over the money, as I am supposed to. My hands are shaking, and in my mind I see River, the way he was last night on the beach.

I had thought for sure he was here. But if he isn't, then where is he? And how am I ever going to find him again?

"Can I help you with something?" Lucas, the sandy one, asks again. I shake my head, clutch the wahoo, and run back out into the parking lot.

"Four minutes and thirty seconds?" Ben says as I get back in his SUV. "Thirty more seconds, and I was coming in." He laughs again, but I think he sounds nervous, the way my mother would laugh when Helmut would tell her that he could smell a storm two days away. I throw the wahoo between our seats, and the brown paper rips a little. "Hey, what did the poor fish do to you?"

"Nothing," I say.

"No, really," he says. "What happened in there?"

"Nothing," I say again. "I bought some fish, all right?"

"All right," he says. Then he turns on the engine and speeds out of the parking lot, back up the hill toward my grandmother's house.

I calm down a little in the few minutes it takes to get back. I take a deep breath and try hard to think. *Think*. River found me on the beach, at night, and all I'll have to do is go back, and then he'll find me again.

But I think of all the nights I climbed out my bedroom window and I went there. The beach was always empty then, no River, no nothing. Those nights, it was later than last night, though, the middle of the night, when my grandmother was sleeping, and maybe River doesn't go to the ocean then. Maybe he sleeps, too, the way everyone else in California does, in a bed. Still, River must be drawn to the ocean the same way I am, though I'm not even sure how he found me to begin with last night. I understand that the Pacific Ocean in California is long and wide, stretching across the beach for miles and miles and miles. But now that he's found me once, I think, he'll find me again. All I have to do is go back to the beach at night, at the same time, and he'll find me.

But I think about the way my grandmother, as Ben called it, was "freaking out" last night, and I'm not sure how I'll be able to make my way back to the beach at night again, at that same time, alone, without her "freaking out" again.

I understand now that I'm going to need Ben's help and that I'm going to have to trust him. I don't have any other choice. "Ben," I say now as he stops the SUV in his driveway and turns off the car. "I need to go back to the beach tonight. You don't need to go with me. Actually, I want to go alone. But I need you to tell my grandmother you are so she doesn't get upset."

"Wait a minute." He holds his hand up. "You want me to lie to Alice and then just let you wander onto the dark beach yourself." He shakes his head, and I wonder what he'd think if he knew about me climbing out my bedroom window in the middle of the night to go there—not that I'd tell him. "Not going to happen."

"I'll be fine," I say.

"You're not on some deserted island anymore. Bad things can happen here. Bad things do happen here." I think about the gun, the shooting in the newspaper. But Mrs. Fairfield told me that place called Iowa is very, very far away from California.

"Fine," I say. "Then you can come with me if you want." I say this because I think it's the only way he'll agree, not because I need him to keep bad things from happening to me. No matter what Ben thinks, I know that the ocean, even here, will protect me, keep me safe. It always has, and it always will. "But you're going to have to keep a secret," I tell him.

"I don't like this," he says. "Why don't you just tell Alice? She's so cool. She'll understand."

"No, she won't," I say.

He frowns. "Why not?"

"Because she hates River . . . Lucas."

"That's why you wanted to go to the fish market? And why you wanted me to wait in the car?" His voice grows louder, and his cheeks turn red; he's mad.

"I'm sorry," I say, though I'm not. "But he wasn't even there. It wasn't him. It was Lucas, the sandy one." I pause. "But I saw him on the beach last night. He was there, right before you came. And that's why I need to go back, tonight. Because maybe he'll come back, too."

He shakes his head. "I don't know. I don't think it's a good idea . . ."

"Look," I say. "You can either come with me and help me, or I'll run again, and then my grandmother will call you and freak out." I pause. "And if that happens, maybe you won't find me so easily in the dark on the beach."

"What are you saying?"

"I know a lot more about the beach and the ocean than you do," I tell him. "I could disappear, let you search for me all night or all week. Let my grandmother freak out." I know it sounds mean, like the words Helmut would spew at my mother when they would fight. He always knew more. Did more. Had more. It was a power he held over her in that way. But we couldn't deny him that. It was true. If it wasn't for Helmut, I'm not sure we would've known how to live on Island. How to survive. We needed him.

Helmut murdered your father. Dr. Banks's voice still hangs uneasily in my head, right there next to River's words. *My mother, too.* And that's exactly why I need to go back to the beach tonight, to find River again.

29

MY GRANDMOTHER COOKS THE WAHOO on her grill for dinner, and as soon as I bite into the dry and flaky fish she's put on my plate, I realize that Mrs. Fairfield was wrong. That this is not the same fish River caught me for my birthday at all.

I don't eat much, but I push the fish around on my plate with my fork, a trick I've learned to make it look like I've eaten more than I have.

"Do you like it?" My grandmother's voice arches expectantly.

I am about to nod and murmur that I do, but then I remember the way she sounded this morning, like she really did want to help and understand me, and I think I should tell the truth, the way my mother always said I should. "It's not the same as the fish on Island," I say.

She surprises me by laughing and nodding. "Well, I suppose not, honey. I don't think anything would be." She takes a bite of her own fish and then clears her throat. "So you ate a lot of fish there, then?" She says it softly, as if her voice is dancing on the crests of waves, uncertain whether they are drowning or floating.

It's the first time she has ever asked me about my life on Island, as if she really might want to know, as if there were things there that were *normal*, and that it was okay that I did them and that I loved them. I hesitate for a moment, but then words spill out of me. I tell her about the fish that River speared for me on my birthday, the one he held out to me as a present, spanning the length of his wide arms. I tell her how we roasted it over Fire Pit until it began to rain, and then we ate it, huddled together in Shelter. And then afterward, we tumbled into sleep holding on to each other, our bellies warm and full.

"It sounds very nice," she says, but I can't tell if she means it, because something about her eyes seems far away, as if she is looking at something I can't quite see. "You know what I gave your mother for her sixteenth birthday?" she asks after a little while. I shake my head. "A bracelet. Perfect pink stones. Do you know what that is, honey?" *A bracelet. Pink. Perfect.* I nod. "Your mother loved that bracelet."

I think of the bracelet my mother made me on Island before she died, a band of pink shells, its sole purpose for decorating my arm. Now I wonder if she'd been thinking of the one her mother gave her when she made it for me, and if she had been, why she didn't tell me then. "What happened to it?" I ask my grandmother.

"Oh, I don't know," my grandmother says. "I wish I had it still, honey. I'd give it to you. But I don't." She reaches across the table for my hand and gives it a small squeeze.

"My mother made me a bracelet. Out of shells," I whisper.

"I forgot to take it with me, when the boat came . . ." I look down, suddenly biting back tears. *When I go back there, it will still be there*, I tell myself. But the thought rests uneasily in my head now. It suddenly all feels . . . I think of Dr. Banks's word: *complicated*.

"You know what's better than a bracelet," she says softly. I look up, and she taps her forehead with her other hand. "Memories. What's in here." She pauses. "No one can take those away from you, you know."

Memories. The stories that Helmut said never happened. But now I'm not so sure.

I remember so much of Island—all of it. The feel of my mother's delicate fingers as she put the shell bracelet around my wrist for the first time, the smell of the salt water on River's skin after he came out of Fishing Cove, the feel of his warm back against mine as we fell asleep. The sound of Helmut's booming voice as he taught me how to check the traps.

Is my grandmother right? That memories are better than a bracelet, that they cannot be lost or taken from inside your head? But then I wonder, if Helmut did not tell us the truth about memories, what else did he not tell us the truth about?

The doorbell rings, and I know it's Ben. Darkness has fallen now, the night sky a perfect black, the yellow moon a perfect circle, arching high above the shadows of the pines.

"Oh, Ben, honey," I hear my grandmother say from the next room. "What a nice surprise. I owe you a check, don't I?" *A check?* I remember the rectangle pieces of paper Mrs. Fairfield showed me and claimed were a type of money, and I don't know why she would give Ben one of those.

"No worries, Alice," I hear Ben say. He clears his throat. "I, uh . . . just came to see if Megan wants to take a walk."

"Now? It's dark outside."

"I brought a flashlight," he says.

I get up from the table and walk to the front door. "Ben," I say too loudly, "what a great idea. I'd love to take a walk." My heart pounds so hard, I think my grandmother will be able to hear it, pounding through the thickness of River's sweatshirt. This lying, it's a very strange thing. And I feel bad about it now, thinking about the pretty pink bracelet my grandmother said she gave my mother once. Maybe she did love my mother, and maybe she is trying, even, to love me. But I need to find River, and I think about what Ben said about her hating him. I know I can't tell her the truth, even if a part of me might now want to.

She pulls her purple lips together, but all she says is, "Well, you two be careful, and don't stay out too long."

———

Since all the vultures are long gone now, we take the front path to the beach, out the front door, past the houses, down the hill, across the coastal highway, and then down the steps to the beach below. Ben's flashlight hangs out in front of us, a low, round circle sun. I've never seen a flashlight before, but then again the stars were bright enough on Island, and something like that wasn't necessary. The stars always guided us in the darkness, even the twenty paces down the hill toward Bathroom Tree if you had to use it in the middle of the night.

"Why is my grandmother giving you a check?" I ask Ben as we walk down the steps to the sand.

"What?" he says.

"A check. I heard her say she owes you one. That's money, right?"

"Uh . . . yeah," he says. "But it's no big deal."

"No big deal," I echo back, trying to figure out if these are good words or bad ones. *Big* sounds good. *Deal* does not. But Ben doesn't yell that they're bad, so I think they must be okay.

Our feet hit the sand, and I take off my flip-flops. Ben leaves his on, and I run past him quickly toward the edge of the water.

"Sky!" he yells after me. "Wait." But I don't.

I hear the ocean, feel the salt against my skin, and I want to feel the water on my toes. Even if it is cold.

"You're not going to run in again, are you?" Ben calls from behind me.

I shake my head, though I think about the way River came in after me last night, and I pull his sweatshirt tighter around me. I put my hands in the center pocket, feeling for the crisp, thin edge of the picture.

I see the circle of Ben's flashlight hit the water, and then he sits down at the water's edge. I take a few steps back and sit next to him.

"So what do we do now?" Ben asks. "Just wait for him?"

I shrug because I don't know. "Can't you go wait up by the steps?" I ask him. "And turn your flashlight off?"

"Why?"

"Because he might not come out if he sees you here."

"So?" Ben says. "That might not be the worst thing." He pauses and tilts his flashlight down, so it makes a low yellow circle across a wave, catching on a slag of seaweed.

"Ben," I say, "I really need to talk to him."

"What if I tell you everything I know?" he asks. "Then can we go back home and give this up?"

No. But I don't tell him that, because I want to hear it, everything he knows. "What do you know?" I ask.

He takes a deep breath, and then he starts talking, his voice measured, even. Like Helmut's. "Okay, back in the nineties, Helmut Almstedt had this cult. This . . . group."

"I know what a cult is," I say, thinking of the way Mrs. Fairfield's voice went up as she tried to explain it all to me earlier.

"All right. So they called themselves the Gardeners, after, you know, the Garden of Eden." I don't know, but I nod, even though I don't think he can see me in the darkness. "Anyway, at first it was kind of harmless, I guess. Helmut wanted to start this sort of utopian society, where everyone worked on the land and they all grew their own food. He and his wife and . . . Lucas, they lived on this big farm up north of here outside LA, and lots of people came to join them."

"My mother," I say softly.

"Yeah." He takes a deep breath. "Anyway, it was all good until one day Helmut decided that there were evil people who'd gotten into the Garden. Serpents, he called them. And so he poisoned their food."

"Poisoned?" I ask, not liking the sound of that word at all.

He nods. "Yeah, he basically put something bad in it, something that would murder them when they ate the food."

My heart pounds in my chest at the word *murder*. The noise rushes loudly through my ears, and it takes me a moment to realize that Ben is still talking.

"Almost everyone who lived on the farm died," he's saying now. "From what we know, there were only a few of you left, and he took you out on his boat and sailed away into the Pacific. The Coast Guard had him in their sights, and they were closing in, but then there was a storm, and, well . . . you know the rest."

His words are so strange, so far away: *poison, evil, murder.* And for some reason I think about my grandmother's question, when she asked me how my mother had died, the animal noise she made when I told her about the mushroom. *Poison?* But that's not how my mother died. She only ate a mushroom. A bad mushroom. *Helmut lied.* River showed me that day on Island, as if he knew, as if he remembered that there was more, before us.

"Well . . . ," Ben says. "What are you thinking?" I stare silently into the ocean, into the round yellow sun of his light, dancing on the waves as they go slowly up and down, the way they always do, the way they always have. "Come on," he says. "Say something, please."

"I can't," I whisper. Because I don't think there are words to say how I'm feeling, and if there are, I don't know them. I think about my mother, the way her arm was limp around my body that morning, her fingertips cold, her lips slightly parted as if she wanted to whisper something more in my ear, but also they were an unnatural blue.

"I don't think he's coming," Ben says now. "And we should probably get back."

I don't want to leave. I want to stay here, right next to the ocean, where there is something, one thing, the rush and pull of the water, the tides, that makes sense.

"Sky." Ben stands and touches my shoulder. "Come on."

I stand and force myself to turn away from the ocean. We climb up the beach, and I stare at the back path, the pine trees, for even the smallest glimmer of River, but all I see are the arches of the pines swaying gently in the night breeze.

"Ben," I say as we climb the steps back up to the road. "There's one thing I still don't understand. Why does my grandmother hate River ... Lucas?" I wonder where River is right now, and if he knows all the things Ben just told me, and if he believes them, and if he's all alone. I want to hold on to him, to hear him whisper in my hair, feel the tangle of his fingers in my braid. I want to tell him that he's not his father and his father isn't him, and that anything that might have happened then has nothing to do with us. And that maybe the entire world is wrong. Maybe they don't know what they think they know.

Ben doesn't answer me, but as we cross the coastal highway and make it back onto their street, he stops first in front of his house. "Come in for a minute," he says. "I'll show you something that might answer your question."

I follow him in through the front, and when we walk in, I'm surprised to hear the sounds of the television box.

"Mom," Ben calls out. "I'm home."

The sounds of the television box fade, and for the first time I see Ben's mother. She is small and thin, and her face is round like Ben's, her hair a little longer, but only at her chin, brown but streaked with gray.

She stares at me and then smiles. "Oh my goodness, Megan, is that really you? I've heard so much about you. Come sit down on the couch. Can I get you an iced tea?"

"Mom," Ben says, "we'll be upstairs."

He pulls me toward the steps, and I hear her calling after us. "Well, let me know if you need anything. I'll just be down here."

"She seems nice," I whisper.

Ben shrugs. "Yeah, she's fine," he says. "When she's actually home."

I think about what Ben's saying and about how much time he said he spent with my grandmother growing up, and it makes me sad that he did not spend every moment of his life with his mother, the way I spent with mine. But also it makes me sad that she is still here, with him now, and my mother is gone. It doesn't seem fair.

Ben turns on the light in his room, and my eyes go immediately to the wall with all the pictures. Then I notice that a new one sits on his table, not yet hung, and I pick it up. A girl, running into the ocean. The waves crashing over her. *Me.* "What's this?" I ask.

"Nothing." He snatches it from my hand and puts it face-down on the nightstand. "I'm not finished yet. Anyway, here . . ." He walks over to a table, opens the box I recognize as *laptop computer.* My grandmother has one, too, and Mrs. Fairfield says I will learn to use it eventually, that it is like the television box, only there is so much more you can do with it.

Ben moves his fingers across what I recognize as letters, and then turns the laptop computer so I can see it.

"What's this?" I ask.

"Google." I see only blank white with some letters I can't read—Google looks like nothingness, like the whiteness that surrounded me at Military Hospital, and I have no idea how it could tell Ben anything. But Ben moves his fingers across the letters on the laptop computer again, and then something different comes before me. Small words that I don't think I can read. And pictures. But unlike the television box, these pictures are still, the people in them unmoving, like the pictures my grandmother has handed to me, only these pictures are behind the laptop computer's window.

There is one of Helmut where he is much younger, standing by a large grassy hill, smiling. He looks so much like River here it's shocking. "How did you put this in here?" I ask as I put my finger up to trace the outline of his face, thinking it belongs to me. Then I think about what Ben said, about the poison, the murder, and I pull my finger back quickly.

"I didn't put it in there," Ben says. "It's just the Internet. Google. Any picture you want, at your fingertips."

I don't understand how that is possible, and yet Helmut is here. Inside Ben's laptop computer. The blank white Google is amazing. And frightening in its power.

"Here," Ben says. "This one." He presses one of the letter squares and the pictures shift, so I see a different one.

A small boy holding on to a basket with one hand and what looks like an apple in the other. He's smiling, and behind him there are people sitting at a very long rectangle table. Their faces are blurry, hard to make out, but one catches my eye, and I think it's possible it's the same man from the picture my grandmother gave me.

"I don't understand," I say.

"This is Lucas Almstedt." Ben points to the boy, and in the boy's face I see a little of the River I know. A very small, short-haired version, but there is a look in his eyes that's familiar, that same look, that same grin, as the one he had when he walked back to Shelter with my large birthday fish spanning his arms. "And this"—Ben points to the basket and the apple—"is how these people were murdered." His finger spans the blurry heads at the table, one of whom might be the man my grandmother claims to be my father. "Poisoned apples."

Ben pushes the letter button again, and there are more pictures. River—Lucas—handing people apples, and then one I have to look away from, rows and rows of the people lying on the ground, certainly dead.

"I don't understand," I say again. "How did all these pictures get in here? How do you know all this if everyone from the cult died or got on the boat?"

"Helmut left some of the pictures behind, I guess." Ben shrugs. "And I think the authorities had him under surveillance for a while. It was like they knew he was going to do something crazy, but they didn't figure it out in time."

Ben closes the laptop computer and pushes it away. But the image stays in my head, little River, feeding people poisoned apples. I don't think for even a second that River knew what he was doing, but even still, I understand what Ben is trying to tell me. Everyone in the whole wide world who doesn't know River the way I do—they believe the worst about him. They believe that he is just like his father: a murderer.

30

I LIE IN BED IN the darkness for a very long time, tracing the path of the moon across the gray sky, my eyes transfixed and open wide. Every time I close them I see the pictures, River, the poisoned apples. And now, for the first time, I have this horrible feeling in my stomach when I think of Helmut: I hate him. And not for the reason my grandmother or anybody else in the whole wide space of California does. I hate him for what he did to River, for the pictures he left behind, for all the Googles and laptop computers in the world that show River—my River— killing people. I hate Helmut.

When the numbers on my clock turn to all bright-red threes, I get out of bed and go over to the window. I can't lie here anymore; I need to go back to the ocean, to look for River again, and if he's not there, maybe I can leave him a message in the sand, draw him a picture the way we used to when we were kids.

I open my window and yank on the screen. And a few seconds later, my feet hit the grass, wet and cool with dew, and I suddenly realize I'm not wearing shoes. I've forgotten to take my flip-flops tonight. It startles me that this thought bothers me now—out of the house without shoes—and I hate how quickly I've become someone else. How quickly Sky has faded away and Megan has appeared. I'm not going to climb back up for them. I did not wear shoes my entire life on Island. I will be fine without them now.

I run through the dewy grass, and then I climb over the fence and run to the pine-filled path, my feet crunching on sharp pine needles. I can smell the ocean so strong in my nose, how close it is, and that's enough to bring me comfort, even as my feet sting against the pine needles.

The beach is still and silent, and the tide has pulled in closer. My feet hit the sand, and I yell River's name as loud as I can, but my voice is swallowed up by the ocean. I yell it again and again and again. But still, I'm alone.

I sit in the sand, and with my finger, I trace the outline of two circles, their round sides connecting midway through each other, and I think about how strange it feels to be drawing without a pencil now. But River and I drew this picture, when we were younger, in the sand. "It's you and me," he always told me.

"That's not what people look like, silly," I said once.

But now, I see it exactly the way he understood it then, River and me, our edges overlapping, connecting, entwined. That's the way we're supposed to be. Without him, I am lost, empty. Just a circle, a deep, empty hole.

When I finish drawing, I stare out across the ocean for a long time. I think about all the many days of my life spent staring out at Ocean, with my mother, Helmut, and River. I think of my mother's story, about the owl and the pussycat, how they sailed out to sea in a beautiful boat. And then they danced and danced on Beach by the light of the moon. It was her story—I always thought it was, no matter what Helmut said about it. She and Helmut, me and River, sailing into beautiful deep blue Ocean in a boat. Island calling to us, a paradise found. But now I'm not sure. The way Ben told it to me, it was as if they were running away from something, something terrible, not running toward something beautiful. And I don't understand how that can be true.

I look up, and I notice the sky is lightening a little now, that Venus now hangs low beneath the moon, just the way it always did on Island. It looks exactly the same here, a bright yellow star. Nothing more.

I think of the song my mother taught us when we were little: *Starlight, star bright, first star I see tonight. I wish I may. I wish I might. I wish the wish I wish tonight.*

What do you wish for? I always asked her.

I wish for you to be safe and healthy and happy.

I always wished for fish, that they would come quickly and easily to my spear the next morning and we would have enough for all of us to feast on the next day. But that night River and I carried my mom's and Helmut's limp bodies into Ocean, I wished for her to come back when I saw Venus. I wished for the water to carry her out and to heal her, and then for the tide to bring her back to me, full and whole again, the next morning.

It didn't. It never did.

I stopped making wishes.

"It's you and me," a voice calls out into the ocean now, riding the crest of a wave in an echo, and I don't know if I'm imagining it or if it's really there. I turn quickly, and it's real. He stands there, by my circles in the sand.

"River!" I yell, and I run to him. He wraps me in a hug, and I hold on to him so tightly. *Like two connected circles*, I think, our arms wrapped around each other, our bodies fitting together the way they always have and always will. "Where have you been?"

"Shhh." He tangles his finger through my braid.

"I've been looking for you, and I couldn't find you," I say. "I thought you were at the fish market, but you weren't. And then I didn't know where else to go but here." I bite my lip to keep the tears from coming, but I can't stop them. They come quickly, and River wipes them away. "I know about everything now," I tell him. "The cult, and Helmut, and . . . the apples."

He nods slowly, and by the way his face turns down, I understand that it's all true. Or at least he thinks it is. He knows, and he believes it.

"Aren't you happy here, Skyblue?" he asks me. "With your grandmother and . . . your Ben, and . . ."

"No," I say quickly. "Are you happy here, Riv?"

He shakes his head and lets go of me. He sits down in the sand, in the middle of one of my circles. I sit down next to him, and I put my head on his shoulder, entwining my arm through his, listening to the soft sound of his breath, his heart, his life. "I'm sorry," he says. "We never should've left Island." I think about that last morning, the way he begged me to go with him the twenty paces up Grassy Hill, the way he swam for me when

I dove back into the water, pulling me back to Roger and Jeremy's boat. "This is all my fault," he says.

"No," I tell him. "You didn't make the boat come, Riv."

"Yeah, I did," he whispers. "I built a fire on Beach that last day. When you were mad at me."

"A fire on Beach," I murmur. River broke Helmut's rules, no swimming past Rocks, no fires on Beach. *These are the things I tell you to keep you safe*, he promised us, and we believed him. And maybe he was right. River broke his rules, and the boat came. And now . . . we're here.

"So you can hate me now," River says. "I did this."

I shake my head. "I could never hate you."

He turns to face me, and his face is so close to mine now that I can feel his breath against my cheek. "I remembered my mother," he whispers. "I did."

I nod because I believe him now. I think about how I yelled at him that time, years ago, when he swore his memory was truth. How I didn't believe him then, and now I wish I had.

Memories, my grandmother said. *No one can take those away from you.*

I wish I would've asked my mother more questions, made her answer me. I wish I could've known her version of this truth, so I would know how much to believe of what everyone else here is saying.

"My mother carried me somewhere once," River is saying now. "I don't know where. But she was holding on to me and running through grass, and the sun was warm and she was laughing, this really nice laugh that kind of sounded like the rain on the rocks." I think of that place Ben told me about, and I wonder if that was where they had been. "My head was on her shoulder, and she had her arms around me. And I just felt . . . safe. Loved." He pauses. "I thought if I came back here, she'd still be here, waiting for me." His voice cracks. "I just wanted to see her again. I didn't know she was dead. All this time, I thought she was still here."

I lean my face in closer so our noses touch. I feel River's shoulders shake against my hands, and I think he's crying. "It's not your fault," I tell him. "You didn't know."

"I fed them the apples," he says. "I poisoned my own mother, and your father and a hundred other people."

"You didn't know," I repeat. I finger the edges of the picture in my pocket. *My father*. He knew me and he loved me, my grandmother said. I think of the blurry image of his face, of River, standing there with the apples. *I poisoned my own mother*, River said.

I think of River seeing those pictures that Ben showed me earlier, and my stomach hurts as if I've been socked under hard by a wave and thrown into Rocks, gutted and mutilated like a fish.

River pulls away from me, and he stands. I'm afraid he's going to run again, so I stand, too, ready to chase him. I'm fast, almost as fast as him. I can catch him. "I promised her I'd stay away from you," he says.

"Who?" I put my hand back on his shoulder until he turns toward me.

"Your grandmother," he says. He looks down, as if he's ashamed to look at me when he says it.

I put my hand on his chin and tilt his face up gently so our eyes meet. "When did you talk to my grandmother?" I ask him.

"At Military Hospital," he says. "She came to see me, and she told me everything then. About Helmut and what he did and what people think of him. And she showed me all those awful pictures with the apples." He pauses and casts his eyes back down to the sand. My toes are tangled in a mess of seaweed now, but I barely notice. "She said I'd only be hurting you by being around you here, and she was right," he says softly.

"What?" I feel an anger so thick it curls inside my body, in my blood, pouring and rushing into my head with the sound of the ocean so suddenly it's hard to hear. The seaweed chokes my foot, and I kick at it, hard, until it flies. River is still talking, but I can't make out what he's saying.

Cold and broken. My grandmother is the worst of all of them. She showed River the pictures. She told him to stay away from me.

"No," I finally say, grabbing onto River's shoulder again. "She wasn't right. She doesn't know anything about me, about us. About Island."

River stops talking, but his mouth is still open a little. I pull my face in close to him and listen for his breathing to even.

I notice the way River's face and mine are almost touching, the way our breathing has evened in unison, as if we are one person. I notice that he still smells of salt water, and that being this close to him, my skin suddenly grows warm even in the cool night air. River is here, the same as he always was. But nothing is the same. I don't feel the same. Maybe this is what my mother meant when she said things would change when we got older?

I want to tell River this, but I'm not sure how, so I stand up on my toes and lean in even closer, and do what I often saw my mother and Helmut do. I put my lips on his and I kiss him.

"Sky." He pulls back. "What are you doing?"

I don't know what I'm doing. Or why. But touching his lips with mine suddenly feels like an instinct for survival. Just like the ones we knew on Island. I need to show him how much I missed him, how empty I am without him. How he can never leave me again. How we fit together. River and Sky. Sky and River.

So instead of answering, I stand up on my tiptoes and kiss him again. I hold on to his lips with mine, and my entire body fills up with warmth from the inside out, as if we are back there again, in Ocean, the beautiful warm water holding us up, carrying us together.

"Skyblue," he whispers, his mouth so close to mine that I think I can taste the sound of my name, my real name, in his voice. Warm and salty and just a little sweet like coconut milk on Island, and like everything I know to be true.

"It's okay," I whisper back. "We're going to be okay."

He hesitates for a moment, but then he smiles and wraps his arms around me tightly, pulling my body to him. He moves his mouth back to mine, and even through all our California clothes, I can still feel his warmth as I always knew it.

There are no words, good or bad, empty or filled with meaning, that could say any more than what we say to each other as our lips move tightly together. They fit, the way those circles I drew on the beach do, as if this is the way they were always supposed to be.

"Come on," River whispers when he finally pulls back. "Come with me."

He holds out his hand, and I take it.

31

RIVER AND I HOLD HANDS as we walk down the beach, and by now the sun is almost up over the tall brown hills. I have the thought that my grandmother will notice the open window in my bedroom soon, that she and Ben will rush to the beach looking for me, and that I won't be there, and she will be upset and worried. I feel bad for a moment, but then I think about what she did to River, and I push the feeling away. For the first time since I left Island, I know exactly who I am and where I'm supposed to be. Here. With River.

"Where are we going?" I ask River after we've walked for a little while. I wonder if he has a grandmother and a "team of professionals" to make him *normal*, but something tells me he doesn't—that here in California, River is all on his own. For one thing, he is not wearing shoes, and for another, I notice now his shirt is on backward and his hair, though shorter, is messy, uncombed.

"My shelter," he says. And immediately I think of the word

house, because that's what a shelter always seems to be in California, and now I think it's strange that River doesn't say this.

But I soon see why. River's shelter lies underneath a long wood structure held up by tall sticks that spans from the high rocks above us, across the beach, out over into the water. We duck to walk underneath the wood, and inside it's darker and smells a little like Bathroom Tree. When my eyes adjust, I see two men a little farther down, sleeping against each other in a pile of dirty-looking clothes.

River leads me to what I guess is his space, along the other end, where he has a blanket and a brown paper bag.

"This is where you've been?" I ask, and I feel a knot in my chest at the thought of him sleeping out here all alone, with no bed, nothing.

He nods, and he says, "It's not that different from Island, really. And I can get everything I need here. If you climb up Rocks there are boxes of fruit and even fish some days."

I think about the fish market, and I think that here in California, you have to pay money for these things, and I don't know if River knows that. But I'm not going to mention it now. "You must be tired," he says. I nod. I am. "Come on. We can sleep, and then we'll figure everything else out later."

He lies down on his blanket, and he pats the space next to him. I lie down, too, and he turns the way he always did on our rabbit pelt mats in Shelter, so our backs are touching, hugging each other. I hear the rush of the ocean close by, and then I close my eyes and fall asleep.

———

When I wake up, my back hurts, and it takes me a minute to remember where I am. I sit up and stretch, and River is already awake, sitting there, staring at me. "I got us some fruit," he says, and he hands me a small green carton filled with strawberries. For some reason I think of that stupid picture Ben showed me in his laptop computer, River holding on to a basket of poisoned apples, grinning, but I push the thought away and take a strawberry. It's sweet, and the juice melts in my throat, even as I think of what my grandmother told me, that it's dangerous to eat fruit without washing it in the sink first.

"Thanks," I say, and I smile at him. He smiles back, and I watch his lips for a minute, remembering how they felt against mine last night, in the darkness, on the beach. I want to feel them again, even though now the thought makes me feel embarrassed, and I think my cheeks might be turning as red as the strawberries.

"Hey." He reaches out for my hand. "Are you sorry you came with me?"

"No way." I shake my head, and I'm not sorry. From farther down, one of the dirty men groans and drinks something from a brown bag, and I quickly look away. "Don't you have anyone here in California like my grandmother?" I ask him, and I think guiltily of the way her voice shook when she talked about my mother and her pretty pink bracelet. But then I think of what she did to River, and I hate her all over again.

He shakes his head. "Helmut has a sister who lives in Temecula. They let me call her from Military Hospital, but she didn't want to have anything to do with me." He shrugs. "I don't blame her. She says this Temecula is pretty small and she has little kids, and, well, everyone would know me there. It's bad enough that she's already Helmut's sister."

"I'm sorry," I say, reaching for his hand and squeezing it.

"It's fine," he says. "I don't even remember her." I nod. "Anyway, they said at Military Hospital that since I'm eighteen they would just let me go, on my own."

"But you're not eighteen yet," I say, wondering if I've missed his birthday. Even though Mrs. Fairfield has shown me the calendar, and I've been making pencil notches behind my bed, it's not the same as Tree of Days, and I have trouble keeping track, especially when some mornings my grandmother would shake me awake after I'd barely slept.

He shrugs. "I am. I have been for a few months, I guess." He pauses. "That doctor at Military Hospital, she told me we weren't counting right on Tree of Days."

"Oh," I say, but I don't know that I believe that. It was easy to count. A notch for each day. And we always made one, every morning. Not like here, where I sometimes get distracted and have forgotten or haven't been able to find my pencil.

"The doctor said that our birthday should count from the day you first come into the world as a baby human. She said the birthday we celebrated on Island—the day Helmut first put us in Ocean and gave us our names—that isn't what a birthday really is."

"Oh," I say again, not sure I believe it. The day of your birth is the reminder of the day the water first cleanses you, gives you life, the day you are named and become one with Island. I was too young to remember being dipped in Ocean that first time, but Helmut always told the story. He told how immediately I swam, even though I was just two, how my head bobbed to the surface and I just knew the water. But how River was four years old and nearly drowned.

"Dr. Cabot said it was like we were reborn. New kids. River and Sky. Not Lucas and Megan. Lucas and Megan have different birthdays, I guess." He shrugs, and I wonder what day my birthday is, at least according to Dr. Cabot, if I am already sixteen or not quite yet.

"Did you remember on Island that you had another name?" I ask him.

He shakes his head. "No. I remember the water part, that first birthday. I remember coughing water, and Petal pulling my head up and hugging me." He pauses. "And I remember things from this other life . . . but not the name. No. Lucas." He laughs grimly now. "He's like this boy I never even knew."

I nod in agreement, so glad I have River here, finally, to share with. And for some reason I think of what Mrs. Fairfield told me about religion. Maybe that thing about Helmut dipping us in Ocean was the kind of thing she was waiting for me to tell her, but I didn't really think of it at the time. And I'm not sure if that dipping meant something else that I never understood. Not that it matters now anyway. I clear my throat. "So, you've been here on your own all this time?" I ask him. "I don't understand how."

"Your grandmother gave me money," he says softly. "When she told me to stay away from you, she paid me what she said would be enough to live with for a while, and she found me a shelter that she called Apartment. But she said I had to promise to stay there, away from you." He pauses. "I tried—I really did,

Sky. But there were so many people there, and they weren't nice. They yelled things at me. And there were all these bright suns flashing in my eyes."

"Cameras," I say, thinking of the vultures at the bottom of my grandmother's driveway and about the fact that River had no one to shield him from them. Helmut was many things, some of which I'm still not completely understanding, but I don't know that he was wrong when he called me the practical one and River the dreamer.

"So," River is saying now, "I found this place. It was close enough to you so I could keep an eye on you."

"Keep an eye on me?"

"Yeah." He shrugs. "I've kind of been following you from a distance. Just watching to make sure you're safe."

"You've been tracking me?" He nods, and I think of the way Helmut used to hunt and track boar when we were younger. He would never let River go with him, because he always said River didn't have it in him to track an animal. The thought makes me laugh a little now. River has been tracking me here in California. "So that's how you found me in the ocean the other night?" I say.

He nods again. "You looked like you were going to drown."

"I wasn't," I say quickly. "I'm a good swimmer."

"I know," he says. "But you looked like . . . I don't know, like you weren't trying to swim. Maybe you wanted to drown?"

"I didn't," I say. "I just wanted the water to heal me, to take me back."

"It doesn't, though, you know." He looks down, and I think he's remembering that morning, how hard it was to drag the bodies of our parents all the way from Shelter to Ocean. How I told River then what I hoped, what I wished, for, and then how Ocean didn't answer me, how it just kept going on and on the way it always had. "The only way to go back," he says now, "is with a boat."

His voice is calm and serious, and I think he means it—that he wants to go back, too. And that somehow in his life here, without his team of professionals, River, the dreamer, has figured out a way. "Do you have a boat?" I ask him, my voice rising with excitement, though even as I say it, I am having to squash the feeling that it could not be that easy. That nothing is that easy here.

River shakes his head. "I just have this," he says, pointing to the paper bag. "Money."

"You need money for everything here," I tell him, and he nods as if he already knows.

"Do you want to go back, Sky?"

"Yes," I say quickly. "Of course." I think about my grandmother and her house and her team of professionals, and then Ben and his nice mother and his drawings and his music. Going back would mean letting go of all of it, and something a little uneasy twists in my stomach at the thought of leaving it all behind, going back to Island, a place that was ours but also once was Helmut's.

River smiles as big as he did that afternoon of my sixteenth birthday when he held out the fish, and I wonder if he still believes what he told me just before we left, that if we stay on Island, we, too, could die. Maybe I could talk to my grandmother; I could make her listen, convince her that River could come live in her house with us. But I think again of what she did, how mean she was to him at Military Hospital, how it was she who has kept him from me in California, and I know that I can't. That I will either be with River or be with her, and I will choose River every time.

River leans in closer and wraps his arms around me tightly. I put my head on his chest, and his heart beats the way it always did. "I can't let you go, Skyblue," he whispers into my hair, tangling his finger in my now-messy braid.

"You don't have to," I whisper back, though even as I say it, I wonder how it's really possible. How we can really find our way back to Island when Mrs. Fairfield couldn't even locate it on her maps.

———•———

River and I spend the rest of the day and the night lying together on his blanket, speaking in whispers. I've missed this, having someone I can trust and tell and ask anything. Though after a little while, my back hurts, lying on the ground this much, and a part of me longs for my bed inside Pink Bedroom. I don't share this thought with River.

"Did you remember?" I ask him instead, after the darkness has fallen and the yellow moon seeps in through the cracks above us in the wood. "About the apples? I mean, did you always know, the whole time on the Island?"

"No," he whispers. "I remembered Eden. That was the farm where we lived. I remembered my mother being there."

"That's where you were when she was carrying you?"

He nods. "I think so." He pauses. "She would sing to me, too, when I was falling asleep."

"What would she sing?" I ask.

"I don't know, but I liked it." He closes his eyes, as if remembering the sound of her voice, her closeness to him. "It was nice there. We were happy."

I close my eyes, too, and I try so hard to remember, even the smallest inkling of it. I think of the grassy hill from inside Ben's laptop computer, and the room with the table where everyone sat, but none of it comes into mind as something real, as a memory. I remember nothing before Island, and I think again that it's not fair that River is older, that he has something more to hold on to.

"I always knew that there was something else," he says. "I just didn't know how it ended . . . that we couldn't come back here because of it. I thought Eden would still be there, waiting for us, you know?"

I don't know. But I nod anyway, my head nudging against his strong shoulder. I think about Island, and I wonder if it's possible, if you can ever really go back to a place you've left behind.

River strokes my hair with his hand. "You knew something, though, didn't you? Deep down you must've suspected?" I say.

"Why do you say that?"

"You knew about the mushrooms. You saved me that night." It's the first time I'm admitting it, even to myself. That Helmut might've known the mushrooms were poison and given my mother the mushrooms on purpose, that maybe he wanted her to die, and maybe she wanted to die, too. That he wanted me to die. All of us. I push down all the anger that comes with that thought and listen for River's answer.

"I didn't know," he says. "Not really. But I just knew not to trust Helmut. Just this feeling in my gut that I was always pushing against him for survival . . . in spite of all his rules. And I knew he was lying about where he'd found the mushrooms."

"You saved me," I whisper, leaning into him.

He turns to face me, too, and our lips find each other again and again in the darkness.

32

THE NEXT MORNING, RIVER'S SHELTER begins to fill with thin smoke wafting over from the dirty men farther down. They don't appear to be cooking anything, and their smoke smells different from cooking smoke, sweet and kind of sickening.

"Come on," River says. "Let's go up Rocks, and I'll show you everything that's up there."

The way he says *Rocks*, I think of the ones at the edge of Fishing Cove, and it confuses me for a moment until I realize he means the steps that wind up from the beach over the tall high rocks up above us. But I say nothing as we hold hands and climb out from under the wooden shelter, walk up the beach, and then climb the winding stairs to the top.

I am without shoes, the way I always was on Island, the way River is, but now the sand scratches between my toes and the hard steps hurt the bottoms of my feet, and I feel strangely naked. River's shirt is still on backward, and it looks funny, with the tag sticking out in the front. I think about telling him to change it, but I don't want him to feel bad, so I don't say anything.

"They have Falls here," River says, his voice filled with excitement, and I look up. He's pointing to what seems to be like the shower at my grandmother's house, though outside in the open. I glance at it uneasily, at the thought of being naked here, outside, where the air is colder than it is inside my grandmother's bathroom. "And there are Bathroom Trees there," River is saying as he points to two wooden structures.

"Good. I have to go," I say, and he lets go of my hand. I wonder if he knows the right way to use the toilet now, but I am too embarrassed to ask him, and I really have to go, so I just give him a small smile and run toward the bathrooms.

Inside the tiny bathroom, there is a small silver bad-smelling toilet, and I go quickly, feeling my stomach turn at the smells. When I'm finished, I flush and look around for a sink, but I don't see one. I hear some noise from outside, yelling, so I forget about the sink and run back out to see what's going on.

A woman stands in front of River, pointing her finger in his face. "You," she's yelling, "you're pure evil, boy."

Evil. I think about the way Helmut always stood at the edge of Ocean waiting for it to come to Island. *Evil.* I never understood what he was waiting for, and I still don't. I think of the way Ben described it to me, that Helmut had decided some people in his cult were *evil*, my real father and River's mother included, and that made him poison them. But then I think of the way Mrs. Fairfield called Helmut an *evil* man. How could they possibly mean the same thing?

River stands there now, seemingly still, like a rock, and I

quickly run over and grab his hand. "Leave him alone!" I shout in the woman's face, and then I tug on River's arm so he will run up the steps with me.

When we've reached the top and we're both breathing hard, River pulls me tight in a hug. "It's okay," he says to me. "I usually just let them yell."

"Usually? This has happened before?" I think about Mrs. Fairfield and Ben and even my grandmother, how hard they were trying to teach me things. I have not been yelled at ever in California, and it makes me sad to think of River out here all alone.

"I told you," he says softly. "That's why I couldn't stay at Apartment." He pauses. "The people with the bright suns would shout things at me."

"Oh, Riv," I say, reaching for his hand. I think about my grandmother, about the way she called them vultures, the way she got out of her car and yelled at them. *She was trying to protect me*, I think. But who does River have to protect him in this strange world? *Me*.

He looks smaller in this California morning light, broken in his backward shirt. I understand now that I need to take care of him here, the way I often took care of him on Island. I am the practical one.

I pull him close to me, stand up on my tiptoes, and kiss him softly again. "You're not evil," I whisper. "None of this is your fault."

He pulls back but still holds my hand. "I'm just so glad you're here," he whispers, his fingers tangling in my braid. Then he grins. "Come on," he says, just like he might have said it on Island. "Let's go catch some dinner."

———•———

At the top of the hill and down the street, there are rows and rows of tables with a large sign that has words that look similar to *fish market*, but I understand they're not exactly the same and I don't really know what the first word means.

I follow River from table to table, where people have set out fruits and flowers of all kinds. "You know you have to pay money for all this, right?" I ask River.

He nods and pulls a messy pile of bills from his pocket. I remember what he said about my grandmother giving him money, and I swallow hard, thinking that this money in his hand is hers.

"But you see that man over there?" River points to a small man with dark brown skin. "He gives me strawberries every morning. He won't let me pay him."

"Why not?"

River shrugs. "He says he feels bad about everything that happened to me. That it wasn't my fault. I was just a boy. He says he feels better knowing I'm eating fresh fruit every day."

"Oh," I say, thinking that maybe not everyone in California is broken. The man nods at River as we walk by, and he stares at me for a moment until I turn away and look ahead.

"The fish is up here," River says, and there is just one small table, not nearly as big as the glass window at the fish market. River begins looking at the fish and asks for what he wants, but

I stop paying attention as something catches my eye on the next table: the newspaper. And there on the front, again, is my picture.

I move closer and struggle to make out the words: ISLAND GIRL MISSING.

Island Girl, that's me, the words Ben had written beneath his drawing. I think of Ben, of the way he said that and laughed as we listened to music in his bedroom.

"Hey," the man from the fish table says. "I know you." I look up, and I realize it's the man from the fish market, not the one behind the window but the one from the back, the owner: Lucas, the sandy one.

I put my head down and grab River's hand. "Come on," I say. "We have to go. Run."

"Hey," Lucas, the sandy one, calls. "Wait a minute."

But I hold on to River and run fast through the tables, down the hill, down the steps, past the rocks, onto the beach. I don't even stop to breathe until we are back inside River's shelter.

————

River cooks the fish over a small fire that he starts with matches. "See," he tells me, and he grins. "Just like Island."

Only it is nothing like Island. Fear wraps itself around my insides, like Helmut's giant hand, clutching and pulling and stretching. ISLAND GIRL, the paper said, and Lucas, the sandy one, saw me. He knew who I was. It would only be a matter of time before they found me, and River, too, and I don't want to think about what will happen then. I think about telling River, but I also think he won't understand it, the enormity of the

California world. The way these people move so quickly in their cars, on their I-5, always going somewhere, always looking for something. So instead I say, "We need a plan, Riv."

"A plan?" he asks, turning the fish slowly to keep it from burning. I think of how this was my job on Island, how even on my birthday I cooked the meat, but I don't offer to do it here, in what feels like River's shelter—his place, his fish.

"We'll need a boat," I say. "But even then . . ." I hesitate, not wanting to tell River about the maps, Island's nonexistence on them.

He nods. "We can get back to Samoa on a boat. Then we'll just find Roger and Jeremy and get them to take us back to Island."

I nod, but I am thinking that my grandmother will find out, that Roger and Jeremy probably can't be trusted, or maybe even found. I'm not sure how big Samoa is, how far away it is from here, and how many different Rogers and Jeremys there are. But I swallow those feelings because I know River can't stay here, and if he can't, then neither can I. What other choice do we have but to find our way back there somehow? And anyway, that's what I've wanted all along, isn't it?

"How much money do you have?" I ask him, though I have no idea still how much you would need for a boat. Twenty dollars for fish, for dinner. A boat has to be more, but I don't even know where we might go to buy one.

"A lot," River says, and I nod, though that means nothing. "Here, fish is done," he says. "And I didn't even burn it." He grins. "When we get back to Island, you might even let me cook the fish now."

The fire still burns, low and small, but the red flames show me his face, every familiar space of it. He looks relaxed, not worried at all about a plan, about a boat. Still the dreamer.

I reach up and touch his cheek. His face looks sure and strong and steady. Like Helmut's, only kinder. "Sure," I say. "I'll let you cook the fish when we get back." It feels like a lie, but I don't mean it to be.

Maybe we can go back. Maybe we really can. Maybe here, in California, I have become a dreamer, too. But I don't care. I want to believe. I want to go back. I want the world to be small and familiar, the way it always was. River and Sky. Ocean and Beach, Shelter and Falls.

We pull at the cooked fish with our fingers, letting the warm meat slide down our throats and fill our bellies. I close my eyes, and Island feels so close. The waft of the salty Pacific, the taste of the warm fish. The feel of River's body against me, our knees touching as we eat.

And when we are finished, we lie together, back to back, as we always did, as we always will, I think. Nothing is certain. Nothing is true. Nothing is real.

Except for this.

33

I AWAKE TO THE SOUND of voices, and when I open my eyes, it's dark with just the smallest curve of moonlight coming in above us through the small wood spaces. I think I'm in Shelter for a moment, that last night when I awoke to the sounds of Roger calling for his mate, Jeremy. I wish I'd been stronger then. That I'd convinced River not to leave, to hide with me at Falls until the men left. I don't believe the cut on my leg would've hurt me there on Island. I'd had cuts and scrapes before, and they'd always healed with the sap of the aloe that grew on the other side of the body of water that shares River's name and the salt water of Ocean. If River and I had stayed, we would've been just fine. The world would've still been perfect.

"River," I whisper now into the darkness, feeling for him with my hand. But when I don't feel him, when he doesn't answer right away, I get nervous, and I sit up. I see the arch of his back, a few paces in front of me: he's perched by the edge of his shelter, staring out onto the beach. "River," I say again, moving forward and putting my hand on his shoulder.

"Shhh," he whispers as he puts his hand on top of mine. "It's all right. Go back to sleep, Sky."

"What's out there?" I try to peer beyond him, but he holds me back with his arm.

"Just people on Beach," he whispers.

But I hear the voices again, see the beams of the yellow flashlights rolling into the ocean. "Megan," I hear someone calling. Someone who sounds a lot like Ben. "Megan," he calls again.

"They're looking for me," I admit to River now.

He nods as if he already knew, as if he's known it all along, and I wonder how, when he didn't see the newspaper earlier. Something curls in my chest at the thought of Ben out in the darkness with his lonely flashlight, shouting my name. But I quickly push the thought away and wrap my arms around River, hugging him tightly.

"You could go to them," River whispers.

"No," I say fiercely, holding on tighter, wishing my arms were longer so they could span the width of him, so they could hold him here, keep him from moving. "I'm not leaving you," I tell him. "Never again." I pause. "And you better not leave me, either." He doesn't say anything, and against the rolling of the ocean, I hear my fake name, echoing in the waves. "Promise me," I say, squeezing him tighter. "Promise me you won't leave me again."

He doesn't say anything for a few moments, until the voices

die down, the beams of the flashlight roll away, and then finally he says it: "I promise."

———•———

In the morning River presents me with more strawberries, and I eat them quickly. I am hungry and thirsty, and the juice is delicious in my throat. I also need to use the bathroom, but I'm afraid to walk out from under the shelter, to go up there now, so for the time being I hold it in.

After I finish the green basket of berries, River pulls a small silver knife out of the brown bag. "If we're going to do this," he says, "you're going to have to let me."

"Let you what?" I ask.

He tangles his fingers in my braid, then puts his hand on my face. "Let me cut it," he says.

I think of that morning, sitting in the car with my grandmother at the place she called the salon, where she tried to convince me to get my hair "shaped." I couldn't let go then; I wouldn't. The braid is mine, my mother's, everything I had left. But now I have River, and I know he's right. My braid is me, and without it, I can be someone else. Not Megan. But not the Sky who came here, either, the one everyone will be searching for. *Island Girl.* "Okay," I say softly.

I close my eyes and feel River's hands moving gently against my back, then the cool whisper of the knife against my neck. I hear him pulling and pulling with the knife, as if my hair were a tree branch, thick and heavy and hard to cut. And then I hear a snap, and I open my eyes. River holds my braid in his hands, the way he always did, he always has. But now it's no longer a part of me.

I reach up to feel for my hair, its absence like a shadow, something I can still imagine but can no longer touch. When I try to hold on to it, I grab only a fistful of air. "It's really gone," I gasp.

"I'm sorry," River says.

But I shake my head, and then I wonder if you have to let go of everything you were just to be everything you are. Is that how my mother and Helmut felt when they first went to Island? The owl and the cat, dancing by the light of the new moon. Starting over again.

I run my fingers through what's left of my hair, and it falls out loosely around my shoulders.

River reaches up to comb through it gently with his fingers. "Come on," he says, putting my braid in the brown bag. "I know where the boats are."

I stand up, and I follow him. We hold hands as we step out of his shelter and onto the beach.

I follow River up the winding steps through the rocks, and after a quick stop at the bathroom, we head into the pines. It's too dangerous to walk on the beach now during the day. But still, I'd much prefer the feel of the cool sand between my toes than the sting of the pine needles. I think again about my silly flip-flops. I'd climbed down the window so quickly without them, and I feel a small pang of regret now. I wonder if I will forget about them, about everything I learned here, once we make it back to Island, but I don't think I will, and I feel a little sad.

I hold on tightly to River's hand as we weave through the pines. I feel lost in the tall green darkness of the trees, not like the paths I knew so well on Island, the trees I could navigate between, even on the darkest of nights.

But River seems to know these trees well, and I imagine that these were the pathways he took as he tracked me all those many weeks. I think of all the times I watched the tops of the pines slant in the breeze from Pink Bedroom in my grandmother's house, and how I had no idea that River was here, so close. So alone.

"Tell me about your Ben," River says now as we walk, holding hands.

"Ben?" I'm surprised that River is asking, and also I feel my stomach clench again as I think about the round beam of his flashlight, the way he called for me, sounding so desperate, last night. I think about his room, covered with drawings, the one of me diving into the ocean. The one he told me was unfinished. Will he finish it now, or will he just throw it out? "What do you want to know?" I ask.

"You like him," River says, not a question but a truth, solid and undeniable.

I shrug. "I don't know," I say. "He was nice to me."

"You'll miss him when we leave," River says, and I think there's something wounded in his voice, like an animal in a trap that's gotten its foot stuck and is crying in pain, knowing, knowing what is about to come.

"I don't know," I say again. "But it doesn't matter now, anyway."

"Yeah," River says, his voice catching in his throat. "I guess not."

He stops walking, and I think we've gone farther than my grandmother's house, or maybe we're right near it. I don't know. And I hate this feeling of being lost, of not knowing my own way. It's the way I felt those first few days at my grandmother's house, when I understood nothing at all of this world.

"Wait here," River says to me.

"What? No way, I'm coming with you."

He shakes his head. "Someone might recognize you."

"But my hair," I protest.

"Just wait here," he whispers, and he leans in and kisses me softly on the lips. "Let me go and talk to the man with the boats. And then I'll come right back."

"No." I shake my head, though even as I say it, I understand he's right. If someone recognizes me and calls my grandmother on her cell phone, she will get into her car and be here, wherever we are, in no time. And if River and I are separated again, I worry we might never find our way back to each other, to Island. "Okay," I say softly. "I'll wait here." He grins at me the way he always has and starts to walk away, but I catch his arm. "Just turn your shirt around," I say. "It's on backward."

He looks at me, confused, and on his face I see the way I've felt so many times since coming to California. But he pulls the shirt off and then stares at it, unsure, as if it is a strange animal he has never encountered before and now he is seeing it for the very first time.

"The tag goes in the back," I say, reaching my hand up and touching the tag to show him. But even as I say it, it sounds silly. Unimportant. And I wish I hadn't said anything at all.

River turns the shirt around, pulls it back over his head,

and offers me a small smile. But even with the shirt on the right way, I realize it doesn't look right on him. It's too big, swimming over his shoulders all wrong, making him look smaller than he is.

"Be careful," I call after him as he walks away, but he doesn't turn to answer.

———•———

It takes River a long time to come back, and I find myself walking back and forth in a small space of pines. *What if something happened?* I worry. And I wonder if I should go after him. But then I think I'll wait just a little longer because I don't want to ruin it all now by being recognized. I find myself wishing I had a watch, like Mrs. Fairfield and my grandmother wear on their wrists, so I could keep track of time, because in the thickness of the pines, it's hard to track the path of the sun, to understand how much time has really passed.

But then at last I hear the crunch of pine needles, the snap of a twig, and River appears as if in a dream, in his too-big shirt. I reach out to touch his face, just to make sure he is warm and real and here. He is.

"What took you so long?" I ask him.

"Sorry," he says. "I was trying not to . . . bring attention to myself." But by the way he frowns when he says it, I'm guessing that he did bring some attention. I think about the vultures yelling at him outside of some empty, soulless shelter—*Apartment*, he called it.

"Okay," I say, and stand up on my toes to give him a kiss. I'm so glad he's here now, he's okay, that any annoyance or worry I felt at waiting for him has already left me. "So . . . did you find a boat?"

He nods, grinning, just the way he did on my birthday when he caught us a fish. "I found a man who said he'd take us to Samoa in his boat if I brought him all my money."

"Really?" I'm surprised. Just like that? River and I could go back, with a man. On a boat.

"Really," River says.

But it feels too easy for this California world, where *nothing* is easy, and I wonder if River misunderstood or if this man was lying to him. I realize I should've gone to talk to him with River, even if it was risky. Because River doesn't understand as much about this world as I do, and I'm not sure if I trust now that he has found us a real way home.

"So we're going now?" I ask. My heart thrums heavily in my chest, too fast, and for a moment, I can't catch my breath.

He shakes his head. "Soon. He said there's a storm coming, and after it passes, he'll take us."

"A storm," I whisper, closing my eyes and thinking as I always do of that last night my mother was alive, the way the thunder rolled like breath, heavy enough to shake Shelter. The way the rain covered us the next morning on our horrible walk to Ocean.

"Yeah." River takes my hand. "He said it's coming soon, so we should get going. He said to come back tomorrow morning with all my money. And then he will take us in his boat."

I nod and I think of how afraid I once was of a boat coming to Island, taking us away. And how now we need a boat so badly. The only thing that can save us. Take us back. We have to be sure that we can trust this man with the boat, that if we give him River's money, he really will take us to Samoa. And now I have a nervous feeling in my stomach. Uncertainty.

But River is smiling so big, so pleased with himself, that I swallow the feeling, and I hold on to his hand through the thick of the trees.

Pine needles stab at the bottoms of my feet, piercing my skin. My soles are thick from years and years of walking through sand without shoes, but not thick enough for pine needles, and they sting and burn until I have to slow down.

———————

Back in River's shelter, the dirty men are laughing. There are more of them now. Three or maybe four. Their smoke tufts in the air, making the space around us sweet smelling and hazy. It makes me feel sleepy. And the bottoms of my feet ache now. I wish for the aloe plants, but I tell River I'm going to walk to the edge of the ocean instead. The ocean heals and soothes, even if the water is colder here.

"Do you want to come with me?" I ask him.

He hesitates for a minute and glances uneasily at the dirty men, then his paper bag, and he shakes his head. "I'll wait here," he says. I glance beyond the side of his Shelter, and I can see the edge of the water. "You won't go in too far?" he says softly, and I know he's thinking of that other night when he pulled me out from beneath the waves.

"And you'll be here when I get back?" I ask, keeping my voice light, teasing him, but not really. I mean it.

He nods, and his hand falls on my back, where my braid

used to be. Its absence feels heavier now than its existence. But I think of what he said, how the man with the boat will take us back soon. To Samoa. And then from there we'll find Island, or Island will find us. The world will be perfect again. It will. In time my hair will grow, and I can forget words like *murder, cult, poison, grandmother, Ben*. I want this all to be truth so badly that I tell myself that it has to be. There is nothing else.

"When you get back from Ocean," River is saying now, "we'll go get more fish."

I don't correct him, tell him that Ocean is *the ocean* here. That even though they are the same—*the Pacific*, really—they are not the same at all. Soon enough, River and I will be back at Ocean again. Together.

I smile at him, and then I run down to the edge of the water, the roar of the ocean swallowing every other sound, everything else. I don't hear the dirty men or smell their smoke. I put my feet in the cool rush of the water. It stings and it chills, and then it soothes. The waves are loud and strong and capped with white. I look up, and the sky, I notice now, is a silver gray.

For a little while, I don't hear anything except for the water. Except for Island calling to me, whispering to me across the loud, strong Pacific. It's still there, waiting. For us. Calling us back. I hear nothing else.

And then, suddenly, I do.

Suddenly the dirty men rush across the beach, screaming.

34

I KNOW IMMEDIATELY THAT SOMETHING'S wrong. I feel it in my chest, a deep sharp pain, like the way I felt when I realized my mother's lips were slightly parted and blue, when I pushed her harder and harder and her body fell limply back at me, over and over again. I just knew. And I know now, too.

I run out of the water, running up the beach as fast as I can. "River!" I shout. He doesn't answer me. "River!" I shout again.

My feet push hard against the hill, the sand, but I run and push back until I can barely breathe. I duck under the wood where the dirty men were, where their dirty things still are, and farther up, near River's spot, I can see only shadows. Two of them. "River!" I shout again as I run closer, and his head turns. His entire face falls, and he shakes his head. I can see it in the depths of his green eyes that I know so well it's almost as if they belong to me. *No,* he's telling me. *Stop. Run.*

But I don't. Of course I don't.

The other shadow turns, too, and I am close enough now to

see it's a tall person dressed in all black, black clothing covering everything except the space of his eyes, a living, breathing shadow. The living part I can only tell from the steady rise and fall of his shoulders.

River shakes his head again, slowly, carefully, but I push forward until I am close enough to touch him, until I grab his hand, feel his warm skin against mine. A relief.

"Don't move," the shadow growls, and that's when I understand what is happening, or I think I do. I see his arm is outstretched, and at the end of his black-gloved hand, there's something else black: a gun. It looks just like the one in the picture Mrs. Fairfield showed me in the newspaper when she tried to explain the shooting to me. I didn't exactly understand how guns worked, but now her words echo in my head, about guns being able to kill people quickly. *Very dangerous*, she told me.

Then why do people have them here? I asked her.

Well—she thought about it—*to hunt, I guess.*

I tucked it in the back of my head, one more silly thing about California, that people here need something *dangerous* to hunt, rather than using traps like the ones Helmut built on Island.

"Give me the bag," the black shadow growls now, and he gestures with his gun to the brown bag behind River. *He is hunting us*, I think.

"No," River says, puffing out his chest, and I realize that he doesn't understand. That he doesn't know what a gun is. That he doesn't know that this small black thing is so powerful it can kill him. Both of us. He's still the dreamer. I'm still the practical one.

"Just give him the bag, Riv," I say, trying to keep my voice even, but I hear the words tremble and break.

"No," River says again. He looks at me. "It's everything we have." The money my grandmother gave him, the money River promised to the man with the boat. Mrs. Fairfield told me about a place called Banks that will keep your money safe for you, and I always imagined that's where Dr. Banks went when she left my grandmother's house each day, as if her tiny gray body could be the keeper of all money in California, which made no sense to me, that everyone would trust her so much. But of course, River doesn't know any of this. River didn't have a Mrs. Fairfield, or a Dr. Banks.

The shadow person moves closer now and grabs my arm, twisting it tightly so that it hurts. I cry out in pain without meaning to.

"Give me the bag," he says to River, jabbing his gun against my shoulder. It is cold and hard, and the spot where he jabbed it stings a little, but it's so small. It doesn't seem like something that could actually hurt me, that could kill me. River eyes it suspiciously, and I know he's not going to give the shadow person the bag now. River, who saved me from the mushrooms, from the scrape on my leg, from the dark, cool depths of the California ocean.

He moves so quickly that for a second I'm not sure what's happening. River's reaching for me and for the gun all at once. *He doesn't know.* He doesn't understand what the gun can do. I want to open my mouth to scream it, to tell him, but everything is happening too quickly, and I can't.

Suddenly there's noise. The loudest, hardest claps of thunder that I have ever heard or felt. Everything is hot and shaking and broken. I'm falling; River's falling. A pearl of smoke whispers in the air.

The shadow grabs the brown bag and hangs above us for a moment. And then it's gone, blackness onto the sand.

I can't move. I am stilled, like a fish hanging on the end of my spear, eyes still open, air still moving through gills, but perfectly and completely still, as if moving is impossible this close to the end. I can't move. The whisper of smoke climbs higher against the top of the wooden shelter.

"River," I shout, or maybe I whisper. I'm not sure, because all I can hear in my ears is the roar of the thunder, not my own words. He doesn't answer. "River," I try again.

I want to stand up and run to find him, but I can't get my legs to work, so I crawl across the sand instead, pulling as hard as I can with my fingernails, clawing my way to him. I reach my arm around and around and around for the feel of his warm body. Our money is gone, I think. I don't know how we'll get back to Island, but we're still here. Together. River and Sky. It will be okay. It has to be.

"River," I say again, and then my hand hits his. His fingers squeeze mine softly, and I sigh, and finally, I can lean up a little bit.

And then I see him. He's lying on his back, a bright red flower seeping across his chest over his too-big shirt, growing and growing. His eyes are closed, and beads of sweat line his forehead.

"River!" I scream.

But I don't think anyone can hear me. It's like we're there again. Back on Island, alone.

35

EVERYTHING NEXT BECOMES HAZY, LIKE the low fog that I now know hangs over the California ocean in the mornings. The marine layer. It hangs in my head and in my heart, covering, weighting, changing. I will never be the same.

People rush under River's shelter, wearing black and white, speaking loudly and quickly. Someone picks me up and carries me, and that's when I realize that I really can't walk, that my legs no longer know how to work, or that they just don't want to.

River is pulled away on a long, thin bed, like the one I was lying on in that newspaper picture I kept under my pillow. I shout for him over and over, or I want to, I try to. *He promised me he wouldn't leave me again,* I think. *He promised me. He made me a promise.*

Someone places a clear triangle over my nose and mouth. I struggle to push it away. "It's just to help you breathe," a voice says. "Don't be afraid. You've been shot, but we're taking you to the hospital."

"So sad," another voice says. "These teenage runaways down here."

They don't know me, I think. *They don't know I'm Island Girl. That River is River.* I can still save him. I can still stop them from taking us away, pulling us apart.

There's a hand on my arm, a sharp, jabbing sting like that morning when Sergeant Sawyer held my arm, and then, again, I'm drowning in blackness.

———•———

In the blackness, there are voices, and loud wailing noises like birds being feathered before they are fully dead. I roll and I shake, and then I climb under the water. It pulls me in and it heals me. It's cold and gray, and then it changes, and it's warm and blue.

River is with me, just beyond Rocks, holding on tightly to me as we bob up and down in the gentle water, our fishing spears in our hands.

"Look," he tells me. "It's not so bad beyond Rocks, after all. The water is calm and warm. And there are fish everywhere." He's grinning big, like that afternoon when I turned sixteen and he had caught me a present.

Our bodies move in the water, skimming the surface of the gentle waves. The fish swim soundlessly through our calves, around our ankles. His strong arms hold tightly against my bare skin, and I hold him back. He's weightless in the water. I can carry him. I move him. I lift him up. He's laughing and falling back down, the water so clear and blue I can see his feet. I can see the bright red flower seeping across his chest.

———•———

I wake up in a bed, the world white and small, unfamiliar. *Hospital*, I think. I'm in a bed in Military Hospital, just like I was when I first came to California.

Above me, my grandmother's pale face looms large, with deep, worried wrinkles hanging around her blue eyes. "Megan." She breathes deeply. And I puff up with hatred for her, for that stupid name that means nothing to me. For what she did to River.

"River," I whisper.

"Oh, honey." She picks up my hand and squeezes it tightly. "You were shot. You could've been killed. But you were so lucky. The bullet just grazed your leg."

"River," I whisper again, remembering my dream, Island, Ocean. River's wooden shelter, the black shadow, the bright red flower seeping across River's chest. I struggle to sit up, but my body is heavy and it's hard to move.

"Shhh," she says. "Just rest. Everything's going to be all right now."

I close my eyes, but even in my hazy faraway world, I understand that she's wrong. That nothing will be all right now. That River and I will never make it back to Island; we might not even make it back to each other.

235

I'm too tired to open my eyes. But still, I feel the tears falling past my lids, marking rivers, oceans, across my face.

I think I sleep, until suddenly I'm aware that my hand is warm, being held. River is in my head and my heart, and I whisper his name again, or at least I think I do.

"Island Girl . . . Sky," a voice says, and I realize it's not River. It's Ben. Ben is the one holding my hand. "Are you awake? Can you hear me?"

"Hmmm?" I murmur, or maybe I don't. My throat hurts, and my tongue feels thick.

Ben doesn't say anything for a moment, and then I feel him squeeze my hand. "You asked me that night on the beach if I was your friend, remember?" I remember, but I can't find the words to make any sound. "And I didn't answer you then. But I should've. Because I am, your friend, I mean." He's quiet for a little bit, and I'm not sure if he's still there until he starts talking again. "But I wasn't completely honest with you. You were kind of like my summer job. Your grandmother has been paying me to spend time with you, to teach you things. She told me not to tell you, because she didn't want you to feel bad. But after you . . . disappeared, I told her I don't want any more money. I mean . . . I still want to spend time with you, but because I like spending time with you. Not because she's paying me. I'll get my job back at Vons."

His voice moves in and out of my head, and I think about the money my grandmother paid River to stay away from me, that the shadow took as he shot us. And the money she paid

Ben to keep me close. How does she have so much of it, and why does it mean so much here in California? I don't understand it. It's just paper. It floats and falls in the breeze like dead palm leaves. How can it mean so much? Everything? Is that what Helmut was waiting for as he stood at the edge of Beach, waiting for evil to come to us on Island? Is that what he was looking for? Paper money, floating down across the horizon, sinking softly into the water?

36

WHEN I WAKE UP FOR real, the room is empty and dark. I feel around for a light to turn on and wind up pressing a red button instead. A woman in a white dress comes in—a nurse, I think. I'm surprised she's not in green.

"Megan," she says to me. "How are you feeling?" I don't answer her, but I nod. "Your grandmother stepped out to get a bite to eat, but I can call her and let her know you're awake."

"Wait," I say, reaching out to hold on to her arm. She smiles at me and pats my arm back, and she has a seat in the chair next to the bed.

"What happened to River?" I ask her.

"River?"

"Lucas." *Lucas*. The name feels thick and hard against my tongue. It's an ugly name, the name of a stranger, a boy who once lived in a place called Eden and handed out poisoned apples.

"Oh," she says. "Lucas . . . well, maybe I should let your grandmother—"

"Please," I say, squeezing her arm with all my strength, which isn't much.

She nods slowly. "He had surgery when they brought him in, and then they moved him to Camp Solanas. For . . . security reasons." I don't know what that means, but I remember the blank white walls of Camp Solanas, quite similar to these blank white walls around me, and I nod.

"I'm not in Military Hospital?" I ask.

"No." She shakes her head. "You're at University Hospital." She smiles at me in a way that tells me she's done telling me anything. "Okay . . ." She stands and starts to leave. "Let me go call your grandmother. I know she'll want to hurry back and see you."

"Wait," I call after her, and she turns in the doorway. "He's going to be okay, right? If they moved him . . . that means he's going to be okay."

"It's still very touch and go," she says.

"Touch and go?"

"We just don't know yet," she says softly, retreating past the doorway.

A few minutes later, my grandmother and Ben turn the corner together. My grandmother looking happy, Ben looking pale and small, like he might throw up. I think about what he told me when I was sleeping, and I'm not sure if I dreamed it. From the look on his face, though, I don't think I did, and I know I should hate him now if it is true. But every bit of hatred in my body curls into a giant, coconut-size ball in my stomach that I wish

I could pick up and throw squarely at my grandmother's head just between the eyes, knocking her out.

"Megan," she says now, rushing to the bed, reaching for my hand. I pull out of her grasp and roll over. This is all her fault—everything. If she hadn't forced River to leave me in the first place. If she hadn't given him that money to begin with. If she hadn't tried so hard to make me into someone who I'm not and I'll never be ... "Honey," she says, her voice breaking on the word. I can hear the chair scraping against the floor as she sits down, though I refuse to turn and look at her. She puts her hand on the back of my head. "You cut your hair."

"River did," I whisper, biting back tears as I remember the way he held on gently, the way he tore across my braid with the knife.

"Did he hurt you?" she asks.

I roll back around hard, and my leg throbs. "I was shot," I tell her.

"I know, honey," she says. "But before that ... ?"

"None of this is River's fault," I yell at her. "It's yours."

She nods slowly. "I'm just glad you're okay," she says. She leans down to kiss my forehead, and as soon as I realize what she's doing, as soon her lips make contact there, in space where my mother's lips and River's have touched, I yank my head back quickly, so my forehead bangs her nose, hard.

She puts her hand up to rub it, her mouth open wide as if she wants to say something, but she's not sure what. Ben stares with wide brown eyes, eyes that remind me of the eyes of an owl perched so high in a palm tree it would never find its way into one of Helmut's traps. We never ate an owl, anyway, because

Helmut said that owls were not for eating. I always thought it was because of the story, the owl and the cat, because Helmut was the owl, but Helmut said it was because owls watched over us at night, their eyes so wide and alert like that.

"I need to go see River," I say now, using all my strength to pull myself up in bed. I let my grandmother keep me away from River before, but only because I didn't know better. Only because I thought River wanted me to be kept away. Now I know. Now I picture him hurting and alone, trapped inside the cold whiteness of Military Hospital. He needs me, and I'm going to go to him.

I pull myself out of bed, and I grimace as my feet hit the floor and my one leg throbs with pain.

"Megan, what do you think you're doing?" My grandmother stops rubbing her nose to put her hands on my shoulders.

"I'm going to see River," I say through gritted teeth. "Even if I have to walk there myself." She tries to push my shoulders to get me back on the bed, but I push forward with every bit of strength I have left, and her small body slides across the room.

She looks at me for a moment, her lips in the shape of a circle, and then she yells, "Nurse!"

The woman in the white dress runs to the door. "Is everything okay in here?" she asks.

"Can't you give her something to calm her down? She's so agitated."

I put my feet on the floor again and try to walk, but I fall, crashing into Ben, who holds me up with his arms. I think about Ben's voice calling for me on the beach, his flashlight beam rolling in the waves. How River asked the next morning if I would miss him. If he meant anything to me. "Island Girl," he whispers now. "Come on."

I shake my head, refusing to look at him, and then I fight with everything I have, everything I am, thrashing my arms and legs wildly, clawing at the air, at Ben, at my grandmother, like a wild animal. But even an animal stops after a little while, after it realizes that there is no way out of the trap, that it's the end. Even an animal gives up when it gets tired.

But I don't stop fighting until the nurse jabs my arm, and the warmth takes over my blood, my body, until I'm falling into darkness again.

———

A wave pulls me under, holding me below the water until I think my breath will disappear, until I think the world will become black and murky and dead. The water is cold, and it saturates my body, making it impossible to feel. The water soaks through my skin until I am nothing. I am emptiness.

And then there are arms, River's arms, pulling me up, pulling me to the top.

Skyblue, he says, *the current's too rough here. You could drown. Maybe you wanted to drown.*

I didn't. I promise.

His arms hold me up, pulling me to the surface, pulling the dead weight of my body to Beach. But just before he puts me down on the sand, he falls, flat, on his back. The bright red flower sprouts across his chest, growing bigger and bigger.

You promised me you wouldn't leave me again. You promised.

The petals of the flower float and grow, and tear away,

falling slowly down his stomach, onto the sand, turning the entire beach red.

"Island Girl," a voice calls to me. My tongue is thick and I try to swallow, but I can't. I move my mouth, trying to make a sound, but I can't. "Sky. Wake up." Ben pushes on my shoulder, hard.

I groan and open my eyes. The room is white and filled with sunlight, not electricity but real, honest sunlight streaming in through the window. It must be afternoon because the marine layer would have to be gone for the sun to seem this bright, though afternoon of what day, I have no idea. Nor do I know how long it's been since they were all here and the nurse was jabbing my arm, poisoning me. *Evil*, I think.

"What do you want?" I finally say to Ben, my voice sticky in my throat now, so my words come out sharp, painful, like the pine needles that stuck in the soles of my feet.

"Come on," he says, pulling my arm up, pulling it over his shoulder. "We're going to get you out of here."

"What?" I rub my eyes. "Where's my grandmother?"

"She's talking to the police," he says, "so you have to hurry. We don't have much time."

His voice rolls in my head, and it's so confusing, so hard to understand. But then I remember his confession to me, that my grandmother was paying him to be nice to me. That he was with her, not with me. "Get off me," I say, shaking away his arm. "I don't trust you."

He sinks down in the chair by the bed and frowns. "I deserve that, all right? I know I do. But if you want me to drive you up to Camp Solanas, then you need to get your ass out of this bed and move quickly."

"River?" I whisper. "You're really going to take me to him?"

He tosses me a sweatshirt and a pair of jeans. Not River's sweatshirt, but his, I'm guessing. "Come on," he says, and he turns away so he isn't looking at me. "Put those on."

I do the best I can, throwing them quickly over my hospital dress. Everything is too big. But it's better than wearing just the thin dress. I notice I still have the tube in my arm, the IV, but it doesn't seem to be connected to anything now, so I cover it with the arm of the sweatshirt, and then I tap Ben on the shoulder.

He wraps his arm around me, and I lean into him this time. Maybe I shouldn't trust him, but I'm not sure now I have another choice.

———— ·•· ————

"Why are you doing this?" I ask Ben once we are inside his SUV and he's pulling out of the parking lot. I notice his hands shaking against the wheel, and he glances behind us uneasily even as he drives. The car lurches and so does my stomach, and as soon as Ben makes it down onto the busy I-5 with cars swarming around us in all directions like crazy, angry bees, I have to close my eyes and breathe deep to keep from throwing up again.

"Why am I doing what?" he asks as he weaves his SUV between and around other, smaller cars.

"You know," I say. "Taking me to see River."

"Oh," he says, as if my question is a surprise. The car slows as all the cars in front of us do, too, and up ahead, there is an ocean of bright red lights glittering on the I-5 like wayward daytime stars. "Well," he says after a little while, "did you hear me talking to you the other night, when you were sleeping?"

I nod. "I think so."

"Did you hear me tell you that I'm your friend, for real?" I nod again. "Well, this is my way to prove it to you, I guess."

"But you hate him," I say. "You think he did horrible things."

"I never said I hated him," he says. "I said Alice did. And that she's a good judge of character." The weight of my grandmother's name hangs in the car, like the weight of the ocean crushing, pulling you under when the current is rough. Neither one of us says anything for a while, and then the cars start moving again. Ben's SUV dances between the other cars. My stomach lurches, and I close my eyes again.

"He talked to me the other night," Ben says softly.

"What?" I open my eyes to look at him, and his face is pale and serious.

"I was looking for you by the pier, and Lucas . . . River, he came out to the beach, and he talked to me."

"No, he didn't," I say, thinking about how I awoke and River sat there, staring at the ocean and the beam of the flashlight rolling across the waves. How he promised me he wouldn't leave me again. *He promised.*

"He did," Ben says. "I swear." I think about that next morning, how River suddenly insisted I cut my braid, how he asked me about Ben as we walked through the pines. "He wanted to know why I was looking for you, what happened," Ben is saying now. "He didn't tell me you were with him. But I knew."

"How did you know?" I ask, and I wonder if the Google told him this, too, if the Google is all-knowing and all-seeing.

He shrugs. "I didn't *know*. But I guessed." He pauses, and he gets off the I-5, turning onto a quieter, smaller street that hugs closer to the ocean. I watch the way the sunlight melts into the water in wide yellow swirls, making it seem warmer, brighter, than it actually is. "I mean I should've just gone under the stupid pier and taken you back home with me, and then none of this would've ever happened."

"I wouldn't have gone with you," I tell him matter-of-factly.

"Yeah, I know," he says. "And anyway, that's not why I didn't do it."

"Why didn't you?"

"I don't know." He shrugs again. Then he says, softer, "I thought that if you were there—with him . . . well, maybe that's where you wanted to be. Where you were supposed to be."

I feel a new warmth for Ben building in my chest, and I put my hand on his shoulder as he pulls into Camp Solanas. "Thank you," I say, and for some reason I think of his unfinished drawing, me diving into the ocean, surrounded by the waves, being swallowed up by them, and I wonder if he's finished it by now.

But I don't ask him, because Ben is stopping the SUV, pulling down the window, and trying to explain to a green man why we're here, what we're doing.

The green man says something about not having clearance, and Ben looks to me, eyes wide again, like an owl's. He planned my escape from the hospital. He drove me here, fighting so many cars on the I-5, and now he can't get the SUV past the small, thin gate in front of us. I lean across him, even though it hurts my leg to put weight on it. "Get Dr. Cabot," I say.

"I can't—"

"Dr. Cabot," I yell, and then the man's face freezes funny, the way my mother's sometimes would when she would bite into a sour piece of fruit, and I think that maybe, even without the braid, he knows me. He recognizes me.

A few minutes later, I see her walking past the gate, dressed in green, her blond hair pulled back tightly at the bottom of her neck. She puts her hand to her eyes, shielding the sun, and she peers into the windows of the SUV. She nods, says something to the man, and the gates open. Ben smiles at me, and then he drives right through.

37

"I THOUGHT YOU GOT SHOT," Dr. Cabot says to me as she helps me out of Ben's SUV and through large glass doors into Military Hospital. They look different than I remember. But maybe it's because last time I was looking out into this great wide, unfamiliar world, and now I'm looking in, back to the blank whiteness, to a place where I was so filled with fear, so lost, so . . . unaware, that I feel a tightening in my stomach at the thought of going back in there.

"It just grazed me," I say, repeating what my grandmother told me. I don't know how that's different from being shot, exactly, but it sounds slightly better. *Grazed*. Like a rabbit chewing calmly on small pieces of grass.

She eyes my leg suspiciously and then walks away for a moment and comes back with a chair on wheels. "Sit," she commands me, and I do. Not because I want to listen to her, but because my leg really does hurt. "And you are?" she says, glaring now at Ben.

"He's my friend," I say quickly, and Ben smiles at me and puts a hand on my shoulder.

"Okay, fine," Dr. Cabot says, holding her hands up. "You push her, then."

Ben grabs the handle on the back of the chair, and then I feel the ground moving beneath me, the white-walled hallways moving past me, spinning sideways, until I begin to feel dizzy.

Dr. Cabot walks beside me. "You cut your hair," she says after a few minutes of walking. Her voice is softer now. And she nods approvingly.

"River did it," I say.

"Oh," she says. "I see."

"That's why I'm here," I tell her. "I need to see him."

She stops walking, and Ben stops pushing, and she kneels down so she is right in front of me, her bright red lips, her pearl green eyes. "I know," she says. And there's a kindness in her voice, in her eyes, that I haven't detected until now, or maybe I was just so confused the first time I was here that I didn't have the time or the depth to understand. In my head, she became one with the tall, gray, annoying Dr. Banks. "But I have to tell you," she says, "it's not good."

"It's not?" I whisper.

"He's in a coma," she says softly. "Do you know what that is?" I shake my head. "He's unconscious." I shake my head again. "It's like a sleep, but a very, very deep sleep that we can't wake him up from."

"But he'll wake up soon, right?" She doesn't say anything, but she draws her red lips together in a small, tight line.

"I'm going to be honest with you, Megan, because I feel you

deserve that after everything you've been through, okay?" I nod, and she stands and reaches out her hand for me to take it. I do. I struggle to stand, and Ben helps to lift me, holding me up under my arms. "I'll take you in to see him now. But you should think of this as your time to say good-bye."

"No," I tell her. "I'm not going to say good-bye."

I think about that morning when my mother and Helmut were dead, how it was River's idea to take them to Ocean. Our whole lives on Island, the water had healed. We soaked sore feet and tired arms, and the salt numbed. The water made the pain better. Helmut pulled my mother in when the monthly bleed came so late that time and wouldn't stop, and the water saved her then. But still, that morning, it felt wrong just to pull them in like that. Just to push their bodies under the waves and let go.

We're not going to say good-bye, River said as he pushed Helmut under the water for the last time. Helmut's face was purple and bloated, his lips pressed tightly together, unlike my mother's. We let go, and Ocean swallowed them down, a wave washing them out far, farther than we would ever dare to swim.

Not good-bye, River whispered. *See you again soon.*

Like me, River dreamed the bodies would come back, wash up on Beach, healed.

See you soon, I whispered then, the waves swallowing my voice.

"Megan"—Dr. Cabot shakes my shoulder a little—"if you want to see him, you need to prepare yourself." She pauses and stares directly into my eyes, hers penetrating mine like spears. "You need to understand," she says softly, "that this will be it."

"It?" I whisper, though now it is not that I don't understand, it's that I don't want to, that I can't. After everything, every day River and I spent together on Island, every night we fell asleep back-to-back in Shelter, all this time we were apart in California, and then how we finally found our way back to each other, where we were supposed to be. Together. *No.* This, in Military Hospital, can't be *it.*

"This will most likely be the last time you will ever see him," Dr. Cabot is saying.

I shake my head. "But he promised," I whisper.

"Come on," she says. She pushes a door open, and inside the room is dark, the blinds closed. Something beeps softly, and in the center of the room there's a bed with so many lines running and twisting out of it. I expect to go closer and see someone else there on the bed. That maybe Dr. Cabot and Ben are just lying to me. *Cold and broken,* my mother said. *Skeletons.*

But as I grow closer, it's him. He's the one who looks like a skeleton. *River.* A line runs into his mouth, and his face is blank, expressionless, nearly unfamiliar. I put my hand above his chest, letting it hover in the spot where the red flower crept and grew. In my dream, on the beach—I'm not sure. It's gone now, or at least I can't see it.

Dr. Cabot gets me a chair, and she pushes it close to the bed. Then she whispers that she and Ben will be right outside the door and that she'll be back to get me in a few minutes.

After they leave, I almost expect River to sit up, to reach for me, to tangle his fingers through my now-short hair and whisper in my ear: *Skyblue. You came. I knew you would. I'm fine. Everything's going to be fine. We'll find a way out of here. Together. The man with the boat is still waiting for us.*

But I listen, and the only sound I hear is the beeping, the strange machines that surround him. They rush and whir, almost like the ocean, pulling him in, pulling him under.

"River," I whisper, "River, it's me. I'm here." I reach for his hand, and I squeeze it. I will him to squeeze back. His hand is warm still but limp, and he doesn't respond. "Listen to me," I tell him. "I'm not going to say good-bye to you. You're going to get better and wake up, and we're going to go back to Island, okay?"

The machine beeps, slow and steady. River's chest moves up and down. He's still alive. He's still breathing.

I turn his hand over, and I look at his large palm, and then with my finger I slowly trace the picture I left for him that night on the beach. The picture he drew for me on Island. Two overlapping circles. Me and him. Him and me. Going around, connecting, together.

"You promised," I tell him.

Suddenly the beeping on his machines gets louder, higher, the beeps closer together.

Dr. Cabot runs in, and she is not alone now. Another doctor I don't recognize runs to River's other side and pushes on his chest. Then another one runs in behind him. "Megan," Dr. Cabot says, "you need to leave." She tugs on my shoulder.

I shake my head. "What's happening?"

"You can't be in here any longer." She pulls hard on my arm so I'm forced to let go of River's hand. It falls limply back to the bed, and now a few doctors surround him, pushing on his body.

"I can't leave him," I say, but she is strong, and my leg is weak, and she pulls hard so that I have no choice.

"River!" I yell. "River." But only the machines answer me, beeping, beeping, beeping so loud that I don't think there's any way River could hear me over them.

"See you again soon," I yell, tears streaming down my face as Dr. Cabot pulls me into the blank white hallway.

Ben and I don't say a word on the ride back to University Hospital. We don't talk about the way River looked lying in that bed, or what Dr. Cabot said, that it would be the last time I'll see him. We don't talk about what it meant when the machines started beeping louder, when the doctors rushed in and pushed on River's chest. We don't talk about how River is a part of me—that he always has been, and he always will be—and that I don't know the world without him. And I understand now I don't want to. That without him, my circle is broken, empty, alone.

I am glad that Ben isn't making me talk, asking me questions, as if he understands that I can't talk, that any words now may break me. Maybe he really is my friend. But what does that matter now, anyway? What does anything matter if River isn't with me?

Ben drives his SUV through the car forest of the I-5, and I lean my head against the window, closing my eyes, opening them again. Wishing every time they open that all this is a bad dream. That when I look around, I'll be lying on the rabbit pelts in Shelter, River's back hugging mine, the sounds of the green birds crying in the distance. But the only sounds I hear are car horns, and something on the radio that I don't recognize, that I don't have the strength to ask Ben about.

When he finally turns back into the parking lot at University Hospital, I see a lot of cars with bright red throbbing lights on the top. "Oh, shit," Ben says.

Shit, I remember, is one of the bad words that I'm not supposed to echo.

Ben stops the car, and a man dressed in black bangs on the glass of Ben's window. "Step out of the car, son," he's saying. I think I hear my grandmother's voice yelling from somewhere in the distance. Or maybe she's crying. It's hard to tell.

"Shit," Ben whispers again. His face is very pale, his eyes so wide. An owl's. A scared one.

He puts his hand on the door to get out.

"Thank you," I say, but the words escape me like a shadow, so soft and shapeless, I'm not even sure Ben hears them.

38

I'M NOT SURE WHAT HAPPENS to Ben after we get out of his SUV, and I know I should care, and part of me does. But it is very hard to think of anything else but River, of the way he looked, lifeless in that bed as the doctors rushed toward him.

I allow my grandmother to pull me back to my room in University Hospital because I don't really have another choice, and I'm tired, and my leg hurts. Back in the bed, I lie there limply, not even trying to fight as the nurse pushes her poison into my arm again. I want it to take me away now. To take me back. I want to dream in Island again, the water and the fish swimming easily through my legs, River's arms holding me up. But I don't. I dream nothing.

I don't know how much time has passed when I wake up again and the gray marine layer falls in through my window. Morning again. In California. But I don't know what morning it is, how many mornings, how long I have slept and slept, lulled into darkness with the nurses' poison.

This morning, a nurse brings food I won't eat, that I haven't eaten in what feels like forever, and she leaves it on the table next to my bed along with a newspaper. I hold out my arm, expecting her to inject me again, waiting for the relief it will bring, the blank and dreamless darkness. But instead she says, "You're going home today."

"Home," I repeat, another stupid, empty word in California. Home is Island. River. My eye catches on the newspaper she brought in with her. My picture is there on the front again, and so is River's. And Helmut's. "What does this say?" I ask her.

"I don't know if I should . . ."

But I know how to read one word: *dies*. Mrs. Fairfield taught me to read it when we read that article about the shooting in Iowa together. *Dies. Dead. Murder. Gone.* My mother and Helmut sinking down beneath the waves, cold and purple and bloated.

The newspaper is saying what I already knew these past few days through my long, dark sleeps. River is gone. River is dead.

I clutch the newspaper so hard that it begins to tear, that my fingers turn black and purple, and the side of River's face has rubbed away because I can't stop touching it, running my finger across it, wanting to make it real, make him come back here.

———————

A few hours later, my grandmother wheels me out of University Hospital and into the parking lot. My fingers still clutch the newspaper picture of River, my fingertips black. She is talking to me as she wheels me out, but my ears are filled with water; my head is numb and heavy.

I hear her say something about adding someone else to her team of professionals, a physical therapist who will help my leg get back to normal. I hear her voice, her words thrumming in my ears, like bees buzzing. A painful, stupid noise. But I am just a shadow now. And I don't care if my leg works or not.

"I need to see him," I say as we get to the car. "Where is he?" My eyes fill with tears, and then her face falls.

"Oh," she says, "honey." She puts her hand on my shoulder. "He has an aunt in Temecula. Dr. Cabot told me that she was . . . taking care of everything."

I think again about how River and I *took care* of my mother and Helmut. River should find the water, too, I think. He should be put in the ocean. I understand that the Pacific might not be able to heal him, but maybe it will. Maybe it will bring him back to where he belongs, the other side, to Island. *See you soon*, I'd said to him. "I want to do it," I say softly.

"Honey." She shakes her head. "I'm sorry. You can't. His aunt is family. That's her job. That's the way we do things here."

"But she hated him," I say. "She didn't want him when he was alive. Can't you go talk to her, tell her? He needs to be in the water, in the ocean."

She frowns but doesn't answer. She puts her hand on my shoulder, and she leans over to help me out of the chair and into the car. My bones shift and move, but that's all they are, all I am— bones. I am the one who is empty and broken now, a skeleton.

Back in the pink bedroom, I go to sleep again.

I sleep for days or weeks or months. I don't know. The notches that I marked for days behind the bed with a pencil are gone, and I understand my grandmother must've found them and made them disappear while I was away. So now time is nothing. It is empty. I don't even try to understand it.

I am *resting my eyes*. I remember when my grandmother said that, and she seemed sad, and now I understand what it means.

My grandmother brings food, and I push it away. I rest my eyes and try to get back there, to Island, to Shelter, with River's warm back hugging mine. I try and I try, and sometimes, in my dreams, it is almost right there, almost close enough for me to grab it in my fingers and pull it back to me. But then it disappears, slipping through my hands like grains of sand.

"Mrs. Fairfield is here to see you," my grandmother says, and I tuck my head tighter under the covers, pretending to be asleep, wishing for it. She tries again later, or the next day, with Dr. Banks.

Maybe I am here, with her, without River. Stuck in California. But they can't make me get out of my bed, I think. They can't make me eat. Or even breathe. I can stay here between these sheets forever, until my skin falls away and my bones peek through. Until my skeleton collapses into the water, and then somehow, I will find them again. My mother. River. Island.

39

I AM JUST ABOUT BACK to Island, skimming the water in Roger and Jeremy's boat, River's hands on my back, Island a small shell growing larger in the distance, when I hear R.E.M. singing in my ear.

No, *shouting*, about the end of the world.

I open my eyes, and River, the boat, Island, they're all gone, and Ben is hovering above me, his iPod in my face, screaming music at my head.

"What are you doing? Stop it." I push the iPod away with my hand, and it falls, hitting the floor. But R.E.M. is still shouting at me.

Ben reaches down to pick up the iPod and turns it off. "Hey, Island Girl," he says softly.

"Don't call me that. And get out," I snap at him. "I'm trying to sleep."

"Sky," he says gently, "do you know what it took to convince Alice to even let me in here to see you?" I think about how he took me to see River, when no one else would, and how mad my grandmother must've been. But if it hadn't been for him, I never would've seen River again. I never would've held his hand one last time, tracing the circles of us in his palm.

"Sorry," I say.

"I brought you something." He bends down and reaches into his bag, and then he pulls out a drawing and hands it to me. I expect it to be the one I saw on his table that day, of me running into the waves. But it's not.

It's a picture of River's wooden shelter, *the pier*, as Ben called it, rising high above the sand, the rocks, the ocean. I touch my finger to the spot underneath where River's things were, where we slept the last time, together. Where the shadow in black shot us. I hate everything about this picture, but also, I love it.

"Thanks," I tell him.

"I did it in fifth period, chem lab." I don't know what he's talking about, so I shake my head. "School," he says. "I was bored in school today, so I drew it for you."

"Oh," I say, understanding now that time has passed, that Ben is in school, that River is gone, and the world has shifted and moved, and yet for me, everything has stayed exactly the same. After my mother and Helmut died, after the storm ended, River and I left Shelter and did the jobs we always did, adding to them the extras done by Helmut and my mother, too. We did it wordlessly, without discussion over who would do what. I caught the fish, as I always did, and cooked it, too, as my mother did. I checked the traps the way Helmut taught me. River prepared the fish and cleaned it in Falls after he'd collected flowers. I feathered a bird the way Helmut would've. River lit the fire in

Fire Pit the way my mother did and extinguished it at night before we went to sleep, as Helmut did. Everything moved and hummed and lived, exactly as it had before. Until time passed, and my birthday came. And River and I were happy there, the two of us, as if that were the way it had always been.

"You know you have to get out of that bed," Ben says now.

"Why?" I ask him. "And how did you get my grandmother to let you up here, anyway?"

"I promised I'd get you downstairs for dinner." He pauses. "And I gave her money back."

"Why?" I ask again.

"Because I liked spending time with you this summer. It didn't feel like a job." He smiles at me. "And she feels really bad about what happened," Ben says, and his face turns, so I think he does, too.

"Yeah, sure she does," I say, and I think about the last time we talked, when I pleaded with her to talk to River's aunt in Temecula and she refused. She told me to accept it. To move on. I can't.

Ben starts to say something, then hesitates for a moment. "Remember that day when we went to the fish market and you asked me about the shooting in Iowa?" he finally says.

I nod, though it feels so far away now, the thought of a gun then, like a boat once was on Island. Something I wasn't even sure was real, though now my leg throbs, reminding me just how real guns are.

"And I said it happens all the time. That stuff like that . . . happens." I nod again. "Well, I started to tell you something, but I didn't think I should. And now I think you need to know."

He pauses. "Do you know why your mother joined Helmut's cult?"

I shake my head, though it feels silly that I didn't think about that before. That I never once considered why she left Pink Bedroom to go live on the farm with Helmut and those other people. *Eden*, River called it, remembering its beauty. Maybe she just loved it there as much as River did.

"Well, something happened," Ben says. "Your mom was pregnant with you at the time, and she went out to lunch at a restaurant. You know what that is, right?" I shake my head, but he keeps talking anyway. "It was crowded. There were a lot of people there. She was waiting out front to get a table or meet a friend or something, I'm not sure. And then some crazy asshole with a gun started shooting. A bunch of people were shot, killed." He pauses. "And your mother got shot, too. She was seriously injured. She was shot in the shoulder, and she lost a lot of blood. She nearly died, and so did you, before you were even born." He touches my shoulder softly, right there, right in the spot, the spot where my mother's deep purple mark burned sometimes. And I feel a stillness in my bones and in my blood, a cold like I felt that night when I ran into the California Pacific. The cold of almost having been dead, of almost drowning but not quite.

Ben exhales and continues talking. "After she recovered and you were born, your mother wanted something else. Something better . . . I guess. And that's when she and your father joined the cult."

I think about the line on my leg, still hurting, and then I think again about the wrinkled purple circle of flesh on my mother's shoulder. It had always been there, her one imperfection, the thing that would sometimes grow hot and send her into Shelter during the day. That was from a gun? I'd asked her about it, and every time, she'd said, *Oh, that? Just a scar from when I was younger.* And she'd shrugged it away as if it was nothing. But now I wonder if it was everything.

"How do you know all this?" I ask Ben, though I guess it's the same way he knew about Helmut. The Google in his laptop computer. And I wonder again if it's all real, entire lives and stories trapped lifeless inside the tiny laptop window. It feels so strange that my life—my mother's life—is out there for the entire world to see and read in their laptop computers as if they know me, everything about me, as if they know me more than I know myself, and maybe they do. That's the strangest part. I only know what I've seen, what I can touch—the water, the sand, River . . . my mother's wrinkled purple imperfection. *A gunshot.*

"Well," Ben is saying, "my mom has told me some of it, and Alice talks about it sometimes. Every year on the anniversary of the shooting, she goes to the restaurant where it happened and brings flowers. There's a small memorial site there across the street now." He pauses. "Even though your mom didn't die when she got shot there, I think Alice kinda feels like she did . . . That she feels like she lost your mom forever that day. You, too."

Everything that Ben is saying falls in my ears, as if it doesn't make any sense. It is not at all a part of the world I thought I knew or would've ever imagined. I think about my mother describing California to me as a place where people were cold and broken, skeletons. And now I think the skeletons she was talking about were not my grandmother or the Bens of California, but the shadow men with the guns. *Bad things happen,* Dr. Banks told me.

But I never imagined something like this happening to my mother, my grandmother. Me.

"Shit," I whisper, Ben's bad word seeming like the only thing I want to say, I know how to say. I can barely understand what I'm feeling now, much less find the words to describe it to Ben.

Ben nods, and I think about what he said, about how my grandmother feels as if my mother died that day so long ago, in a time when I wasn't even born yet. Now I see a glimmer of Island as she must see it, something ugly, something that took my mother and me away from her forever. And as much as I want to hate her for what she did to River, I feel something else for her now, too, a deep sorrow that tugs in my chest, holding me under like a strong wave.

"Come on," Ben says now, nudging my shoulder. "Alice is grilling wahoo for dinner. I picked it up fresh after school."

"I don't even like wahoo," I tell him, but I give him my hand, and I let him help me up out of the bed.

My grandmother seems smaller than I remember when I see her sitting at her kitchen table, not at all like the kind of person who could destroy someone, or who would even want to. *I just wanted to help*, she once told me. *I don't know what to do. There are no rules for something like this.*

When she sees me, walking unsteadily into the kitchen, holding on to Ben, she jumps up. "Honey, finally," she says.

"It's just dinner," I tell her, though my voice falters.

"Yes," she says, and she smiles. "You're exactly right. It's just dinner."

40

EVERY MORNING, THE SUN COMES up, and at night, it sets again out over the ocean, earlier and earlier now that it is fall. In some places, Mrs. Fairfield tells me, the air grows colder in fall, the leaves on the trees change color and fly to the ground. But not here, not in California. Not on Island, either. *California has no seasons*, Mrs. Fairfield says, but I don't agree. *Seasons*, she tells me, means change, shifts in the air. But even the air feels different now that River is gone. Heavier.

Every night, I look out my bedroom window, watching the moon. It still puffs and it grows, until it breaks the sky in a bright yellow ball, and then once again, it's small, just a sliver of light, Venus hugging close below it.

Each afternoon, Marta, the physical therapist, comes to exercise my leg, and it's beginning to feel better now, stronger. The graze of the bullet is just a thin pink line. I think it'll turn to a pale purple eventually, like the circle my mother always wore on her shoulder, though I wonder if mine will grow hot sometimes, too, even after years and years pass, if it will always ache and hurt, the way it does now.

"It'll fade," my grandmother tells me. "In time it does, honey. It won't always feel as bad as it does now."

I want to believe her, but I'm not sure whether I do, whether my pain really will lessen the way she seems to think hers has.

Still, every day, I work hard with Marta to get my leg back to what it once was. My grandmother has kept me in the house, away from the beach, from the world. For now, she says. For my own safety, she says. Until I get better, she says.

I have dreams about the shadow person still, the gun thundering in the air and the red petals of blood exploding on River's chest. I am afraid still, in a way I never was on Island. But not of the beach, the ocean. I long for them. And I know once my leg is strong enough, I'll be able to remove the screen and climb down the tree again and make it back to the ocean on my own. That's all I want, just to hear the whisper of the ocean, to feel the water against my toes, dancing there, a memory of what once was. There is still so much I don't know, I don't understand. But what I do know is this: the ocean heals and it soothes. The water is home.

———•———

One night, as I am planning my climb down to the beach while my grandmother sleeps, she comes into my bedroom just after dinner. I'm sitting on the bed, listening to music on the iPod that Ben has filled with songs. I see him less now that he's back in school. But he still comes over for dinner a few nights a week, when his mother is working late. I think my grandmother has forgiven him from the gentle way she hugs him when he walks in the front door holding a brown paper package from Sandy's Fish Market, but then, aside from talking about my leg healing, nobody talks about what happened over the summer. Not about the money. Not Camp Solanas. And especially not River or Island.

She knocks softly on the door now, and I look up and see her perched there like a fine thin bird. In her hand she clutches a book. *The* book. The one she wanted me to read once. The one she promised me was filled with everything. Answers.

"Can I come in?" she asks me, and I remove my headphones and nod. She sits on the edge of the bed and offers the book to me, the way River offered me the fish on my sixteenth birthday—a gift.

I take it in my hands, and it's heavy, overfull, the edges of newspapers hanging out the sides. "I know you probably have heard it all by now, one way or another," she says. "But it's all in here, too. Why don't you look through it, and then you can ask me if you have any questions or need help reading anything. Okay, honey?"

I don't know if I want to. The book is filled with things I can't understand and probably never will. In my lap now is a piece of the past, and how will it change me if I know more, if I understand more? My life on Island is gone. River is dead. The world pushes on. The tides pull back and forth. The sun rises and falls. The moon expands and then quivers to a thin yellow feather.

I hand it back to her, but she pushes it back on my lap. "No," she says. "You keep it. You'll read it when you're ready." She smiles at me and moves toward the doorway.

"He saved my life, you know," I tell her now. "River." And as soon as I say his name, I see her smile evaporate, like puddles of rainwater on the beach on a hot, hot day. It goes so fast you're not even sure it was ever really there at all. "He stopped me from eating the mushrooms on Island. The ones my mother ate." I pause. "He couldn't kill. Not even the rabbits. I was the one who did it. I was the one who snapped their necks. I skinned them and took their pelts for us to use, too." Tears well up in my eyes as I remember Helmut showing me how to do it, how to remove the pelt with a sharp stone. How River hid his head in my mother's hip.

"Oh, honey," she says, walking back over to the bed and again sitting carefully on the edge.

"Ben showed me the picture with the apples," I tell her. "That's probably in your book, too, isn't it?" I hear the sound of my voice, angry. But I'm not angry. I just want her to know that her big, heavy book can't mean something. It can't mean more than what I know and what I remember. Whatever Helmut did when he was here, well, that was not my life on Island. That was not him. Or River.

"That picture was everywhere," she says, her voice cracking. "After you vanished, it was all you saw. In the newspaper, on the news . . ."

"But you know that wasn't really him, right?" I tell her. "You know River didn't even know. He thought Eden was still here, that he'd be able to go back and be with his mother." I need her to know this, to understand this. That River was everything good that I was, that I am. That I loved him, and that she was wrong about him. That he saved me, that he would've given anything to save me. Even himself.

"Now I do," she says, and her voice is thick and filled with something I don't recognize, an emotion that didn't exist on Island but seems to exist everywhere here, in all the adults around me.

She reaches up and wipes a tear from my cheek, and then she leans back in and hugs me. "I'm sorry," she whispers into my hair. "I know you loved him. I know that now." She pulls back and holds my face between her hands. "And I'm sorry for everything that's happened. I really am."

She lets go of my face, but I can still feel the impressions of her fingers on my cheeks. She has tears in her eyes, too, and there is something about the way she's looking at me now that makes me think maybe she's telling the truth.

"I might have gone about it all wrong, but I really did just want to protect you." She pauses and shakes her head. "Just the way your mother thought she was protecting you once by taking you away from here, I guess," she says, and she sighs. "I never wanted him to get hurt . . . I never wanted anyone to get hurt." Her voice breaks a little, and she takes a deep breath. "I was just thinking of you. What I thought was best for you . . . I thought I was helping him, too. With a little money, an apartment . . . It was stupid. Seeing how much help you needed here, I should've known. I just . . ." She pauses and stares out the window for a minute. She seems to be looking very hard for something, though I'm not sure what. "I've lived in California my entire life. Sixty-six long years," she says.

"You'd think I'd know everything there is to know by now. But sometimes I wonder if I know anything at all."

I think about what she just said. Is it true that you can live in this place, in California, for sixty-six long years, and still not understand anything about it? I lived on Island for fourteen years, and I knew everything there was to know. Almost. Except for what to do when the boat actually came.

"I've been thinking about how you asked me about him when we were leaving the hospital," she's saying now. "And how hard this must be for you." She pauses. "So I've been trying to call his aunt in Temecula. I've left her a few messages. She hasn't called me back yet, but hopefully she will soon . . . I know how hard it is to lose someone you love so much. I do, honey. It was terrible the way I lost your mother and you. Not knowing. Then just thinking you were dead, all that time, and not even having anywhere to visit you." She pauses. "Maybe if we could go out there. See where he's buried. Bring him flowers . . ."

I think about what Dr. Banks called my *brutal honesty*, and I think I understand it now, the way the truth feels as if it has punched you hard in the gut, so hard that it hurts. *See where he's buried*. River, in the ground. In some strange place called Temecula.

I know how hard it is to lose someone you love so much . . .

"Thank you," I whisper, and she looks at me, her face turning in surprise. "For calling his aunt."

She nods and squeezes my hand and offers me a small smile. She stands, hesitates for a moment, and then leans in and kisses my forehead. I think about how when she did that at the hospital, I pulled so hard I smashed her nose. Now I stay still.

"Now that your leg is stronger," she says softly when she pulls back, "Ben offered to come over tonight after he finishes his homework to walk you down to the beach for a little while." I glance at the window, and she says, "I had it bolted shut while you were in the hospital. You can't be climbing down there. It's just not safe."

"But I have to." The words collapse against my throat, the thought of being trapped here forever, even after my leg is completely healed.

She nods. "I know," she says. "I know how much you miss the beach—I do. So any time you want to go, you can, okay? But you have to use the door. And just take Ben with you, for now. Until you get a little stronger." She pauses. "From here on out, I'm going to do everything I can to make sure you're happy here." Her voice is so soft, so honest seeming, that for a minute it almost reminds me of my mother's.

Ben and I take the front walk to the ocean tonight, and I'm glad, because even the sight of the pines twirling in the wind from my window is too much to bear. It reminds me too much of River, of our last morning together, when he led me through the path in the pine forest he knew so well, when he beamed with our plan about finding a boat, going back together. If I squeeze my eyes shut tightly enough, the roar of the ocean calling to me in the near distance, I can almost hear him whispering my name: *Skyblue.*

I want to remember it forever, the sound of his voice, the feel of his fingers through the tangle of my braid. But already, I can feel him slipping away, the way my mother started to after just a little time of being gone.

Ben takes my hand and laces his fingers through mine. It's a nice gesture, the way he is holding on to me, trying so hard to be my friend, to help me. I'm glad I have him here.

I hold on to his hand as we walk and breathe deeply, taking in the cool, salty air as we walk past the last of the houses, toward the steps that will take us to the beach below. The sky is a pearly blue gray now, the sun a yellow-orange ball dropping so far on the horizon that it seems to be floating on waves in the distance.

"Can I ask you something?" I say, just as we walk down the steps to the sand below. "What happened to the person who shot us?" I take my flip-flops off even though my leg hurts a little without them. I want to feel the sand between my toes, to remember that in one way, the world is still the same, just as it always was.

"I don't know." Ben shrugs. "I know the police were looking for him, but they never found him. The money in the bag was just cash—bills," he clarifies, "and they weren't traceable or anything. So I guess he got away with it."

"Do you think they'll ever find him?"

Ben shrugs again. "Probably not. Unless he does it again and gets caught. It sucks, I know." He sighs and holds on to my hand tightly as if he's afraid to let me go too close to the water, as if he understands this inclination I have, I always have, to run in, to dive under the waves, to let them swallow me and carry me home. To Island. Except Island without River wouldn't be Island at all.

I roll up the bottoms of my jeans and let my toes touch the edge of the water. It's still cold enough to sting, but I don't care. The wind blows hard, whipping my short hair in my face, pushing the water up my legs in curls, seeping into my thin pink scar. The Santa Anas are here, just as Mrs. Fairfield promised me they would be as she tried to explain it to me, the regularity in this California world. Every October, Santa Ana winds. *The normalcy.*

I try to imagine it again, across the giant space of the Pacific. Island. I don't know what will happen to it, now that we've left it, now that it's going on a map. Mrs. Fairfield guesses that tourists will want to see it, that cruise ships will stop there on their way to Fiji. She laughs when she says it, as if Island, my life, is something that amuses her. I don't want to let it go, any of it, but maybe I have to.

The past is now a giant, heavy book waiting in my bedroom.

But it's also the shimmering memories I have of a beautiful life on Island. Of my mother. Of River. Even of Helmut.

Ahead of me, there is the same ocean. And yet everything about it is different: the color, the temperature, even the beating of the waves against the shore.

The tide is coming in, and we have to move back so the water doesn't take us. "Can we walk a little down the beach?" I ask Ben.

"We probably shouldn't, Sky," he says. "It's getting late."

Sky. I think of that girl I was. With River. *I can't be her anymore,* I think. Island is gone. My hair is gone. My mother is gone. River is gone.

But I can't be Megan, either. *Megan.* This baby who once

lived on a farm called Eden, who once rolled around in her mother's belly during a shooting. *No.*

I am the girl with the thin pink line on her calf, the girl who doesn't know who she will be and what she will do without River. The girl who understands loss and love, survival and death, but who still doesn't understand money, where it comes from, why everyone wants it so much. I am the girl who could stay here in California and maybe learn to love her grandmother. And also the girl who still dreams in Island, and wants to find a boat to make her way back to the place she still thinks of as home.

I want the ocean to tell me, as it always has. I want the ocean to call to me, to heal me and save me, to protect me and feed me. I want it to offer me answers, the way it once offered fish and pretty pink shells.

"Can you give me a minute alone?" I ask Ben now. He hesitates, and then I say, "I'll be right here. I promise. I'll meet you up on the steps in a minute." He nods, and he walks back up toward the steps.

The Santa Anas blow, and the sand swirls behind me in the wind as I watch him go. When I turn back, I see the sun has almost fallen below a wave, and the sky has turned a pale blue, surrendering to the whole moon, to Venus twinkling just below it.

Starlight, star bright, first star I see tonight. I wish I may. I wish I might. I wish the wish I wish tonight.

I wish for the ocean to tell me who I am and where I belong.

I stare at the ocean, listening to it carefully. The waves crash and turn, and crash and turn again. The tide has pulled me closer in and also caused me to drift down the beach a bit. I take another step back. This time, without looking first, and my foot hits something hard, a shell or a stick, or a piney branch. I bend down to pick it up, and then my eye catches on something in the sand.

It is hard to see at first, and the water comes in again and washes over it. I wait for the water to recede again, and I kneel in the wet, cold sand to have a closer look.

The last moments of sun shine down across the sand, illuminating the top parts of two circles that were connected once, through the middle. The bottoms are missing, drowned already by the high tide, but the top parts remain, still connected, in just the smallest way. When they were whole, before the tide came in, they were exactly what I drew that night when River found me here. But that was so long ago. These drawings are new, fresh. Exactly what I traced in River's limp palm in Military Hospital. Two circles, running through each other, together, around and around. Forever.

You and me, River told me.

See you soon.

"River!" I shout his name into the ocean now, and then turn and shout it again into the pines. The Santa Anas blow, twisting the treetops. The ocean roars, higher and higher up the beach. The tide is almost at its height. "River," I shout again.

The ocean answers back, the waves falling, crashing against the sand. Rushing over these circles, erasing them a little piece at a time as the tide comes in.

I feel a hand on my shoulder, and Ben is back, standing there behind me. "You all right?" he asks. "I heard you shouting."

"River is still here," I whisper to him.

"Yeah." He squeezes my shoulder. "I know. The ocean reminds you of him, doesn't it?"

The trees rustle behind me, though for a moment, I do not feel the wind pushing against my cheek. I turn quickly, but the rustling stops, and then in another moment, the winds are back, cresting the tops of the pines like waves.

Promise me you won't leave me again, I said to him that night underneath the pier.

I promise, he said.

"Come on," Ben says. "We have to get back."

"Not yet," I whisper.

But he tugs on my hand. "Come on," he says again. "We can come back tomorrow."

As we walk up the beach together, I keep on looking behind me, back toward the ocean, toward the circles disappearing in the waves of the high tide. I'm pretty sure they're completely gone, erased by the water, by the time we climb the steps.

But now, from higher up, the Pacific begins to glow in the new light of the full moon, the waves bright and dancing, and suddenly, filled with hope.

Acknowledgments

Thank you to my agent, Jessica Regel, for her support and guidance and for encouraging me to take a chance on Sky and River. I'm so lucky to have her championing my work, which she did in this case even through a hurricane! Thank you also to everyone else at JVNLA, especially Tara Hart and Jennifer Weltz, for all their support and hard work on my behalf.

Thank you to the entire team at Bloomsbury, whose enthusiasm for this book has been amazing, especially my wonderful editor, Mary Kate Castellani. Thanks to Mary Kate for all the time, hard work, and editorial guidance, and for loving Sky and River just as much as I do! Thank you also to the Bloomsbury UK team and my UK editor, Natalie Hamilton, for giving this book a home in the UK.

Last but certainly not least, thank you to my friends and family who read my work, encourage me, and keep me going on a daily basis, with biggest thanks to my husband, Gregg, who plotted this book across the kitchen table with me and who took over the real world while I delved into Sky's world.

Jillian Cantor wrote her first story, about a talking hot air balloon, at the age of nine and has been writing ever since. She is now the author of several novels for teens and adults, including, most recently, *Margot*, a reimagining of Anne Frank's sister's life, had she survived the war. Jillian lives in Arizona, USA, with her husband and two sons.